RAVEN EASTON

windy city wild!

CHAPTER 1

THE LAKE MICHIGAN BREEZE HAD BEEN ODDLY INSISTENT

THE LAKE MICHIGAN breeze had been oddly insistent that morning. Like it was trying to tell her something.

Chloe Manning shook it out of her hair and sat down.

∽

Chloe Manning was unhappy. She was unhappy a lot lately.

The mere state of being unhappy, in turn, made her even more unhappy because there was no good reason for her to be unhappy in the first place. She was young and smart and rich and influential and she turned heads wherever she went.

And today, she was wearing *super*cute shoes.

Happiness should follow like a cat follows a cricket.

At that moment, however, she was sitting in a roomful of lawyers at a major Chicago law firm. That was seldom a happy state of affairs in Chicago or anywhere else.

One doesn't sit in a roomful of lawyers because something wonderful has happened. One sits in a roomful of lawyers because something is broken.

Sometimes, Chloe Manning thought, *it's you.*

This meeting, which she had requested, would not be addressing her recent feeling of vague unease, of something missing in her life. This meeting would be all business, her business. It had a definite, narrow goal, the only kind of meeting she would attend these days. She told herself to get focused.

Today, though, something was tugging at her heart that she knew she should tend to, but she couldn't name it and she couldn't picture it and she couldn't hear it. But since that something was not killing her, she told herself to put it aside for later consideration, along with whether to redo the kitchen or to care about who the president is.

But as she sat there in the moments before one or another of the lawyers would start talking to begin this meeting, she felt that heart-tug return.

She thought about the lousy first and last date of the evening before, the latest blessedly short chapter in what seemed like an endless novel full of unsatisfactory men. This one was already beginning to fade, some Jason or other who had a bunch of hot sandwich franchises, a setup she had reluctantly accepted to humor a girlfriend.

On evenings like this, she had thought as she watched him sip his beer much, much too slowly, the only thing worse than being lonely is not being lonely enough.

Where did all these men come from? How could they all have grown up to be so *ordinary*? Is it possible a whole generation of fathers modeled tedium for their sons? Even the cute ones, dull as a stick. Even the rich ones. Even the cute *and* rich ones. How has the species survived? What woman would want to have sex with some of these slugs? What woman would want all those mundane chromosomes wriggling around down there, swimming hard to be the winner in the derby to make more mundane boys? Is there a God? Is He this tiresome?

Is it me? No. Is it?

Focus, Chloe. Focus.

Not everything is about men. So why is she thinking about them sitting here with these expensive lawyers with far more pressing business at hand? She had called this meeting; *let's get our mind off men, shall we?*

God had a son. He was interesting. I'd rather go on a date with Jesus than this latest batch. He probably wouldn't stare at my chest all night.

Focus, girl. Forget about last night's drink and vegan sliders with Jason Nothing.

She checked her look in the mirrored back of her phone, smoothed the last breath of that morning's breeze out of her hair, and directed her attention to the collection of attorneys who had gathered to try to make her happy.

᪥

Chloe Manning was particularly unhappy that a major lawsuit brought by a construction contractor against her company Barbiron was still hanging around. The contractor, owned by a couple named Robert and Lorna Philbrick, had failed to complete a major building project for the company – it seemed like they barely even started it – and Chloe had fired them. Instead of conceding their failure to keep their own promises, they sued Barbiron for millions of dollars, claiming that by firing them Chloe had breached the construction contract.

Barbiron was paying big legal fees each month with no forward movement that Chloe could perceive. Chloe did not like things that did not move forward. She especially did not like things whose lack of movement was costing her money.

"If you're not dynamic, just stay in your hammock," she said to her operating teams. "It's a stupid saying, but stupid sayings tend to stick in the mind." In case that particular couplet threatened to fade in her employees' memories, she set up a hammock near a busy office intersection and tossed competitors' brochures into it.

She had arranged this meeting to kick some urgency back into Barbiron's defense of the Philbrick case.

Barbiron had not been entirely her company since she began to bring in other investors, but she was its founder and chief executive officer and still its largest shareholder. Since Chloe had started the company the year after she got her MBA, Barbiron had increased its annual revenues to over $800 million. Its line of traditional hardware – hammers and drills and saws and ladders and whatever other manly tools Barbiron thought ripe for a makeover – were redesigned with attention to size, materials, weight, and ergonomics for the female hand and frame. And with attention as well to the female eye: Chloe had involved artists and sculptors in the design process to ensure that that each item, from garden trowels to leaf blowers, possessed a distinctive appeal in line, shape, color. If cars can be art, Chloe demanded of her design staff, why can't tools? The designers' visions had challenged Barbiron's engineers to innovate to accommodate the handsome new looks. Chloe insisted that each tool be beautiful as well as tough.

Which, perhaps not so coincidentally, described the public Chloe Manning herself. The private Chloe Manning was much more than that – and, she felt, sometimes much less – but, by her choice, known to few.

Barbiron's products were revolutionary and even sexy, and Chloe was the company's sexiest product and its very public face.

She was tall, and in the lofty heels she favored there were few men she could not look in the eye or beyond. Legs, long; waist, high and narrow; hips, slim and gently flaring; bust, inspirational.

Her backside when she passed by was the author of more wrenched male necks than a hundred-car pileup.

A face out of Donatello's dreams; flesh, out of Michelangelo's.

She wore her glowing golden hair in loose natural waves down to her very serious shoulders. On those shoulders and hips were draped the most sophisticated and flattering business and evening fashions.

Her eyes were large. Persian through the corners, Bacall green.

Not an inch of her had felt the surgeon's blade.

No one looked like Chloe Manning. Men and women dreamed about her, but their dreams were not the same.

She was interviewed and photographed by all the leading business publications, and she was beloved by women's lifestyle and fashion magazine editors as a can't-miss cover story. Designers flocked to her; she'd even done a spread for *W* mag, "CEO, Windy City Style," where she had been dressed by Herrera, McCartney, Ford, and Wang, posing in the foreground of the city's attractions like she'd been raised in Avedon's studio. She had even been featured in *Good Housekeeping* and *Women's Day*.

She did not think of herself as a by-the-book feminist; her success, she felt, had nothing to do with any ideology other than one favoring hard work and brains. As Barbiron's market share grew, though, she found herself celebrated as the model for a particular species of the successful woman of business, strong and smart but spectacularly female.

And, for a dash of intrigue, spectacularly single. She was sometimes photographed on the arm of some big deal, but his deal must not have been big enough because the next time it would be someone different. With most of them, it looked like they were on her arm.

When she felt like thinking about the broader arcs of her life, she talked it out with her cats. They seemed sympathetic, although she had to admit the sincerity of their interest appeared to wane as feeding time approached.

"It's hard to describe," she said to Gloria the Chocolate Siamese after an evening out with an airline pilot. "He was nice enough and good-looking and wasn't a jerk and I only caught him staring at my boobs a couple of times. That's within boob-staring tolerances. But he just isn't what I've imagined for myself, you know? I could feel it in about five minutes."

"Of course," Chloe continued while she removed her makeup as Gloria sat on the counter, "I can't really tell you what I am imagining for myself. Just not him. So Bandit," she said to her Blue Point, who was doing his late-night walking-talking act signaling his requirement of a pre-bedtime treat, "what do I say when this guy calls or texts again? You're a guy, what's the nicest way to be let down? Although I guess your social life went down the drain when, you know, snip-snip."

It was a good life, if a sometimes lonely one. To keep it good, she zeroed in on unexpected twitches in Barbiron's expense statements like an owl on a field mouse. It had brought her to the law firm's offices today to see if something could be done to speed the resolution of the troublesome Philbrick lawsuit.

Lawyers. Like any other profession, there were good ones and bad ones, lawyers whose breathtaking fees you were happy to pay for the value their skills added to your bottom line, and those who should not be representing a sack of asphalt. Chloe had her pick of Chicago's best. Barbiron was a bright spot in Illinois' dismal economic picture; every law firm in the city wanted to be in the spotlight that followed its charismatic CEO around. Barbiron's locations employed over a thousand people in its design and fabrication facilities, most of which the company had renovated from abandoned industrial facilities in and around the city, and firms were keen to be associated with this conspicuous example of civic loyalty. They also wanted to charge top hourly rates for the sophisticated litigation and transactional work Barbiron required.

Today's audition was to be performed by the 275-lawyer firm of Rockwell Morton & Gilles LLP.

Before they headed to the meeting, Chloe spoke to her utterly devoted and could-be-attractive-if-she-tried young assistant Amy, who knew everything – almost everything – about Barbiron's operations and its leader's comings and goings. "What are the fees so far on the Philbrick case?"

Amy tapped at her tablet. "A little over $37,000 billed," she said.

"Have we paid all of it?"

"Last statement is pending."

"Hold that one," Chloe said. "We may be reassessing."

Jesus Christ. Well, maybe the fees she was burning today would get some people off their asses.

Or she might hire some new asses to see if they could get some results on the Philbrick case.

Chloe looked around the conference room and considered how much this meeting was costing her. Rather, how much it was costing Barbiron. Chloe felt an almost motherly sense of protection over Barbiron's cash, which she knew was really its shareholders' cash. As Barbiron's largest shareholder, it seemed like her own money was going into the pockets of these lawyers.

Across from Chloe sat Barbiron's current lawyer on the case. Lisa Blazier called herself "The Flamethrower" because she fought every case hard and loud and made herself so unpleasant that the parties and counsel on the other side would settle for more (or, in the rare defense case she handled, less) than the case was worth just to get her out of their hair. She had also curated a very striking personal presentation that drew the eye and piqued the imagination. Her surgically-improved bosom on most other women would have seemed comically oversized, except that nobody laughed at Lisa Blazier. Her shoulders-back carriage and careful selection of outfits drew attention to those assets, usually tastefully, although when the occasion required she could tart up to spectacular effect. Her hair changed seasonally in shape and shade, but was always some version of red that approached her own fiery hue. Juries were intimidated and fascinated by her. Some judges, too, at least by reputation. Chloe had hired her for this difficult case because she saw The Flamethrower as a version of herself, smart and strong – and impossible not to notice – and not afraid to stare down the challenges that smart and strong women still continued to encounter in business and the professions, no matter how noticeable they were.

She was charging Barbiron $725/hour.

But Lisa the Flamethrower had made no progress on getting rid of the Philbrick case.

Next to Lisa sat a young associate from her firm who was assisting her on the case. Chloe could never remember her name; even after they were reintroduced on her arrival today, Chloe had already forgotten it. One of those J names. While the J-girl was quite pretty she was not nearly as attractive as Lisa, and it occurred to Chloe that no associate of Lisa's ever would be. What, maybe $375 an hour for her?

Over a grand an hour right there between the two of them.

Chloe was throwing a little flame of her own today. She had asked Lisa to come to a meeting at Rockwell Morton ostensibly to explore the possibility of that firm joining the Philbrick case as co-counsel with Lisa. That fooled nobody, least of all The Flamethrower, and Chloe had not intended it to. Lisa was fuming at the implication that she wasn't handling the case properly and might need help from another firm – or worse, that she might get fired. Chloe didn't care. She liked Lisa but this was business. She wanted to light her own fire under the damned Flamethrower, convey her impatience in a dramatic and, she hoped, constructive way. She wasn't committed to demoting Lisa, but maybe she'd see something she liked at Rockwell Morton & Gilles.

That firm, in the person of senior founder Nelson Gilles, was excited to host this unusual meeting with Barbiron's celebrated chief executive. Chloe had met Nelson at a luncheon following one of her speaking engagements. Silver-haired and thick-bodied, he used his age and size to convey authority and confidence. He was seated at her table – *how did he swing that?* she wondered – but instead of chatting her up the way men always tried to do with her, especially men who wanted to do business with Barbiron, and even more especially men who wanted to do business with Barbiron and entertained the notion that there was some chance in hell that they might sleep with her, he spoke only once. Rising to excuse himself before dessert, claiming a hearing to attend, he bent to speak softly to her as he passed:

"Your earrings – Armentas, are they? – with those Christian Louboutins, perfect."

And he was gone. Chloe made a mental note to give him a shot if she decided to add to Barbiron's collection of law firms. Not because he'd nailed her earring and shoe choices, but because he'd had the sand to try that minimalist, off-center approach and had pulled it off with a hit-and-run flair she'd never before encountered.

Nelson had brought two Rockwell Morton lawyers to the meeting. Chloe assumed that Brian Accardo would serve as the hotshot trial attorney Nelson had selected to take the lead should Barbiron favor it with a case. "No relation to Tony 'the Big Tuna,'" he would say when asked about the late organized crime boss of Chicago, "that I know of." Nice-looking; intense, but with a dark Mediterranean warmth about him. Wedding ring.

And, of course, there was The Woman – all the professional firms seeking work with Barbiron made sure to include The Woman in their presentations to Chloe, these days usually The Two Women. This one was fourth-year lawyer Oona Karras, strong Greek features and that delicious skin. Amazing thick black hair you could do anything with. Chloe noted that Oona's big-bonedness and an unfortunate choice of eyeglass frames were overcome by a lovely smile that conveyed a sincere delight at being the low woman on this particularly exciting totem pole topped by Chloe Manning.

In the dog-and-pony shows firms would stage for Chloe, one of The Women was almost always a partner, sometimes the frontline lawyer being proposed for the deal or the case. As long as she was going to be patronized in this way, Chloe liked it that Nelson was patronizing her with one younger, slightly shy lawyer in whom they had obvious confidence rather than some stylish tough broad they hoped Chloe might bond with.

That concluded her survey of the room. She figured Nelson, Brian, Oona together, what, another grand-and-a-half? Together with The Flamethrower and what's-her-name, if Nelson billed her for this getting-to-know-you session, that's two-and-a-half large per hour down the drain and who knows how many hours?

This had shaped up to be one costly afternoon. But if it got the damned Philbrick case moving the right direction, it would be money well spent.

❦

Chloe seldom got involved in the litigation that every large company faced – wrongful termination, employment discrimination, the occasional vendor or customer dispute. She had not hired an in-house general counsel, instead letting her chief financial officer deal with the law firms on these routine disputes and contractual matters. The cases would burn some legal fees and eventually get settled apparently without much relationship to the merits of the dispute. An expensive nuisance, but Chloe had better things to do than crusade to change the laws that encouraged weak claims against prosperous defendants. Instead, Barbiron responded by spreading its business between several firms whose competitive jostling kept fees reasonable and quality high.

The Philbrick case presented a more dangerous risk and required a more thoughtful response. Barbiron had awarded the Philbrick company the contract for the conversion of an old warehouse on West Grand Avenue into its new corporate headquarters. The Philbricks were a husband-and-wife team who gave an impression of true marital equality in their business. They came across as salty/earthy types, but with some sophistication and entrepreneurial energy. They knew their way around a PowerPoint without seeming too slick about it. Chloe had liked the Philbricks' portfolio of their prior projects and she visited a couple of the sites to confirm that they looked as good as the photos in their presentation. She was impressed that they had the insight to speak directly to her vision for the project rather than to try to impress her with their own ideas. And as the Philbricks were a low-overhead operation, Chloe imagined that their low bid did not include rent on fancy offices or a bureaucracy that wasn't going to be building anything.

Barbiron's facilities managers and director of corporate operations had warned Chloe that the Philbricks were too small for the job, but the idea of giving the business to a local creative couple appealed to her. In Barbiron's early years she had been told many times that her company was too small and that she was too inexperienced to launch one major initiative or another, and she liked the idea of throwing the business to a venture she could take a chance on the way others had taken a chance on her. Besides, she figured, subcontractors would be doing most of the actual work.

The Philbricks struck her as having the energy and focus to lead the different subcontractor teams to a successful and timely project completion.

She was wrong.

The project was behind schedule from the first day of demolition, what little construction that took place was shoddy, subcontractors complained of non-payment, systems failed. The Philbricks offered little besides endless excuses and requests for advances on progress payments. Worst were the failed periodic inspections and code violation tickets from the Chicago Department of Buildings and the raised eyebrows from the city officials Chloe had so carefully cultivated. Chloe quit paying and fired the Philbricks. They sued for breach of contract claiming millions of dollars in damages for loss of the contract and the destruction of their business.

Chloe thought the case was complete bullshit. All you had to do was look at the near-empty shell out on West Grand. That hulking mess should have opened as a beautiful new headquarters a year earlier. But not only was the case still hanging around and burning legal fees, Lisa the Flamethrower had called a few days earlier to tell her that the Philbricks' lawyer had served a notice to take Chloe's deposition.

Chloe called Nelson Gilles.

CHAPTER 2

THE MEETING BEGAN AWKWARDLY

THE MEETING BEGAN awkwardly, as Chloe had intended. Too bad. *Out of discomfort comes creativity* was her motto, which she had just that minute made up.

"Thanks for bringing us together, Chloe," Nelson said. "We do appreciate the opportunity to meet with you, but I probably don't have to tell you that in Lisa Blazier you already have excellent representation."

"I know. This is not about Lisa," Chloe said, although it was, more than a little. "I just felt like before we started down the road of depositions, and in particular my deposition, I wanted an independent consult. Not a second opinion exactly, but maybe just a brainstorming session with a fresh pair of eyes. Looks like I got three pairs," she said, smiling at the Rockwell Morton team. "I certainly don't mean any offense to Lisa," she said. Which was, again, only partly true.

"Thank you, Nelson," Lisa said, acknowledging his diplomacy but barely concealing her anger at having to sit there and listen to her work reviewed by other lawyers, especially that old warhorse Nelson Gilles. "We did what we always do. We looked at the legal issues raised by the complaint. Jessica did legal research that I reviewed and I agreed with her conclusions on the applicable law and her recommendations on how to respond." Jessica, Chloe thought, that was that associate's name. So many Jessicas in that generation, no wonder it didn't register.

"And of course, we investigated the factual allegations with your people, Chloe," Lisa continued. "You remember Jessica's visits to your offices to interview your operations and facilities guys." Chloe did not remember. "We did not see any grounds for a motion to dismiss the case at this stage. We made sure we filed an answer on time that contained the technical defenses we saw potentially available to us. We denied the factual allegations of the complaint that we could truthfully deny, and we denied that Barbiron had any liability. We're also looking at filing a counterclaim for the damages the Philbricks have caused Barbiron if we can't get the surety company to make good on the completion bond."

"We only got a copy of the complaint a few hours ago," Nelson said, addressing Chloe, "so we have not had the opportunity to look at the matter as thoroughly as Lisa and Jessica, nor, I should add, have you engaged us to do so at this time. I will say that the answer Lisa filed looks good, as I would expect it to. Material allegations denied, affirmative defenses listed, jury demand, it's all there."

He paused. He was trying to be nice to that blasted Flamethrower but the whole room could tell she was boiling. "Chloe," he said, "I'm sure I don't have to invite you to speak candidly, but I'm also certain you are aware that there's some discomfort in the room on all of our parts."

"Not mine," Chloe said. Her parts were functioning in perfect comfort. A little unsure as to what they wanted from the world, maybe, but operating as intended for purposes of discussing the Philbrick case. Lisa visibly bristled.

"All right, but perhaps it would be helpful if you could just give us your thoughts, what you want us to accomplish here," Nelson said. "I'm not going to BS you. Yeah, Rockwell Morton would absolutely love to work with you and Barbiron on any project, and with Lisa in this case if that is appropriate" – he nodded and smiled at Lisa but got nothing back – "but just sitting here with the complaint in front of us for the last couple of hours and no other real background, we're not in a great position to come up with anything creative that would add to what Lisa and Jessica have already done. Brian, Oona, you see anything we could add at this point?"

They both shook their heads no.

Nelson leaned toward Chloe and lowered his voice, reminding her of the way he had approached her at the luncheon. "I feel there's something your gut is telling you that we need to hear. Clients frequently have a personal and even an emotional perspective that lawyers miss. We need to respect that and maybe that can spark some discussion that will move us down the road here."

"I don't see why a case where I'm the wronged party is

taking so long and costing me so much," Chloe said. "They screwed me, not the other way around. I've been in lawsuits. I know it's easy and cheap to file a lawsuit, and I know it's expensive to hire attorneys and expert witnesses and all the rest, and the whole process takes time, blah blah blah. But this one . . . no one who knows what went on with these people could possibly think I owe them a cent."

Brian spoke for the first time. "It is regrettable," he said. "A party may know perfectly well the right and wrong of a situation, but the system gives the jury the final say. Juries don't have to agree with you no matter how right or how nice or how truthful you are, so the only way for the wronged party to get a vote is to be extremely careful and thorough about, number one, getting all the facts out, and number two, putting it all together for them in a clear and persuasive manner. Both take time and money."

"I know all that," Chloe said, aggravated at the unnecessary lecture. "And I'll tell you something else. Nelson said something about my gut and my – what was it? – my emotional perspective. I'll admit it. I do have an emotional perspective on this. Everyone told me these Philbricks might be good with the limited corporate office build-out projects but they did not have experience with major full-scale renovations like this one. That's what people said about me when I started up, said I was just one woman, I could never build a business manufacturing men's tools for women, and I showed them they were wrong. I thought my people were wrong about the Philbricks, too. I wanted to give them the chance my first investors gave me when I was the little guy.

"But it was me that was wrong to hire them. And

although I like it when my people are right, I don't like being wrong. And I don't like a public record of being wrong, and now it's like I'm wrong twice – once for hiring them, which everyone now knows because that West Grand property is sitting there like something from 'The Walking Dead,' and once for firing them, which is sitting in that complaint in the case docket down at the Daley Center for everyone to gawk at after they're done gawking at the Picasso."

Her voice had been rising, but now she took a breath and calmed herself. "Okay, I suppose the complaint is not exactly a big tourist draw down at the Daley Center. I guess what I'm telling you is that I know I'm having a little tantrum here. I know I'm being a little unreasonable, I know it's just a stupid contract case, and I know I can't always get my way just because it is my way, but my gut is telling me there's a way . . . to break out, put some heat on them . . . or maybe something we haven't thought of yet."

Nelson, then Brian, then Lisa all nodded thoughtfully and had no idea what to say to her.

Oona broke the silence: "We could run it by Jon."

"I was thinking the same thing," Brian said.

"Who's Jon?" Chloe and Nelson said at the same time.

"Jon Rider," Oona and Brian said at the same time.

Lisa groaned a little.

"Same question," Chloe said.

"Oh," Oona said, and smiled that wonderful smile. "He's like our resident . . . ." She rolled her eyes. "I don't know how to describe what he does."

"He sees things other people don't see," Brian said.

"What," Chloe said, "like he sees dead people, like that kid in 'The Sixth Sense'? I'm not getting this, what's the deal with this guy and why are we talking about him?"

Oona couldn't hold back. "I think he's brilliant," Oona said. "And he's fun, and he's funny and he's . . . ." She stopped, realizing she was saying more than might have been appropriate to say at a client meeting. But she rolled her eyes again and a spot of color rose in her cheeks. "Brilliant, that's all."

"I was debating whether to use the 'b' word," Brian said. "But it fits."

Nelson turned to Brian. "Why don't I know him?"

"You know him," Brian said. "He's the guy who worked that . . . ."

"Wait," Nelson said, "is he that tall guy that did the . . . ?"

"Yeah," Brian said. "That's him, and he also did that other thing where we filed that . . . ."

"Sometimes I think this firm has gotten too big," Nelson said. "But I do remember this Rider if he's the guy who got us . . . ."

"He used to head up cases and try them up until a couple of years ago," Brian said, "but some things changed for him. Personal stuff. Now we just kind of borrow his brain. He deflects credit, doesn't want his name on briefs. He's not interested in developing new clients. At this point in his career he just wants to help the teams, think and write and go home."

"Is he here today?" Nelson asked.

"He's here," Oona said. "He helped me with a jurisdictional issue this morning."

Typical lawyer solution, Chloe thought, *just throw another lawyer or two at it, we're up to three grand an hour. And now we're getting this pencilneck Poindexter, some kind of antisocial law nerd, who's going to piddle and diddle with technicalities. Well, he couldn't do any worse than all these good-looking people I'm paying now.*

"All right, nothing to lose at this point," she said, although a fleeting vision of dollar signs with wings popped into her head. "Let's get this mystery man in here."

Brian got up to get him and returned with the report that Jon would join them in a few minutes.

Nelson and Lisa exchanged some law-biz small talk while Chloe and Amy bent over Amy's pad reviewing Barbiron's receivables. *Hey, since when did Target take more than 90 days to —*

CHAPTER 3

CHLOE FELT A JOLT

CHLOE FELT A jolt, like lightning had struck nearby. Something almost electric was disturbing the flux in the conference room atmosphere and teasing her flesh. Amy tensed and straightened beside her. Across the table Lisa and Jessica snapped to something like attention.

Oona beamed.

Even Nelson and Brian sat up.

Jon Rider had entered the room.

Chloe felt herself bring her shoulders back, smoothing her blouse and jacket over her breasts.

The man who stood before her had not yet looked her way. Accustomed to sizing up men quickly, she took a quick census of what she saw. Tall, maybe two inches, no, three, over six. Slender but not skinny, not obviously muscled up, either. Hard to tell about his body because unlike anyone she had seen at Rockwell Morton that day, unlike anyone she had seen at any professional office in the last few years, he was wearing a suit. A Canali, maybe? *Wait, why am I thinking about his body?* Jacket, tie, the whole bit; navy suit, subtle houndstooth pattern in the weave, tie matching nicely with his light-blue shirt, knotted up to his neck, with a perfect dimple beneath.

He knows how to make a perfect tie dimple. That's interesting.

Was he handsome? Was he? Why couldn't she tell? He was standing right there in front of her. He was no movie star, no model. Or – was he, now? Maybe. Why couldn't she get a clearer read on this guy? There was something about that lean face, chiseled but somehow bemused, and that body that seemed happy to be wearing beautiful man-clothes.

No, really, why am I thinking about his bod – shut up, let me enjoy this.

She felt an excitement she had not felt in a long time rising through her body. It started in her thighs, crept into her belly and shot up to her chest, she felt it in her heart, in her breasts, it raced to her face. Alarmed, she glanced at Amy, who was blushing and smiling and licking her lips. Chloe felt warm, too. And she felt herself smile for the first time that day.

There was something else. Her expectation of what she expected to see had been defeated, and this confused her. Something in the room was out of joint, something in her brain said *uh-oh*.

Her heart, so far, was not telling her anything. But from somewhere in her person she was hearing *let's go with this, give it a chance, put the grumbling on hold, see what this tie-dimple man can do. And you can watch.*

"Nelson," Jon Rider said, nodding to the Rockwell Morton team. "Brian. Miss Oona, we meet again."

"Hello again, Jon," Oona said. She looked a little pink behind her can't-help-it smile.

He moved down the conference room table to Lisa and held out his hand. "Ah, the Thrower of the Big Flame. No, don't get up. Lovely to see you again, pleased to see no permanent damage from our last encounter." Lisa took his hand but didn't seem ready for the heartiness of the shake he gave it. She opened her mouth but nothing came out.

"Hi, I'm Jessica," her associate said when Lisa failed to introduce her.

"Pleasure, Jessica," he said, and shook her hand.

"Please say hello to Chloe Manning with Barbiron," Nelson said, "and her assistant Amy West."

Jon turned to face Chloe.

Chloe was accustomed to looking into the faces of powerful men, of wealthy men, of handsome men. Some of those faces wanted things from her, some of the faces just wanted her. But she wasn't ready for what she saw in the face of Jon Rider. She wasn't ready for it because she wasn't even sure what she was seeing.

Was he handsome, or wasn't he? *Why am I having trouble getting a fix on this guy? And why do I care?* Why couldn't she decide, why couldn't she make a judgment about this face, much less about the man behind it?

The eyes. It was the eyes. The eyes demanded her entire attention. She could see nothing else. They were ice-blue;

they seemed to possess their own secret illumination, something smoldering that lit them from deep within his person. They spoke, they demanded she listen: She felt kindness, humor, serenity – and *seeing*. They looked right into her. They – he – seemed to know her.

She wrested her focus away from his eyes and she sensed he was doing the same with hers. There he was. The kindness and gentleness and knowing she saw in his eyes was of a piece with his entire person. His face, which she now felt fully for the first time, was a sonata of symmetrical even features, not too big, not too small, but assembled into a manface that could top a president, a model, a prophet, or a lover. He wasn't handsome. *Handsome* doesn't describe men like this man.

He was beautiful.

She became aware that he was holding out his hand. She took it, matched his grip as she did with men, held it a beat, two beats longer than she normally allowed a new man to touch her in greeting.

"Of course I recognized Ms. Manning," he said. "I read your interview in last month's *Chicago Business Reporter*. I thought your observations on how tax incentives backfire in the long run were quite astute, and, I must say, original. It's a great honor to meet you, and I'm happy to try to lend a hand today. A pleasure to meet you too, Amy." He shook Amy's hand.

Amy said, "Oh, yes, thank you, me too, a pleasure, I mean, to you too, a pleasure back to you."

Chloe thought, *I know just how you feel.*

"I thought this place was business casual these days,"

Chloe said. Both Nelson and Brian were in shirtsleeves and tieless.

"I'm business," Jon said, "but I'm not casual."

"Good answer," Chloe said. *He gets it. When everyone looks J. Crew, Neiman Marcus rules the room. Hey, that's **my** strategy.* "The meter's ticking. Let's get down to it."

Jon Rider sat down and the room seemed to exhale. Chloe sat back, relaxed, waited. *Something is going to happen here. This guy is going to shake something loose out of all this legal gobbledygook.*

"Brian brought me up to speed a little," he said, "and I'll tell you the same thing my colleagues here told you, something I can tell you from my own experience, and that is that Lisa is a great lawyer. I'm happy to give it a whirl as we sit here today, but I can't be encouraging that we're going to find the golden key to unlock this case with just a couple of pleadings to review."

"I've been thoroughly advised on Lisa's reputation and skills," Chloe said. Good lord, she had never seen lawyers so reluctant to steal business from another. "I just want to make sure we've considered everything there is to consider."

"All right," Jon said. "Fair enough, as long as we all know how we're feeling about this. Anyone got hard copy of the complaint?"

Brian slid a copy of the Philbricks' complaint across to him. Jon started to read through it, slowly at first. He looked at the pages as though he were thinking of something else, not even really seeing the words on the page. *Oh, great*, Chloe thought, *he's got nothing*. But after less than a minute he looked up and asked for a copy of the answer

Lisa had filed. He placed it side by side with the complaint and paged through them together, checking to see how Barbiron had responded to the individual allegations. His face did not betray much reaction, although occasionally he would frown a little, or an eyebrow would hop. A couple of times he looked up and stared at nothing in particular. A few times he squinted as he read.

Squinting, Chloe thought, *and staring. That's good. That's at least something.*

The room was quiet as Jon continued to flip back and forth in the complaint and answer, comparing pages, reading certain things more than once. He seemed oblivious to the fact that seven other people were in the room with nothing to do other than check their phones and watch him.

Chloe watched him.

As she studied him now sitting across the table from her, the excitement that had overtaken her earlier returned in a more refined and controlled way. This man had something. What it was, she wasn't quite sure. Wrong – she wasn't sure at all. Whatever it was, it was something that reached out and offered to fill a need that was deeper than she had known, a need she had buried and which she could not describe. But now that she felt it, she knew she'd had it for a long time.

It made her a little uncomfortable. She was accustomed to being in control and knowing what was coming next, knowing it before other people did. But she tamped down her nerves and let herself bask in the unexplainable craziness of it, enjoying the feeling of release of command while she gazed at him.

He spoke without raising his eyes from the papers. "The complaint makes reference to an Exhibit A, which is apparently the construction contract. Do we have a copy of that here?"

"It's 80-some pages," Lisa said. "I didn't bring it."

"We didn't print it out this morning," Brian said. "With all of its schedules and attachments it's around 150 pages."

"I have it here on the tablet," Amy said. She tap-tap-tapped the screen and handed the tablet across to him.

"You're going to sit here and read all that?" Lisa said.

"No," Jon said. "Just looking at a couple of things." He looked carefully at the first page and scrolled quickly to the end. "It says in the complaint that the Philbricks had to file for bankruptcy after you fired them. Is that right?"

"I think so," Chloe said. "Yes, I believe they did go BK sometime later. But they were already a bum outfit when I hired them, I didn't drive them —"

"Oona," Jon said, "get into the Northern District bankruptcy records and see if you can pull up a docket for Robert and Lorna Philbrick."

While Oona typed on her laptop, he said: "Just thought of something. Rockwell Morton hasn't been hired, has it?" Nelson shook his head.

"Ms. Manning," Jon said, "do you have a dollar?"

"I have lots of dollars," she said. "But none with me." It had been a long time since she carried cash.

Amy was already digging in her purse. "I got a dollar," she said, handing one to Chloe.

"Good," Jon said. "We'll keep this nice and narrow. Ms. Manning, say to Nelson, 'Will your firm represent Barbiron through the end of the day today for the purpose of assist-ing in the Philbrick case?'" She repeated the phrase.

Nelson picked up Jon's intention and said yes.

Chloe handed Nelson the dollar. "You're hired," she said.

"Great, thanks," Jon said. "Sorry for the little playlet there. Just wanted to make absolutely sure we had formally established an attorney-client relationship so that any kind of advice we gave you, and anything you would say to us, will be privileged and confidential. And we're not stepping on Lisa's exquisitely polished toes any more than we already are by having this meeting in the first place." He smiled at Lisa, who seemed not to take offense at the toe remark; in fact, she smiled. "Brian, you checked for any conflict of interest before today's meeting? Good."

"Got it," Oona said.

Jon walked around the table and viewed the Philbricks' online bankruptcy docket over Oona's shoulder. "This should just take a minute or so." He took her mouse and scrolled. When he found what he wanted, he clicked it open and scrolled down. "Here we go," he said. He looked at the screen for a few seconds and pointed to something he saw there. Oona looked at him and nodded. He did a couple of CTRL-F searches in the document. He closed the document and scrolled the docket for a few more seconds, then straightened.

"I need to check on something," he said. "Might not be a bad time to break for a few minutes." He picked up the complaint and walked out of the room.

Within thirty seconds, all five women were adjusting

their hair and makeup in the ladies' room mirror. Nobody spoke.

⊷

"Sorry to keep you all waiting," Jon said, although he was only gone for about ten minutes. He had left his jacket in his office.

Chloe thought: He's found something.

Lisa looked unwell.

He's found something and I'm liking this no-jacket look quite a lot. Why don't you go out again and come back with your tie loosened and your cuffs rolled up a little? Or maybe no shirt.

"Couple of interesting things," he said. "First, this contract, Exhibit A to the complaint, contains a universal mandatory arbitration provision. Buried in the back in the miscellaneous provisions. This case should not have been brought in a trial court at all; their lawyer should have served a demand for arbitration. I saw in the answer that we did not raise this as a defense, but I assume Lisa has a good reason for not raising it, probably because she's magic with juries and preferred a courtroom trial to arbitration. Certainly a rational strategy."

No, Chloe thought, she just missed it. This Jon Rider is just being nice. Which is nice, him being nice. But this was at least something, more than they had a half-hour earlier. She sat up and scooted her chair closer to the table.

Lisa nodded. "Right," she said, "exactly." Damned Jessica, her job to read these things carefully, even the fine print and the boilerplate stuff. Lisa glanced at Jessica, who was starting to mist up.

Jon found himself addressing his colleagues and Lisa. He even turned to Amy once or twice. He avoided eye contact with Chloe. He could feel her mind moving with his; he wasn't going to interrupt that connection with anything like the mutual eye-zap they'd had when they met. Even if she didn't know exactly where he was going, he felt that she had climbed aboard and strapped in.

"In any event," he continued, "that would not get rid of our claim. At best it would just move the case to an arbitrator instead of a judge and jury. So let's get to something more important." He held up the complaint for them to see. "First, see that the plaintiffs are listed as Robert and Lorna Philbrick."

"Those are their names," Lisa said, irritated.

"Right," Jon said. "But look at the contract." He held it up. "The contract is with "Robert and Lorna Philbrick, *LLC* – limited liability company. Obviously, like most businesses, they have organized themselves as a company to limit their personal liability for their actions as a business. So if we look only at what we have before us, we can say at a minimum that the wrong entities have filed this case. Based only on the evidence of the complaint and the contract, it is clear that the people who filed the breach of contract complaint were not parties to the contract Chloe and Barbiron are supposed to have breached."

Lisa started to say something, but he stopped her. "But let's assume that the right party, the company itself, had filed the complaint. Maybe naming only Robert and

Lorna personally was just an oversight and the lawyer really intended to show the plaintiff as Robert and Lorna Philbrick, LLC. Easy mistake to make, and it would be easy for him to correct even if we filed a motion to dismiss on this ground. If you look up the bankruptcy records as Oona just did, you find that, in fact, the bankruptcy was filed by the company, and not by them personally."

"So what?" Lisa said.

"So this," Jon continued. "When you seek protection under the bankruptcy laws, you have to list your assets because those assets now more or less belong to your creditors. The assets can be converted to cash to pay the people to whom the bankrupt owes money. Now in this complaint against Barbiron, they're claiming that you breached the contract and that they made a written claim, a demand letter from their lawyer, against Barbiron before they – rather, their company – filed for bankruptcy."

"That's true, they did," Chloe said. "We told them to pound sand." *He's got something on the line*, she thought. *I almost know . . . .*

"We sure as hell did," Lisa said. "I might even have used the phrase 'pound sand.'"

"The point is," Jon said, "they believed that their company had a claim against you at the time they filed for bankruptcy, even though they hadn't filed a lawsuit yet. It's called an unliquidated claim, a claim that hasn't yet resulted in any cash coming into the company."

"I'm still saying so what," Lisa said.

Jon ignored her. "Here's the important point: You might intuitively think that their problem with Barbiron would be a liability for them. But it's just the opposite at this point. Even though they had not yet filed a lawsuit or received any money" – he paused – "that claim against Barbiron is actually an asset of their company. It is worth something to creditors even though not yet reduced to cash; the possibility of a future cash recovery has value to the company, and therefore to creditors, even though no money has come in at the time of bankruptcy. There's a specific place in bankruptcy filings for listing the bankrupt's unliquidated claims, and when Oona and I went to that section of their schedules, what do you think we found?"

Oh, man. "Nothing," Chloe heard herself say. "You found nothing."

That feeling in her thighs . . . .

"We found nothing," Oona said. "No mention of a claim against Barbiron."

Jon aimed his eyes away from Chloe. *She's almost there,* he thought. *She knows where I'm going. She's come along.* "No mention of a claim against Barbiron," he said. "But that's a gigantic problem for them, because you can't swear one thing to the bankruptcy court and your creditors – that you don't have a claim, with the intention to mislead them – and then, after the bankruptcy is over, swear just the opposite to the trial court when you sue – that you do have a claim. They didn't tell their creditors about their claim because they wanted to keep any future recovery all for themselves after the bankruptcy was over and not have to satisfy their creditors with it. Basically, the trial court will view a bankrupt's failure to list its claim with the bankruptcy court as a waiver of that claim – an admission that it doesn't have a claim at all. It's got a fancy lawyer name, judicial estoppel."

Chloe sat up even straighter. *I knew it. Yes, go, go you Rider-man.*

"But wait," Lisa said, sensing she was in as much trouble as the Philbricks at the hands of this damned Rider. "This is all hypothetical. You started out assuming that the company is the plaintiff here, which it isn't. Maybe they assigned that claim from the company to themselves personally, formally transferred the claim from the LLC to themselves. They could do that. Which would make Robert and Lorna personally the proper plaintiffs in the lawsuit, and they wouldn't have been the bankrupt party with the problem you're claiming."

"Lisa, you are one hundred percent correct – actually, only fifty percent. It's possible they did execute an assignment of the claim from the company to themselves personally. But no can do in this case. Companies that are insolvent – unable to pay their creditors – are not allowed to move assets out of the company even if they haven't filed for bankruptcy yet. That would be what's called a fraudulent transfer, a transfer that cheats creditors. It's like trying to hide cash during a bankruptcy so your creditors can't get it. A transfer like that is illegal and voidable by the court and by creditors under the Illinois Uniform Fraudulent Transfer Act and the U.S. Bankruptcy Code. It's almost like it never happened. The company is the only proper plaintiff."

Chloe started to fidget in her chair. *Ride it, ride it, you Rider-man.*

"But Lisa, you're absolutely right to raise that

possibility," he said as she slumped a little. "Who knows what really happened here? I wondered whether there's some explanation for all of this, something they can correct with an amended pleading or something. Maybe there was some special order in the bankruptcy court that let them bring the claim personally outside the bankruptcy. Maybe they had some side deal with the creditors to pursue that claim separately at their expense and split the recovery. You never know. I didn't see anything like that on the docket when Oona and I were reviewing it, but we were skimming, could have missed it, or maybe it didn't make it into the docket.

"I know the Philbricks' lawyer a little," he went on. "I had a case with him a couple of years ago. Decent guy, okay lawyer, high-volume practice. Maybe we missed something, or . . . maybe he did."

"Oh my god," Chloe said. "Oh my god."

There she goes, Jon thought. *She knows what I did. No wonder she can sell chainsaws to debutantes.*

"Oh my god."

Everyone stared at her. "You OK?" Nelson asked.

"You called him," Chloe said.

She's got it, Jon thought. *Something cooking under those blond waves.*

"I called him."

"Oh my god," Chloe said. "Oh my god."

She's all the way there, Jon thought.

"Chloe?"

"Oh my god," Chloe said. "You –"

"The case is over," Jon said.

"Oh my god," Chloe said. "God *damn*." Amy was the closest high five and they smacked each other one. "I *knew* it."

"I told him we'd been retained to consult on the case and then sketched out for him what I just told you. He had never thought to check the bankruptcy documents themselves and agreed that if they didn't disclose the Barbiron claim on the schedule after already making a written demand on Barbiron, they were sunk. There was no assignment of the claim from the company to the Philbricks, just sloppy pleading in the case caption. And he knew they couldn't properly have transferred the claim out of the company to themselves and that if they kept pressing the claim in this lawsuit he'd have all their creditors banging on his door screaming fraud. Not something he signed up for, and a loser to boot. I started to say something about sending him a demand to dismiss the case or face sanctions for filing a frivolous lawsuit, but he told me not to bother. He said he'd double-check the bankruptcy filings, but if what I said checked out, he'd advise the Philbricks and file a voluntary dismissal within the next day or so. I sent him a couple of cases on point in case he had second thoughts."

"You got rid of the case without telling me?" Lisa almost shouted. She immediately sensed the absurdity of her remark and sank back in her chair.

The room was silent except for Chloe's squeaking chair. She could not keep still. *I'm the CEO of a big-deal company and I'm bouncing on my ass like a schoolgirl who just watched Jon Bon Jovi write a song and sing it to her.*

"Nice work, Jon," Nelson said. Although he seemed a little sad they weren't going to get the case.

"He sees dead people," Brian said.

"I thought you might dig something out," Oona said, pleased that she had been the one to suggest bringing Jon in.

Jon seemed not to notice the stunned faces – Lisa and Jessica stunned into mortification, Chloe and Amy stunned into delight.

"Anything else?" Jon said. He stood and reached to shake hands with Chloe and Amy. "You owe Amy a buck," he said as he took Chloe's hand. He tried not to let his gaze linger on her as their hands slid slowly apart.

He nodded to Lisa and the associate – Jenisse? "Really nice to see you again, Lisa. Thanks for being cool with all of this, you're a class act. Anyone could have missed that stuff. Maybe we could catch up sometime?"

And he walked out of the conference room.

Chloe did not notice the slight pause that became a stumble, and his turn to look back into the conference room, finding her for just the slightest moment before the glass door automatically whooshed shut behind him.

"What just happened?" Chloe said. *Come back, Rider-man, and bring your eyes with.*

"Chloe," Lisa said.

"Later," Chloe said.

᷂

Jon Rider hoped his quick departure following the bombshell did not seem too melodramatic, but he worried that it did. He did not care about personal praise and did not feel the need to stick around to receive it. In fact, it made him uncomfortable. He was happy to leave Nelson, Brian, and Oona to soak up the client's redirected gratitude, and maybe soak up a Barbiron engagement for other work. And he had no desire to show up The Flamethrower any more than she and her poor associate – what was her name, Jessamyn? – had already been shown up.

But that was not why he got out of there as promptly and as graciously as possible.

He had not wanted to say anything, do anything, or permit any part of his face or body to react or move in any way, that would betray how – excited? disturbed? enthralled? frightened? – he had been upon experiencing the shimmering intellect wrapped in the exquisite packaging of Chloe Manning.

He thought he had hidden it pretty well. He had talked. He had looked at everyone but her. He had kept the jokes to a minimum. He had gotten out of there. Gotten out of there twice. Almost fell down only once.

But the only thing that getting out of there accomplished was to free his mind to consider what to do about the rubble now cluttering his always-orderly emotions.

∾

Chloe thanked Nelson and Brian, and gave Oona a hug. She told Nelson she'd be in touch soon, told him to keep an eye on his texts.

In the elevator lobby, Jessica was on the verge of a full-on cry.

"We all have bad days, girlfriend," Chloe said. "Look,

those three big Rockwell hotshots in there had the same documents all morning and they didn't think of any of that stuff, either. It's Friday. Suck it up, go home and have a margarita, make sad eyes at your boyfriend and get some comfort."

This prompted a new round of choking back tears. "OK, forget the boyfriend, just have an extra marg."

"Chloe, I –" Lisa said.

"You and I both need a stiff one or two ourselves," Chloe said. "Did anyone press 'down'?"

≼

Chloe had conducted the meeting as the brass-tacks executive who demanded results without emotion or a lot of fooling around. But something had changed for her in that room. She was leaving it, she felt – was this possible? – a different person. Still a tough woman of business, but one a little more welcoming to emerging, long-suppressed feelings, one willing to offer a little more good will all around. Even toward lawyers. Even toward Lisa.

That man. That man with the on-demand dynamism softened by his everyman ease – so they make them like that, still.

The thought pleased her.

As they walked out of the building, Chloe noticed that the Chicago morning breeze had risen to wind, and shifted.

CHAPTER 4

JON RIDER RETURNED TO HIS OFFICE AND STARED

JON RIDER RETURNED to his office and stared. He did not stare at anything in particular. There was nothing much in his bare office to stare at.

He was confused.

What just happened?

He, Jon Rider, was the King of Being Squared Away. He was the man in control, thinking through from the beginning everything that required thinking through, seeing the end as clearly as the beginning, and achieving clarity and resolution while others were not even sure what the problem was, or whether there was even a problem.

Emotions, you sit over there in the corner and be quiet.

But his emotions were not obeying. They were running around the room like unruly children, making noise and running into the furniture, knocking over his orderly thoughts and shattering them into chaos.

Being confused was a very foreign and uncomfortable feeling for Jon Rider.

But not only was he confused, he could not put into words why he was confused, except it had something to do with that woman who drank in their mutual gaze – he might have gotten a little drunk himself – and knew before any of the lawyers in the room what he had done.

He thought about that, how quickly she had seen the endgame, and how excited it made her. And how excited that had made him.

So – what? What's to be confused about? Gorgeous women can be smart. What did that have to do with him? He wasn't star-struck by the lovely Manning; he was pretty sure of that. In fact, as he thought about her celebrity and fortune, his memory of their connection – if that's what it was – began to recede, the day's drama beginning to segue into a delicious daytime fatigue.

So he sat in a back-neutral position in his squared-away mesh-backed office chair with the adjustable lumbar support, folded his arms over his squared-away tie with its squared-away dimple, placed his feet flat on the floor, and, having composed his physical person in a way that neutralized all potential ergonomic stressors that might interrupt his concentration, he proceeded to concentrate on nothing in particular, and was out for his usual twenty minutes.

✎

When he snapped to, he discovered that he was looking at an empty Google home page, that big white space with the colorful letters embedded in a cute daily animation and the empty address bar with its blinking cursor, tapping its foot and waiting patiently for him to tell it what information he needed.

He wasn't sure.

That woman.

A stunner. Those blond waves were real. The fine pale eyebrows told the tale.

Cheekbones – custom-designed by – hell, there had to be a God – to support those vast deep green anime eyes.

She had never stood during the meeting. He didn't care. Didn't need to see her body. He wasn't a boob guy. Within reason. Wasn't a tiny waist guy, wasn't an ass guy. Ditto, ditto. Liked the leg, but the woman didn't have to have endless stems or supermodel calves. Just not too calf-like.

Oh, he liked beautiful women. Fact was, he liked women generally. Liked to be around them. Liked to look at them. Liked to love them. But – within reason – he did not require cinematic good looks.

Looks were not an issue with Chloe Manning no matter what the conference room tabletop had been concealing. He'd seen the whole package on the covers of *Forbes* and *Chicago* magazine and even flipped through a *Cosmopolitan* at the grocery checkout line. Nice interview and photo essay on her days of work and nights of – well, more work, and the occasional dress-up hangout with the girlfriends. Her references to men were playful and teasing – *Cosmo* stuff – but guarded.

The whole package was thoroughbred.

And there she had been in his very conference room, one of those women who is more magnetic and lovely in person than even after the most artful lies of lighting, makeup, and software.

But the world is full of beautiful women. Big city like Chicago, they were not hard to find. Apparently, he thought, neither was he. When he got together with friends at the local watering holes, back when he was doing that, attractive women found their way over to him. Within the past few months, friends began to set him up with women who, he had to admit, were lovely without exception. As time went by, he agreed to these dates less and less frequently, finally declining them altogether. A couple of the foxy local TV news reporters were always calling him for on-air interviews on legal topics, and they had both suggested a post-broadcast cocktail more than once. Anna Kendrick had stepped on his foot at Gibsons. A young actress famous from fantasy movies approached him at the Trump International bar and asked in a most charming British accent if he might direct her to the Statue of Liberty.

"Take Wabash north to the Ontario connector to 94 south and 90 east, flip over to 80 when you get to Youngstown" he told her. "Set your odometer for about 800 miles, only about six states away. Don't drive into the harbor. Look up, can't miss it."

"I see," she giggled. "I was misinformed."

He appreciated all the beautiful women, was flattered by their attention.

But female interest was not a rare event in his life, so he was not the sort to be dazzled by fame or celebrity. Or even beauty.

Her, though. Something. Something else.

Brains.

Liked brains.

Ah, well, he wasn't going to see her again.

So he shooed those emotions back to the corner, and satisfied himself that the mess they made was a temporary thing. Time to tidy up.

Right.

Now what?

The Google address bar was in no hurry. Take your time, the blinking cursor said. You know what you want.

∽

Some days, he thought, the gods of law rained down their blessings on the receptive practitioner. He had a reputation as one of their favored children, but he believed it was undeserved. Other lawyers had complete responsibility for cases, for a lot of cases at the same time. They were required to draft pleadings, take depositions, go to hearings, argue motions, butt heads with opposing counsel, keep clients happy and witnesses in line, write briefs, and go to trial. And in addition to all that, find time to go out and schmooze clients for new business, and to bring new clients to the firm.

Jon Rider used to do these things, and he was good at them. He made partner quickly at Rockwell Morton. But in the last couple of years he had managed to shift all of his primary case responsibility to others. He quit trying to develop new clients. The firm was not happy about his withdrawal from these most visible activities that bring value to a law firm, but they indulged him after Amelia died.

After Amelia died . . . .

He lost his taste for the daily battles that used to engage him. He found new sources of satisfaction in the mentoring of younger attorneys and friendly support of the secretaries and legal assistants who really kept the place running. His interest in the practice of law acquired a scholarly bent not often found in busy law firms, but as time went by his colleagues began to value his reflective attitude to case strategy. Brian teased him to his partners that Jon would strip to a loincloth in his office, fire up a few sticks of incense, chant Steely Dan lyrics, and immerse himself in the minutiae of a case until he achieved Zen-like enlightenment on procedural arcana or a lie hidden deep in an opponent's reasoning.

And in fact, he did become known as something like a guru other lawyers would come to for advice on difficult cases, or when they encountered something they had not seen before. Trial partners began to invite him to affiliate with them on cases more like a consultant than a working lawyer. He separated himself from the biases of an advocate, identified unjustified assumptions, and decluttered a case until its outline of evidence and law was pared to the bone.

He didn't consider himself any smarter than Brian or Oona or Nelson or any of his colleagues, or even that crazy Flamethrower (who was actually quite intelligent, he thought); he just had the luxury of time to dissect cases and read the entrails. Sometimes they spoke to him and revealed their secrets; sometimes they just stank. Today those few pages he reviewed had opened up to him like spring's first peony.

That he had seen the problems in the case almost instantly was not, he believed, the result of any inherent braininess. He had cultivated a habit of close observation, a luxury his very smart and very overworked colleagues – heck, even media stars like Lisa the Flamethrower – seldom had. Meanwhile, he could sift through the fine print and overlooked verbiage to find the booboos. Today, for reasons he could not identify, the booboos just seemed to lift from the pages and gather before his eyes.

In the end, it was all about booboos. Who made them, who found them, who found them first.

Jon Rider continued to stare at the Google page. He thought about booboos. People thought he was a squared-away guy. They were wrong. The booboos, they were many.

Take today, for instance.

The professional way, the classy way to have presented the arguments he saw, would have been to explain directly to Chloe Manning what he had found and why it was help-ful to Barbiron's cause, looking her in the eye. That would have accomplished exactly what Ms. Manning wanted, to move the case off square one and toward a favorable resolution. She might have hired Rockwell Morton to co-counsel on the matter, but in any event the firm would have put on exactly the right kind of show to attract the next case Barbiron generated. A near slam-dunk defense in a multi-million-dollar case for a buck, and it wasn't even her buck. He could have shown courtly graciousness to Lisa the Flamethrower, offering to provide her with case support for his argument for her own use in browbeating Philbricks' counsel to get rid of the case.

Those would have been the actions of a pro. Those would have been the actions of a classy guy.

There was another name for what Jon Rider was that day.

Show-off.

He was showing off for the beautiful, brilliant Chloe Manning. Without thinking about it, really without even knowing it, his body and brain instinctively focused on giving this woman even more than she bargained for. His actions addressed the room, but his aim found Chloe's frustration, and a need he saw in her eyes.

He knew he had made an impression on her with his no-prisoners attack.

What he didn't know was why he had tried to do so.

He really had read the interview with her in the *Chicago Business Reporter*. And he really had been impressed with her views on tax incentives.

And, today, with the beauty behind which she slyly camouflaged those brains.

He felt honored to have been in her presence.

He felt something else, something stirring within him, that didn't have anything to do with honor.

A quiet little voice, barely perceived over the riot of feelings the day's events had produced, told him that today's impulsive grandstanding might well prove, in time, to have been a booboo.

Was he about to make another one?

In the Google address box, he typed "Chloe Manning."

It reported 8,090,000 results in 0.43 seconds.

∽

He closed quickly out of his Chloe Manning search results – he had been scrolling through many screens of Chloe Manning thumbnails in Google Images — when he sensed Nelson Gilles and Brian Accardo at his office door.

"Quite a performance," Nelson said.

"I'm remorseful," Jon said. "I should have handled it less dramatically, and more diplomatically with Lisa and – what was her associate's name? — sitting there."

"Jennifer," Nelson said.

"Jessica, I think," Brian said.

"Jessica, Jennifer, got a feeling she won't be an associate for long," Nelson said.

"Anyway," Jon said, "if I hadn't been so all-fired eager to try to hit a home run with that bankruptcy information, Manning might have hired us for the case, even if only to wrap it up alongside Lisa."

"I wouldn't worry about that," Nelson said. "Chloe was pretty much blown away by your, shall we say, direct approach. I'm certain we're going to get some work from Barbiron, probably the next case of any substance." He dug in his pocket for his vibrating phone. "Ha. She's already texted me to set up a lunch. I'm going to set her up with our corporate finance guys as well."

"Half our corporate finance guys are not guys," Brian said.

"Yeah, well," Nelson said, "I don't care where they fall on the gender spectrum, such as it is these days, but a goddam eunuch can bill close to a grand an hour for major deals, and you know Barbiron's got to have some in the hopper."

"She put that Flamethrower in a bad spot," Jon said. "Wonder if that's how she treats all her professionals, playing them off against each other."

Nelson snorted. "Couldn't have happened to a nicer weapon," he said. "Anyway, I'll worry about that after I've sent Barbiron a few invoices."

"Ah, Lisa's all right," Jon said. "If you let her know you don't take her as seriously as she pretends to take herself, she drops some of the nonsense. And she's an absolute Satan with juries. She's, uh, gotten to know a few judges along the way, too. You should give some thought to having Rockwell Morton merge with her firm."

"You still say that after you found three gigantic holes in her case analysis in less than five minutes?" Nelson said.

"We didn't find them, either," Brian said.

"You sweet on that Flamethrower, Rider?" Nelson asked. "You teased her in there and she didn't even flinch."

"No," Jon said.

"Anyway," Nelson said, "thanks for waving your magic wand on this thing, they're going to love that story at the executive committee meeting tomorrow. And, by the way . . ."

Jon noticed a small smile crossing Nelson's face.

"I got the distinct impression that Ms. Chloe Manning, Chief Executive Officer and Chairman of the Board of Barbiron Industries, Inc., and world-class Chicago hot, was extremely grateful for your contribution. And when I say extremely grateful, I mean *extremely* grateful in a way that one might think could lead to expressions of extreme gratitude if played correctly."

"Don't be ungallant," Brian said. "Manning's a classy dame."

"What'd I say?" Nelson said. But he chuckled.

"She was grateful it only cost her a dollar," Jon said. "I barely spoke to the woman and besides, with any luck she'll become a client and her gratitude will be in the form of settling her invoices within 30 days. And those anti-sexual harassment training videos Human Resources makes us all watch discourage getting too close with clients in a non-professional sense."

"You watch those? The firm has been known to wink at relationships with clients in the name of good client relationships," Nelson said, "whatever the hell I just said. Discretion is the better part of profitability."

Nelson left. Brian came in and shut the door. "Nelson's not wrong," he said. "The whole room could feel it. That's not an easy woman to impress, she came in loaded for bear and after you left she was grinning like a chessy cat and thanked Oona and me and even Nelson, who wasn't entirely sure he knew who you were at first, about five times each for bringing you in. She didn't even seem upset that Lisa had billed her damned near forty thousand dollars to accomplish nothing."

Jon Rider did not respond.

"Well?"

"Well what?"

"Well, what are you going to do about it?"

"What am I going to do about what?"

"My god," Brian said, "you dig instant victory out of the fine print but you can't see a chance for romance with the most sought-after woman in Chicago whom you just dazzled with your special brand of razzle."

"About that," Jon said. "I should have discussed this with you and Oona and Nelson before I – before I – "

Brian laughed. "Before you made five of the best lawyers in the city, including your best friend me, look like bar exam rejects. Don't worry about it. We expect rabbit-out-of-the-hat stuff from you, and you obliged in spectacular fashion."

"Still, I – "

"Come on," Brian said. "I didn't just get off the banana boat. You were trying to impress the lovely Manning. If I were single, and if I were smart, and if I could even remember how to tie a tie, I would have been riding my bike with no hands in front of her, too."

So it had been that obvious. "She is impressive."

"So impressive you nearly fell over leaving the conference room."

Jon thought he had covered that bit of gracelessness pretty well. Wrong again.

"Look," Jon said, "it was a fun moment, but it's hardly the foundation for a relationship, and I'd feel like a sleaze trying to leverage a favorable legal result into a date. She doesn't owe me a thing for doing my job. More to the point, I have no reason to think she has the slightest interest in me. And let's not forget that Barbiron is probably going to become a client of the firm. Nelson may not take the don't-do-the-client thing seriously, but I do."

"Rider," Brian said, "don't get all dreary on me. Men all over the country drool over that woman."

"Why would I want a woman with a bunch of guys' drool all over her?"

"You're evading the question."

"You're asking a question aimed way wide of me."

"OK," Brian said, "now you're being deliberately obtuse. You can't deny the attraction, and you can't deny that it was mutual."

Jon was silent. "I don't know," he said.

Brian leaned in closer. "Look, man, I'm not going to patronize you or try to tell you I know how you feel. I don't, I can't. And I wouldn't do a thing that would diminish Amelia's memory. But time passes, brother. Time passes, and denying yourself a chance at happiness, or even a chance for some fun or even some drama in your life – it doesn't do you any good and, if I may be so presumptuous, it only turns her memory into a negative thing."

Jon flared, softened.

"You're right," he said. "You're right. You're right. I should . . . start getting out there again, I guess. But what a drag, that dance where you circle around each other, each trying to figure the other out."

"Attaboy," Brian said.

"But we're talking about starting over beginning with Chloe Manning! That's like coming back after falling off a horse by trying to mount a tiger."

"Interesting imagery," Brian said. "But if the tiger has

shown some interest in this mounting process you're talking about . . . ."

"Look," Jon said, "she's a beautiful woman. A man
would have to be crazy not to be attracted to her. I am not
crazy and I am attracted to her. It's not just her looks. Hell,
it's not even primarily her looks. There are looks all over
the place in this city."

"Yeah," Brian said, a little wistfully.

"And not to brag, but from time to time I attract the
attention of said looks, although I must say, Chloe Manning
is singularly striking. This is going to sound politically correct, which you know I am not, but in fact the intrigue
here is her intelligence. She's quick, and I think she's kind
of deep, in an entrepreneurial sort of way."

"I don't know exactly how entrepreneurial deepness
would get anyone's pants dancing, but –"

"You know what I mean," Jon said.

"Yes," Brian said. "Your type. Life of the mind stuff."
Amelia, Brian thought.

"Right, but her intellect is aimed at practical things,
building things, making life better for her customers which
makes life better for her shareholders, her employees, and,
let's be clear, herself."

"And you, if you don't screw things up."

"Well now, there's the problem, isn't it?" Jon said. "How
not to screw things up, when you don't even know where
the screwdriver is or whether you need a Phillips-head or
a flathead or how to get the damned screw started in the
screw-hole."

"Another vivid metaphor," Brian said.

"The point is that aside from its womanlessness – womanlessness? – my life is good. I think about things I like to think about. I do what I like to do. Along with work, those things take up all my time. I don't look around for stuff to do. My clothes are arranged in my closet in a certain way, which may seem fussy, but I like it that way. And they take up the whole closet. In my three-car garage I have two cars, three bikes, a workbench, and an unassembled foosball table. No other car, bike, bench, or foosball table will fit in there."

Brian looked up from his phone. "Huh. 'Womanlessness' is a word."

"Listen to me. Until an hour ago, my life was not confused. I have a budget and I keep my spending within that budget. And I have an emotional budget and it's balanced, too. And now, here comes along this dazzling comet of a woman streaking across my field of vision and as she whooshes by I'm completely blinded by her tail."

"That tail can definitely cause blindness," Brian said. "It's like if Medusa had a nice ass."

"Medusa turned people to stone."

"Well, if you're turned to stone you're blind, right?"

Jon ignored him. "Did you hear what I said? I'm confused. I don't like being confused. Have you ever heard me say I was confused? Have you ever known me to be confused? It's a very uncomfortable feeling for me."

"Oh, we can't have discomfort, now, can we, not in a grown man, poor guy." Brian made a dismissive farting sound with his mouth. "Don't be such a puss. And I don't think she's short on her own closet and garage space."

"I'm serious. I feel like a kid who hangs out with his buddies but then some girl looks at him and he's forced to reconsider the concept of fun. I'm messed up like that. Ten minutes, ten freaking minutes and I'm scared to death I'll have to risk having some hot feelings. I'm all . . . disordered. Also . . ."

"Also . . . also . . . ?"

Jon Rider smiled. "Also kinda thrilled and turned on and excited and thinking I might need a haircut."

"Your hair is perfect," Brian said. "What are you going to do?"

"Dunno. Think about it, I guess. What I do, right? What would you do?"

"Do like the Euro space agency did. Send a probe to land on that comet."

"Christ," Jon said, "you one-upped me on my own metaphor."

"We've made progress here," Brian said. "We've gone from 'you gotta be kidding' to 'blinding ass.'"

"Tail," Jon said. "Blinding comet tail."

"Whatever," Brian said. "As long as I can watch. I want to watch. The two smokinest-hot people in Chicago about to collide like elementary particles at Fermilab, who knows what kind of quarks you two will throw off?"

"Let me think about it. I don't see a clear path to some kind of date. And I also need to get past the ickyness of it seeming like I'm seeking a payoff for getting rid of the case."

"Don't think about it too long. Comets streak across the sky, flash that tail, then they're gone. Strike while the metaphor is hot."

"Men and women," Jon said.

"You said it," Brian said.

"Women and men."

"A mouthful you said there."

"Women."

"Ah. Point well taken."

"Why do they make us crazy, why do they make us think about them constantly, why do they make us do stupid things, why do they constantly get in the way of our ability to accomplish great things for humanity and the world and the universe and muck up our closets?"

"Because they can," Brian said.

CHAPTER 5

LISA ORDERED A CARNEROS NAPA CAB, CHLOE SCOTCH NEAT

LISA ORDERED A Carneros Napa cab, Chloe scotch neat.

"Look at me, Gayla," Chloe told the server who had rushed to their hightop. "You pick the brand and the age. Nothing too girly, nothing too young, and nothing too cheap. In a rocks glass, please." Lisa had already given Gayla her Blue Business Amex card.

Chloe liked this place. High-end steak joint with a big bar in River North. Floor-to-ceiling windows looking out on the Chicago street scene and the Lambos and Bentleys getting a spot near the door for the price of a valet's night-making tip. The cops winking at the parking regulations. Live pianist playing the standards most nights, trio Friday and Saturday. Lots of hightops and small tables where you can do business, conduct a private flirtation, have a conversation without shouting. Keep an eye on the male talent crowding the bar. Barkeeps and servers who make enough on tips to stick with the job; they remember your name, and you remember theirs.

"Scotch?" Lisa asked. "Neat?"

"I had to schmooze a lot of purchasing officers in the early days," Chloe said. "With some of the hard cases I found it paid to know my dark liquors." She laughed at the memory. "I even initiated an after-dinner cigar once in a while, back when you could smoke in bars."

Lisa fidgeted. She needed to get some closure on the drama at Rockwell Morton. Jessica, damn.

"Chloe," Lisa said, "I really, really have to apologize. These days you have to push the work down to the younger lawyers, but I should have supervised her work more closely, I should have cross-examined her on whether she'd gone over everything with a fine-toothed comb and really thought hard enough about what defenses we might have, other avenues for attack. You have every right to be totally pissed but I'm really hoping we can keep working together, and I'm going to refund every penny —"

Chloe held her hand up *stop*.

"Jon Rider," she said.

❦

"Jon Rider," Lisa said.

"Jon Rider," Chloe said.

"Jon freakin' Rider," Lisa said.

"Jon goddam freakin' Rider," Chloe said.

"What about him?" Lisa said.

"You know him."

"Yeah," Lisa said, "I had a couple cases against him two-three years ago."

"Tell me everything."

"I don't know much. He's just one of those guys, you know?"

"One of what guys? I don't know," Chloe said.

"One of those guys who's so charming that you have to like him. Not charming like oily Latin-lover charming, but charming like, hell, I don't know, think of some charming guy you know."

"Don't think I know any," Chloe said.

"Looks you in the eye. Listens. When you say something, he actually responds rather than tries to turn it into something he's interested in. Grooms and dresses for himself, you saw that today with that gorgeous suit he had on when the rest of the office is wearing chinos and no-irons. He's also smart as hell, but he doesn't hit you over the head with it. It just comes out naturally. He seems to know something about everything, but he has a way of boiling stuff down, zeroing out all the crap. Smartest guy in the room, like they say, you know? But gentle about it. Clever funny."

"I wondered if you might be interested in him yourself," Chloe said. "For claiming not to know much about him, sounds like you're a student of the man. Are we going to have to mud wrestle for him?"

Lisa the Flamethrower laughed. "We could sell out Soldier Field for that." The pianist started to play the Coltrane intro to "All the Things You Are" while the drummer and bassist set up. "You saw him," she said. "He's a total piece. No, he's not on my radar now; but there was a time. Son of a bitch, he was just so smooth and gorgeous and quick I didn't want to have to mess with him in front of a jury. I probably settled for less in those cases than I should have. He was hell with female judges, too. I remember once we were in federal court before Anne McDaniel and the place was packed because they were going to arraign some aldermen who'd been indicted on conspiracy charges. The jury box was full of artists who were there to sketch the proceedings for the local and national news. The prisoners hadn't arrived yet so she called the civil docket first. Rider had some kind of little dink routine motion looking for an extension of time to file something or other, but I was being a jerk and refused to agree to let him file it unopposed, so he had to appear personally to present the motion to the court. We walk up there and he says, 'Your Honor, I'm delighted to see the press here to cover the presentation of my motion to extend time. The problem is that the artists are all over here to my right, but my left side's my best.' Judge McDaniel, she looks at him and says, 'Mr. Rider, I'm sitting right in front of you, and that's your best side.' He and I ended up on pretty good terms. I tried all my asshole tricks but he just laughed them off, didn't take offense, didn't rise to the bait. Most lawyers don't even want to talk to me, other than the ones who want to cheat on their wives, but he'd call me up just to check in, josh me up, soften me up to settle. The guy actually had the nerve to *tease* me, because he could sense that I kinda liked it, actually. From him, anyway. Gotta say, charm offensives usually just roll off my back, but I wouldn't have minded getting to know him better. But he's too buttoned-down for me, you know? We wouldn't have worked; he would never have argued with me, so no make-up sex. Anyway, he was married then, not that that would have made a lot of difference to –"

"Whoa," Chloe said, "I heard the m-word in there."

"He's a widower. She died a couple-three years ago. I don't know anything about her except I heard he was really beat up when she passed. Brian Accardo told me about what happened. He quit trying cases. He just kind of retreated back into the routine of Rockwell Morton and they let him do it because he problem-solves, finds the soft spots, helps people out. Like today, goddam him. Mentors youngsters like Oona. Kind of a waste of his talents, if you ask me."

"Girlfriend?"

"Don't know. Today was the first time I'd seen him since he quit running cases."

They sipped their drinks.

"Kids?" Chloe said.

Lisa shrugged. "So, with all these questions and acting like you just got asked to prom back there, I assume you're interested?"

"What's that supposed to mean?"

Lisa was checking out the men who had started to assemble around the large square bar. They left empty chairs hoping women would ask if the seats were taken.

"It's supposed to mean, and actually does mean, that it was quite apparent to those in attendance that Mr. Rider had made, shall we say, a favorable impression on the guest of honor, and that said guest would like to clean his pipes."

"Lisa! That's ridiculous," but she had to laugh.

"All right, I'm being dirty because I'm a dirty girl and also because I know you want to clean his pipes. So confess: You're more than interested, you're besotted. It happens. He got to you."

"I don't know. I do know. Yes. Yes."

They reflexively checked their phones. Chloe had a text from Amy that a messenger had delivered a personal and confidential envelope for her. The Flamethrower had seven messages from men, three of which related to pending cases, two of which suggested a drink after work, and two of which attached selfies their senders incorrectly believed to be alluring.

"God," Lisa said. "I need to change my image. There have got to be some classy pants left somewhere."

"We should at least consider whether guys are saying the same thing," Chloe said.

"Nah," Lisa said.

"It's funny," Chloe said. "It's been a long time since I've had a really great time with a guy, even longer since anything serious. I've been getting cynical lately with all the duds that seem to come my way, and I don't like myself like that. I like romance. I like men, I really do. I like being a woman and I love being a woman being loved by a fine and loving man. I mean, I do know how that feels. I've had those relationships. None of them stuck, I was probably too focused on Barbiron, or getting my MBA. I probably drove them away or neglected them. Either way the relationships ended, but I have really, really good memories with some of those guys. They were cool, they were good men. They let me go, or I let them go, really without much in the way of hard feelings. By the time I was established and ready for something permanent, I looked around, but they'd moved on. They have kids, I get Christmas cards . . . ." Her voice trailed off. "I like kids." She sipped her scotch. "Since then – maybe the herd has thinned, I just haven't had a good feeling about a man in a long time."

"Until . . . ."

"Until today!" The sadness that had crept into her speech vanished. "Ooo, I need this girlfriend talk so bad! My old crew – I don't know what happened. Time commitments, mine and theirs, boyfriends . . . just hard to schedule stuff."

"I can be a girlfriend," Lisa said. "Special girlfriend rate of zero dollars per hour."

"I just don't want the day to end," Chloe said. "I couldn't just go home and tell the cats. I need information, I need advice, I need applause, I need a slap in the face and I need another one of these." She tapped her glass.

The trio was playing "My Foolish Heart."

"Okay, but while we're on the subject of rates I still need to talk to you about what we've charged you," Lisa said. "I love girlfriend talk, but the way things turned out today – that whole thing's hanging over my head and I feel terrible and I've got to resolve it."

Chloe shook her head. "Keep the money and treat it as a credit against future fees, work it down. With all the stuff going on at Barbiron I'm thinking I'll use you as a consigliere, help me keep an eye on our legal work. Whisper in my ear if I go off track. Keep track of your time and if you want to make me happy about the arrangement give me a break on the hourly rate. I understand about Jeanette –"

"Jessica."

"Don't fire her. Our recent grads all suck too. They don't *know* anything, just a bunch of conceptual theory BS. No skills, and entitled as British royalty." She waved off that topic. "I don't want to talk about that. I want to talk about – I want to talk about – god, this sounds so girly – my feelings."

"Girly is good," The Flamethrower observed. "We can have it all, right? Woman stuff, girl stuff, and if we play our cards right we can have man stuff, or a big piece of it."

"I know, but to talk about feelings is so . . . feely."

"Feelings are good, too. I have them sometimes." The trio began to play "Meditation." "You just gonna talk about *having* feelings, or are you going to talk *about* them?"

Chloe would have been happy to talk about having feelings if it meant she could put off having to describe them. "My feelings are – *I don't know what my feelings are.* They're all over the place. God! He's good-looking and all, but when he looked at me when he came in – I want to say we made a connection, but that's not – that's not, I don't know, not *enough* of what happened. *Connection* is too gentle, like there was some reaching out between us, like we *agreed* to be attracted to each other, but it was not that. It was not that. It was – it felt – God, I'm having trouble with this – it was *primitive*, it was *elemental*, I felt this incredible male energy. All right, I'll say it, male *sexual* energy, washing over me and through me. I mean, I reacted. My body actually started to react in a sexual way. I felt that tingle up and down my body and I'll tell you, that is not the kind of tingle you want to be tingling in a business meeting. There was a look in his eye, I *know* he was feeling something, too. But I didn't feel manipulated, you know? I felt like maybe he was just reflecting my own, my own – my own enchantment back at me. Thank God we broke it off."

The Flamethrower touched their server's arm as she passed their hightop. "Bring her another Johnnie Blue. And one for me."

"I make it sound all swelling violins and breakers on the beach," Chloe went on, "but there was also something really simple and fun about the feeling. It took me back, like back to high school. Do you remember your first huge crush?"

Lisa drained her cab. "Yep," she said. "Lonnie Rupp. He was an idiot – cute and muscles, but an idiot – and two classes ahead of me in high school but all the senior jocks were going after the sophomore girls because all of the senior girls had ignored them when they were all sophomores because they wanted to go out with the senior guys with cars, see. Lonnie had a car, some old land yacht Chrysler thing his dad didn't want anymore. Thing smelled like stale Marlboro Lights and puked-up Old Style, I'll never forget it. I thought I loved him because he would make out with me even though I was too young and poor to invest in any decent boobs. I fantasized about us being married, little cute idiot kids with muscles running around. He graduated, barely, and went to some school way out of state and next time I saw him, home for Christmas, he'd put on 40 pounds of gut and his scalp had retreated like Napoleon from Moscow. It was like he'd spent four months eating his hair." She shook her head. "There was a lesson there," she said, "but I forget what it was. But yeah, I do remember that great cool feeling when you thought some new guy was interested in you, like maybe you just possibly weren't a worthless piece and life wasn't going to be a total suckpile after all."

"Yeah, yeah," Chloe said, a little dreamily, "that's it. Do you think we can still get crushes?"

"That's all I get. About one a week, they seem to hit on Fridays at Gibsons after work. Apparently, it's become a substitute for true love."

"BS alert," Chloe said. "Dung beetles in Ethiopia are checking flight schedules. But that last thing you said about the feeling you get, that's how I felt today. I felt renewed, like something was beginning again. And as I sit here right now thinking about it, I feel like an adult woman who's just had some kind of delicious love appetizer and the main course is going to be *amazing*. But at the same time I feel like a teenage girl with that same feeling of – this sounds all new-agey, but that feeling of *affirmation* you were just talking about with Lonnie Muscles.

"I mean, my god, look at me," Chloe said, "I'm famous and hot and never look at shoe prices, but that damned man made me feel *like someone*, like a female human being feeling like a female human being is supposed to feel at least once in her life. So in the space of just a few minutes today I'm hit with this teenager thrill but also this woman hunger and none of it, *none* of these crazy feelings that have completely ambushed me have *anything* to do with who I've become, or at least who I'm supposed to be, Miss Big

Deal Barbiron CEO Cover-Girl Boss. I'm conflicted, which is bad, and giddy-happy, which is good, at the same time. Am I making any sense?"

"Oh yeah," Lisa said. "Way too much sense."

"What does that mean?"

"You're way overcomplicating this," Lisa said. She paused while the waitress arranged their fresh drinks on the hightop and cleared their empties. "Let's talk about that tingle," she said. "You can marvel about the fun and beauty and cool weirdness of your feelings all you want, you can try to harmonize all those crazy thoughts all day long, but at the end of that day they all come down to sex."

"Well, sure, two genders, men and women getting together, moving the species along, but –"

"No but," Lisa said. "I mean, very specifically, the sex act. Your body and your mind are trying to bust through all the woo-woo starry-eye stuff to get you to go out and fuck with the best genes you can possibly find. They're pointing at this big handsome bag of DNA with the smart brain and nice tie and screaming at you that you found some great chromosomes and please go fuck 'em ASAP."

"But that's so, I don't know, clinical. It's no fun."

"Sex isn't fun?"

"Sure, but what about the dance? Can't that be fun? Can't that keep that good feeling going and growing? Getting to know a great guy? Him getting to know you? First kiss? Feeling his admiration grow into love, feeling your crush ripen into a glow you feel when he's around? Helping each other with life's little things? Company! Talking! Not being lonely. Looking forward to coming home from work. Throwing a dinner party as a couple. Just *being* a couple in a world of couples. Hoping you have a funny little text from him."

"Hoping he's texted you a shot of his junk."

"Stop!" Chloe laughed. "I know you're not serious. You know it's not all orgasms and erections, come on."

"Not all? Lately, not *any*," Lisa said, but she laughed. "Maybe global warming has taken its toll on the male libido. Maybe we've talked too many guys into going vegan, men not getting enough protein. Maybe I need a boob tuneup."

"You do all right," Chloe said. "Maybe we need to work on you getting those old feelings back, but right now we're talking about me."

"Yeah, maybe I need to review my castoffs, see if one of 'em might be worth another throw. Hey, you were complaining about your guys last time I saw you. Look at us! Two major hots and we're boo-hooing about our man collections."

"I think about that sometimes," Chloe said. "I look at women who . . . could use a little help in the boyfriend department and think maybe I should be grateful that I don't really have a big problem getting guys interested. Then some guy with too much product in his hair starts telling me about shorting sorghum futures in Bulgaria or something and I think nope, not grateful."

"What is sorghum? Do they grow sorghum in Bulgaria?"

"I don't know," Chloe said. "Maybe in the future. I don't care. I just want to get to know Jon Rider."

The bar was full and noisy. The trio had launched into

its Elton John medley. The Billy Joel medley would launch when things had thinned out a little.

"Chloe," Lisa said, "what do you want?"

"A perfect man, of course," she said.

"Yeah, well, I'd like Idris Elba locked up in my basement, but he's got other commitments. Also, I don't have a basement. Or any locks. Come on."

"I don't know," Chloe said. "How do you know until he comes along? I want a man who is kind and smart and –"

"And good-looking."

"Yes, and good-looking, and funny, and independent, and –"

"Not too independent, but with dough, right?"

"Yes, all right, financially independent, if we have to get mercenary about it, and age-appropriate and healthy and –"

"Killer-diller in the sack," Lisa said.

"Yes," Chloe said, with some hesitation. "But you know, if I could get everything else, I might settle for diller. Oh, and wants kids."

"'Everything else.'" Lisa looked at her. "Do you realize you haven't mentioned loving him, and him loving you, both of them for the right reason?"

Chloe took a moment. "No," she said, "I did not realize that."

"Listen," Lisa said, "if anyone can have it all in the man department, it's you. But is that really what you want? Scouring the world for Mr. Perfect and never being quite sure if maybe another guy will check one more of your boxes? I know, some of my choices barely move the needle on the guy-o-meter so I may not be the best person to be giving advice, but don't move the bar too high, or at least don't keep moving it after you find a man who truly loves you.

"But you know the best thing you can do?" she continued. "Don't have a bar at all. Don't have requirements above the minimum – you know, living, breathing, true love. Let it happen! Lose the recipe! Fall!"

"It's hard," Chloe said. "I'm not a good one to follow advice to let go."

"Jon Rider," Lisa said. "My little lecture may all be moot. I don't remember all of your boxes, don't know about kids, but all the rest seem possible."

"Yeah, yeah," Chloe said. "Gotta find out, though. I was in his presence for what, a half-hour? And we barely spoke. A little premature, but I can't deny that he knocked me off my grumpy pins a little."

"So, you're open?" Lisa said. "Okay, what's your strategy?"

"My head is still swimming from this afternoon. I'm still enjoying that crush buzz, although maybe it's this scotch. You're the man-vacuum, I thought you might have a strategy for me. And remember, I got first dibs, so no stealing my man before he's even my man."

The Flamethrower tapped her glass and thought about it for a moment. "I don't know what I would do if I were you."

"What would you do if you were you, which you are most of the time."

"Well now, here's the thing, isn't it?" Chloe said. "You're assuming he's interested, all that stuff you said wasn't a connection but obviously was *something*. Right? I mean, he'd have to be crazy or a cyborg not to be interested in you. You're who you are, *the* Chloe Manning, Miss Eligible Chicago, gorgeous, rich, boobs, ass that would make the Pope faint. Any man with a healthy self-image, which is to say every man who has ever lived, is going to go into instant fantasy mode and think maybe he has a chance if you so much as acknowledge his existence. And Jon was obviously, obviously, showing off for you."

"Did you think so?" Chloe said.

"Sister, I know a peacock move when I see one. Of course he was showing off. So – do you think he's interested?"

"He hardly said anything to me the whole time. He really only looked at me when we met."

"Classic male misdirection play." Lisa sipped her scotch and let the taste evaporate into her sinuses. "You were the audience for his performance, not his co-star. He meant for you to watch, not constantly be reacting to him. What I'm trying to say is, he was purposefully *not* flirting, or at least not wanting anyone to think that he was. I'll ask you a third time – do you think he is interested in you?"

"When you put it that way . . . ."

"I do," Lisa said. "So there is your answer. When was the last time an interested guy who thought he might have a chance with you didn't initiate something, call you up, plan to run into you somewhere, get a friend to run interference, whatever? Answer is: never. Sit tight, it's his move."

"But what if he doesn't? What if he's shy? What if he thinks I only date wealthy handsome celebrities?"

"Many answers: First, maybe we're wrong about him being interested. Second, based on what you saw today, did he seem shy to you? Third, so what? It's the twenty-first century, girl, pick up the damned phone. Call him, text him, invite him out for a thank-you drink, send him a naked selfie, any little thing to get your face and figure in front of him again. I know Brian Accardo from a case, he'll give me Rider's cell number." The vapors from Lisa's scotch had summoned a few tears and she dabbed them away. "Fourth, introduce me to some of those wealthy handsome celebrities."

"Have you actually ever done that?" Chloe said. "Sent a guy a nude selfie?"

"Only once, and that was after he sent me one of himself, so neither of us could blackmail the other. It was that kind of relationship." Took a sip. "He was like a third-rate college – small endowment – so I wasn't too worried. Anyway, I looked good." She laughed. "I had another guy take the picture with my phone. Tinyman never asked how I got a full-length selfie."

"Uch," Chloe said, "why does getting going have to be so hard?"

"Hey, you're the one who was talking about how wonderful 'the dance' was. Maybe you're coming around to the tingle theory – we're basically talking sex here. Just go get him, jump on his ass, absolutely demand that he do you at the earliest convenient time and if it's good enough, then forever. Boom. Romance."

"No, no, I'm not that cynical," Chloe said, "Yet."

But what The Flamethrower said made her think about who she was. She had always fought to get what she wanted. She did things women weren't expected to do. Why should her approach to Jon Rider be any different? She had never taken no for an answer, at least not a final answer. She walked in the doors of purchasing executives at the Aces and Home Depots and she never, not one time ever, walked out those doors without asking for the order and if she didn't get it on the terms she wanted, she didn't leave until she at least had a commitment for another meet. *I'm sitting here mooning like some adolescent, 'ooh, what if he doesn't like me, boo-hoo.' I'm an executive; I'll execute. I'm an entrepreneur; I'll innovate.*

"Get me that number," she said.

⤝

"Don't get too high," Lisa said. "Jon is a cool, cool guy and you guys would make a great couple, but just remember that he is a guy, he freaked when his wife died, and his disappearing act after he zapped the Philbricks was kind of weird, didn't you think?"

Chloe nodded as though she were listening to what The Flamethrower was saying. "I haven't felt like this in years," she said.

"All I'm saying is: Have fun. Enjoy it. The chase, the dance, the rutting, all the brainiac stuff, the laughs, just enjoy it. And then tell me about it so I can have some vicarious fun. And if it ends –"

"Don't say that."

"— it's not the end of everything. We women need to be smart about our choices, and I can't believe I just said that as the queen of not-smart choices. Just be careful with the stars-in-the-eyes stuff. We're not kids anymore. I didn't know you were such a romantic."

"I am," Chloe said, "but I'm going to invade his scene with a plan that will make D-Day look like checkers."

Lisa laughed. "He's a goner."

Chloe straightened. "Don't look," she said. "There are a couple of guys at the bar who keep looking over here."

"Which ones?" Lisa said.

"The ones with the spiky hair and scruff beards."

"Got news for you, sis: First, every guy over there has spiky hair and a scruff beard, except the guys with no hair. Second, they've been looking over at us since they walked in. Third, *all* the guys at the bar have been looking over here."

"Well," Chloe said, "that's what we get for being hot and not sitting in some dark corner. I hope they stay put."

"If I see anyone head this way, I'll pick my nose like I'm digging out a *T. rex* and let my Tampax case peek out of my purse," Lisa said.

The trio played "The Days of Wine and Roses."

A young girl appeared at their table. She had flat blond hair past her shoulders parted in the middle and was wearing a Shawn Mendes tour sweatshirt. She seemed uneasy. "Excuse me," she said, "Ms. Manson, may I have your autograph?" She held out a bar menu and pen.

Chloe smiled. "Well, hello. Sure, why not." She took the menu and pen. "What's your name?"

"Whitney," the girl said.

"Whitney, love that name. How old are you?"

"Twelve."

"Do you actually know who I am?"

"Somebody famous? I don't really know," she giggled.

"Are you here with your mother?"

"My dad," she said.

"Your dad," Chloe said. "I see. Which one is he?"

"He has his hair kind of gelled up and kind of a beard like he needs a shave."

Chloe found a blank spot on the menu and wrote:

Whitney –

Best of luck! Dream big! THE STARS ARE YOURS!!

Dad –

You got no shot.

Chloe Manson

"Thank you," Whitney said, relieved that the lady had been nice and her mission had concluded successfully. She turned and walked back into the crowd.

"Honestly," Chloe said, "sending your twelve-year-old out to pimp for you at a bar. That's really disgusting."

"Aw, she was sweet. Hold on," Lisa said, watching over Chloe's shoulder as Whitney made her way back to her father. "Hey, Dad's really cute."

"Lisa."

"He's reading what you wrote. Now he's looking over here and laughing and shrugging his shoulders." She laughed and signaled Gayla for the tab.

Chloe wondered if this was an omen. A reminder of what men will stoop to. Of course Lisa was right when the matter was considered technically; ultimately it's about sex, especially at a bar like this where, she had to admit, women didn't visit to meet brilliant beacons of sophistication and kindness, and the men did not arrive in search of their intellectual equals unless they had big boobs. But it wasn't right. We shouldn't be like that to each other. We should appreciate the preliminary pleasures that contemplating intimacy settle on us like a gift. Even though, she had to concede, she checked out the men when she visited the joint, her eye drawn to the tall, the well-dressed, the confident, and whoever might be connected to that Ferrari out front.

Jon Rider, though – can he provide it all? Life of the mind, good-hearted, plus tingle? Gonna find out. Gonna pin that man down and find out what's up with him. Sexual attraction alone is so, so temporary, so base, so messy.

So . . .

"So why?" Chloe said. "Why have I been dating gorgeous rich men who are uninteresting, self-centered, obnoxious, unfaithful, materialistic, tasteless, shallow, flashy, aggressive, overfit, and oversexed? And they undertip. I mean it, Lisa! Why do I go out with these successful good-looking guys with personalities like Vladimir Putin, but without the warmth?"

"Because you can," Lisa said.

✦

Lisa tapped at her phone. "Your Uber's on me. Sylvia will be here in two minutes with a lux SUV."

"Aren't you coming?"

"I'm going to go over and say hi to Dad," Lisa said. "I sense sweet young Whitney needs some career advice."

"You're kidding," Chloe said. "You're going to talk to that sleaze?"

"He's a cute sleaze. He's Friday-after-work hot." Lisa the Flamethrower turned and looked directly into Chloe's eyes: "Listen to me, girlfriend: There is one, and only one, lesson that women absolutely must learn."

"And that is?"

"We never, ever learn." Lisa laughed and pressed a Hamilton into Chloe's hand. "And thank God for that. Tip the trio on your way out. Tell Ken his Flamethrower says hello, and please play 'The Lady Is a Tramp.'"

"Don't forget to get Jon's number," Chloe said. Lisa gave her a thumb's up as she moved away over to Dad's table with an exaggerated hip-check runway walk, a performance Dad observed with approval as she approached.

CHAPTER 6

THE ONE IS WAKING

— THE ONE is waking, Bandit said.

— Yes, said Gloria. She will put the Food down soon.

— I will go to hurry the waking, Bandit said.

— The One does not nap long enough, Gloria said. I will stay.

Bandit stepped carefully across the folds of the blankets and peered into the face of The One.

"Ee-yower," he whispered.

"I'm alive," said The One. "Don't eat me."

"Ee-yower, rrrup?" he asked, his call rising with impatience.

"Oh, Bandit," said The One, "you jerk, go away and let me sleep."

Bandit looked back at Gloria.

"Miara-ah," said Gloria.

"You too, Gloria?" said The One. "You're usually my

quiet girl. So, I guess I got hungry cats today. In stereo. In-late-up-late equals cats hungry." The One got out of bed and put on her robe.

Gloria and Bandit jumped from the bed and stood by the bedroom door. This was a favorite time for them. The One looked down at them.

The One said: "Food."

– *Food! said Bandit. The One says Food! It is a Food morning for me!*

– *The Food always comes after The One has her long deep nap in the dark, Gloria said. She always says Food to us after the waking. There is no need to act the idiot cat.*

Still, Gloria was very pleased that there would soon be Food.

Bandit ran toward the large pantry where Food would be. He stopped and ran back to The One. "Yower-ow-ow-ow" he hollered. He ran into the pantry again and ran back out again just in time to see The One reach down to Gloria.

Gloria pressed her face into The One's long, giving fingers, and felt them trail down her back as she moved through them. She smelled their salt and oil and heard The One's everymorning cloudsong above her:

Oh Gloria, sweet Glory, my glorious feline

Oh Bandit, Bandito, to his breakfast a beeline

The One popped the lid off the round can and spooned the Food into two bowls. She picked up their water bowls, wiped them out, ran fresh water in each, and placed them near the eating.

Gloria ate how much Food she wanted and lap-lapped water. She went to the bathroom, where she sat on the edge of the tub. She left Bandit behind to finish her Food. With wide eyes, Gloria watched The One at the sink. When the One returned to the kitchen, Gloria followed and jumped on the counter, still watching The One. Bandit came into the kitchen, licking the last of the Food taste from his face.

    – *The One is different, Gloria said.*

    – *She is the same, Bandit said. I remember from yesterday's Food. And I smelled her at the waking. She is the same One.*

    – *She is the same One, but her face is smiling. She stops and looks at nothing. She has not looked at the talking-tapping plate. She always looks at the talking-tapping plate after the waking and the Food. Often before the Food.*

    – *No, said Bandit. She must be the same to know the Food.*

    – *You do not have understanding, Gloria said. Come up here with me. You will see her face and her eyes.*

    – *No, said Bandit. I stand here on this floor sunpatch to warm from the night. I always stand here after the Food when the warm light comes.*

    – *Look up! Gloria said.*

    "Ah-yow? Ee-yower-ah!" Bandit cried.

    "Oh, Bandit, I didn't mean to kick my sweet boy! I'm so sorry," The One said. "Come here, everything's good."

    The One reached down but Bandit turned and moved

away without looking back. The One looked at Gloria on the counter.

– *He is not hurt, Gloria said. He will love you again with Food. He is an idiot cat.*

Then Gloria sang:
– *But you, O my One, what makes your face bright today? Why do you lift your feet from the floor and move quickly to the Food and the bathroom and the kitchen and kick Bandit in his sun-spot with your eyes high and away? Why does the talking-tapping plate hold no interest this morning? Why do you free your golden twirly mane from the stretchy ring before coffee and shake it to your shoulders and look so long and still in the mirror with shining eyes so quick awake and thinking?*

The One chucked under Gloria's chin. She felt the *rrrrrrrr* deep inside Gloria and stroked her coat. "Big stuff, Gloria," she said. "Big cool stuff coming up."

The One unplugged the phone and stroked it, too. She tapped it and smiled when it came alive with something that pleased her.

– *You know it too, my One. You are different.*

∽

Chloe smiled at the phone. Lisa worked fast; she'd already texted Brian Accardo, who gave up Jon Rider's cell without hesitation. A good sign – let's get a conspiracy going. He won't stand a chance against Team Manning.

A horrifying thought brought her up short: Is he allergic to cats? She thought that some who claim a cat allergy just didn't like cats, and she also thought such persons could go straight to hell. Wait, what if he really didn't like cats? No, that is not possible. He is too much like a cat. Comes, gazes, strikes, leaves, depositing in the consciousness an image of grace and strength. She shook it off.

I will not be creating relationship problems before they are problems.

I will anticipate and imagine the good memories I will have before we actually experience anything to remember.

I have always done that.

She felt the tingling rising through her thighs as she imagined – no, not imagined, imagining is not real.

No, she remembered in advance his real hands on her real body.

Real soon, she hoped.

✒

Chloe texted her friend Lily from the Chicago Women's Entrepreneurship Council:

> Met a guy. Could be.

> Give. Who. Where.

> Jon Rider. Lawyer at Rockwell.

> Dont know him.
> You can do better than atty.

> Brilliant, godface, widower. Dont

be prejudiced guy won my case
sitting in the conference room
Lisa Blazier had been screwing
around with months.

Just dug a win out of the case
like magic.

Looking up Rockwell bio now.

OK wow. Take it back. This cute?

Headshot is OK but chain lightning in person.

Got anything going?

When do I get to meet?

Not yet. Not yet.

Does he actually know
about this relationship?

Not yet. I dont know. I felt his
interest. May need girltalk, Lisa
giving me advice.

Like getting career advice
from Lindsay Lohan.

Agree but shes fun.

We betcha need to catch up.

Have your people call my
people if I had people.

Give dates.

Will do. Later.

Chloe texted Jordan, a sorority sister in Rancho Santa
Fe who had married well. The two of them vacationed
somewhere fun every two years.

Got to tell someone! May
explode! Possible guy.

Great! If hes not a guy
what is he? HA.

Lawyer who killed a case against
Barbiron just from looking
through some papers. But more.

More what? Come on. Start with
name then why he may be a guy.

Jon no h. Real good looking
giant brain but something else.
Hard to describe.

I wouldnt say this to anyone
but you but we were young
together. Youve felt love at first
sight no? Or what you thought
was love?

        And I wouldnt admit this to
        anyone but you sistah but yes.

        Maybe more than once.

        Not sneering at that.
        Well this is fun.

Widower. Maybe a little sad
around the edges. But I feel
kindness?

        Do you know what he feels?

No but I sensed an interest.

        You are not going to sit around
        waiting for the phone to ring.

Got that right. Met him yesterday. May call him this
morning to set up a cocktail
thing or something.

Youre leaving something out.

??????

You have never ever texted me
about a potential man. Cant just
leave love at first sight sitting there.
Articulate me baby.

That's the problem I cant! Ive
never felt this way and Im not
processing. Can I not just go
with it?

Sure. Dont know what to say just
dont want my sweet brilliant friend
stepping in it with some shyster.

I know. I have to be careful all
my stuff is always a candidate
for the front pages. Kind of a
delicate time for the co also. But
it has been a long time. What
can I say he was just a cool guy. I
want some fun!

Yeah you want something
else that starts with fu!

No doubt! Hey give me some
dates Jan/Feb and lets make
some plans.

Chloe looked at her phone, took a deep breath, looked at it a little longer, and texted her mother:

Hi Mom. Just wanted to
say hello.

Cant you call? My fingers are too
old and fat to do these messages.

This is just a short check in
making sure youre OK. You are
not old and your fingers are not
fat. Do you remember how I
showed you how you can talk
into the phone and it converts it
into type?

No. That was too hard.

OK Im sorry. Next time Ill call.

You can call me now.

Ill call you real soon. I was just
going to tell you about a man I

met but I should probably wait
until I know him better anyway.

                           Where?

It was at a meeting in a law
office. Hes a lawyer. Its not a
big deal I just thought youd
like to know I might be pursu-
ing something.

              I hope hes not pursuing your $$$.

Nothing like that at all. He
is successful.

                   Good. I hope he is nice.

I think he is but I will find out
soon. Are you doing OK?

                                    Yes.

I love you and I promise I will
call soon.

                              I love you.
                   Do you have your bc pills?

I love you.

Mom!!!

Yes.

Love you.

Good.

❧

As Chloe went about her Saturday business paying bills, picking up some groceries, and checking the 150-plus work emails that had piled up in her inbox – there had to be some way of getting that under control, maybe time to hire a chief operating officer to wrestle with the day-to-day – the scene in Rockwell Morton's conference room was not far from her mind. Despite the cats, she'd had a good night's sleep; if what she felt yesterday was just a temporary thrill from the shock of the unexpected destruction of the Philbrick case, the crisp, clear late-fall sunrise should have illuminated any illusions.

But from the minute she rose, thoughts of Friday's events washed over her like a cleansing rain. She was relieved. She wanted it to happen; "it," hell, she wanted Jon Rider to happen. Yes, it confused her, it confused her to feel emotion rising up her body from some unknowable place down there when all her success in the world was the product of her granite intellect, her strength, her gifts from the neck up. She could tell that her visceral hunger and her smart head were going to be fighting, meeting on the battle-field of her heart. She felt as though she were regarding the coming fight for her soul from some ways off. No, not a fight; a game, a contest.

Something fun. Something crazy.

Chloe did not really expect that texting with Lily and Jordan and her mother would clarify anything for her. She was a big girl; she could sort her feelings out for herself and get some strategy going.

But why did she need a strategy at all? He's a guy. He liked beautiful women because all men like beautiful women, right? And she was more than beautiful. Smart, with money. Available. Interested. He was going to like her. He couldn't not. Why did she need some kind of conversational or social gambit or faked-up meeting or something like that to get herself in front of the guy?

But . . .

He'd hardly spoken directly to her the whole time. He'd only looked at her once or twice, when he got there and when he left. Yes, those were magic moments, but they were only moments.

Maybe she was wrong about his reaction to her. Maybe Lisa was wrong that he was showing off. Maybe she was about to be severely mortified.

OK, maybe, so what? You gotta ask for the order.

Just pick up the phone.

Just pick up the phone.

Pick up the phone, Chloe.

Do it.

She had never called a man before.

This was fun. This was crazy. This was terrifying.

She tapped to Lisa's text and punched his number.

CHAPTER 7

BEFORE THEY HEARD IT, GOODBOY AND GOODGIRL FELT THE DEEP PULSE

BEFORE THEY HEARD it, Goodboy and Goodgirl felt the deep pulse of Man's V-8 thrumming in their bellies as it pulled into the short driveway.

Goodboy and Goodgirl rose together and went to the door.

The door went up. Their excitement was great.

The car went in the garage. Their excitement grew.

The pulse, grown audible as the car pulled in, stopped.

– *Man comes to Pups! Goodboy said.*

– *I love Man! Goodgirl said.*

– *I love Man! Goodboy said.*

The door went down.

Goodboy and Goodgirl pressed their noses against the crack where the door would open.

Man opened the door, the security chime chimed, and Goodboy and Goodgirl launched themselves into Man's legs and stomach, their wagging tails jerking their hindquarters every which way as each tried to find a way in to Man's touch.

"There's my good boy and good girl," Man said. "Who are these good pups? Huh? Who are these love pups?" Man reached down and scratched their necks and slapped their bellies as best he could as the Pups danced and leapt.

"All right, all right," Man said. "Give me a minute." Man went into his bedroom and emerged wearing baggy shorts and a Princeton sweatshirt and soft shoes. A band around the top of his head. He stuffed some plastic bags in his pockets and stood near the front door.

"Hey Teeko, Bridey, get your pup buns over here," Man said. Goodboy and Goodgirl ran over and circled him and jumped up and down.

Man crossed his arms and looked sternly at them, and they sat and settled still before him.

"W–," the man said, making a soft sound that was almost nothing but air.

The Pups' eyes got big.

"Wuh," Man said. Goodboy couldn't sit still. He shifted his weight from haunch to haunch. This was his *favorite* game.

"Wahgh?" Man inquired. Goodgirl haunch-shifted so excitedly that she ended up turning sideways to Man. This was her *favorite* game.

"WALKIES!" Man shrieked, dangling their leashes, and the Pups jumped in the air together.

"Sit still," Man said, "gotta hook you guys up. OK, let's go. Teeko, be a good boy now, stop circling my legs or we'll end up in a heap. Look at Bridey, how she stands and waits like a good girl. Why am I talking to dogs? Let's go."

Jon set off at a jog – not too fast, not too slow — through the Dearborn Park streets. Told himself he wanted to get the dogs some additional exercise but not wear them out, but he acknowledged the truth that he was applying the same consideration to himself. Teeko and Bridey trotted before him without straining the leashes.

"How you guys doing?" he said. They each briefly turned to look back at him but kept going. "I'm going to take that as an 'okay, man.' Talking to dogs, Jesus."

– *Man active and energy,* Goodboy said.

– *I like when he talks to us,* Goodgirl said. *He does not do it so much ever.*

– *I like when he walkies before other things when he comes home,* Goodboy said.

– *He never walkies before other things when he comes home,* Goodgirl said.

– *I wonder if something is wrong for Man,* Goodboy said.

– *Not wrong,* Goodgirl said. *Active and energy and talking is not wrong.*

– *Good for Man, good for Pups!* Goodboy said.

"Whoa, red light," Jon said.

The Pups heard a woman voice say, "Oh, what adorable dogs. May I pet?"

"Yeah, sure, go ahead," Jon said. "They're very friendly."

While she bent down to scratch and pet Bridey and Teeko, Jon looked over the young Asian woman with interest. Although dressed for the spring sundown chill, her compression tights and Lululemon workout top managed to fail to hide her spectacular figure, all the more spectacular because she was short and even a little slight – tiny but perfectly proportioned.

A Shetland person, Jon thought.

Flawless skin, shining coal-black hair pulled back into a knot but with lots left over to spill down her back. And that irresistible facial symmetry that suggested both mystery and an almost sculpted agelessness.

"I've seen you out with them before," she said. "I'm Kira, short for Akira, by the way." She held out her hand and Jon shook it.

"Jon," he said. "I believe I've seen you out and about."

Brian's lecture must have shaken something loose. He was enjoying this easy flirtation. He thought about Chloe but mentally scheduled thinking time later in the evening for further thinking about her.

"Oh yes," she said, "I'm in those new apartments over on Wabash but I like to come inland a little bit sometimes."

"I'm in one of those new stand-alone rowhomes over on Plymouth Court."

"I know," she said, "the ones with those cool tandem garages." She giggled. "I'm not stalking you, I just noticed you coming out with the dogs one day."

– *I like Man is talking to this woman*, Goodgirl said.

– *I like Man is talking to this woman, Goodboy said. But she does not give good scratchies and her smell is like bathies.*

– *She is not so interested in Pups or scratchies, Goodgirl said. More the talking.*

Jon considered what to say next. He settled on: "This is Teeko and Bridey, by the way."

"Wow, Teeko sounds Japanese. What a good boy."

"It's just – just a dog name," he said. He could scarcely believe his next words, which were: "Which way you headed?"

"I don't know," she said, "which way you headed?"

"We need to stop over at the park where the pups usually relieve themselves," he said, "which is more or less in your direction."

"Let's go," she said, as the light changed.

– *Let's go! Goodboy said.*

– *Let's go! Goodgirl said.*

– *Walkies right away, talks to us, active and fast walkies, talks to the woman, Goodboy said. You say good. I don't know.*

– *Maybe Sadness is over, Goodgirl said.*

⁕

"Well, what did you doggers think of that?" Jon said.

– *What is doggers, Goodboy said.*

– *There is only Goodgirl, Goodboy, Pups, Goodgirl said.*

– *Not doggers, Goodboy said.*

"Ah, pups, I wish you could talk. I'm sure your opinion would be of interest and of great value to me."

Goodboy and Goodgirl turned their heads to look back at him but did not break stride. Man had increased the pace as they headed home.

— Our words is small, Goodboy said.

— It is small but enough, Goodgirl said. We live and we are happy Pups with Man. This walkies is happy.

"On second thought, probably just as well you mainly bark and some whining, and not much of that. That seems to work for us. I'm also glad you don't have opposable thumbs. Why am I talking to you pups?"

— So much words I don't know, Goodboy said.

— So much words I don't know, Goodgirl said. So much words Man never says to us.

— Doggers, no. Talky woman. Walkies even faster to home. Never fast walkies to home. I think Man has trouble.

— Good trouble I think, Goodgirl said. Happy trouble.

Man had been sad and quiet at home for a long time, since his Woman.

— Good happy trouble for Man to end Sadne—

— Squirrel! Goodboy said.

— Squirrel! Goodgirl said.

Man held their leashes tight as they leapt and strained after the squirrel, who had run across the street before them nearly a block distant and disappeared into an alley. "Neither of you pups has ever caught any kind of a varmint," Man said, "and that one is already in Cicero. We're almost home, and then it's supper. And why, I ask you, why am I talking to you? And why am I even asking that question out loud? And then that one, too?" Man laughed softly.

Goodboy and Goodgirl only heard one word of Man's talking but Goodgirl hoped all the newly musical words meant the end of Sadness.

– *Supper! said Goodboy and Goodgirl together.*

∾

Jon Rider thought about what Brian Accardo had said to him. Brian had been right to suggest, gently, that it was time for him to snap out of it. Amelia had been gone a long time. His sorrow had been profound and long-lasting.

But as he sat staring at his list of Saturday errands, he found his thoughts wandering far from getting the Jaguar washed and picking up the dry cleaning. Life on earth – there is so, so much of it, and it so little notices even the great tragedies of its small actors marking their minutes across sunrises and sunsets until their little shows each come to an end. The sadness, the solitude – yes, he was beginning to perceive, it was pointless, it was wasteful. More than that, it was selfish. Since Amelia died, he was making no one happy, he was making no one a better person, and he was not allowing anyone else to make him happy or better.

Yes, there were his colleagues at Rockwell Morton. He had value there. He taught the young lawyers. He supported the staff. He forged jumbled evidence into magic bullets for the trial teams and mined the case records for winning motions. That's not worth nothing. A paycheck appeared in his checking account twice a month. But if he winked out of existence on Monday, the firm would briefly note that circumstance with regret before resuming its assembly of billable hours and courtship of insurance companies. Not much of a contribution.

It was time to think about his emotional legacy, his spiritual footprint. Doing for others, doing for the world. Doing for himself.

It was time to think about the true meaning of sojourning in the world of women, of what emerges after you have wandered in that uncharted forest of feeling – lifelong commitment, shared closets, unpleasant relatives. Love.

And – sex. And babies maybe sometime. No, for sure babies.

Oh, man, this was going to mess up his life something fierce.

Or make it incredibly great beyond the power of human language to express.

He smiled.

It was time to think about Chloe Manning. He formed an image of her in his mind. He remembered what she wore, what her hair looked like, the smile in her eyes with just a hint of the apprehension that comes with unexpected desire, the ever-so-slightly lingering handshake when they met and parted. He remembered that she had jumped right along with him as he pieced together his attack on the Philbricks, so damned smart she was. That, now that was sexy, how excited she got when it all snapped in place for her. She bounced, that was – it was cute! He remembered how aware he was of her presence even as he directed his attention to others in the room.

She liked him. He liked her. He should have a date with her. One date wouldn't bring the firm's don't-romance-the-client policy to its knees. Two dates? More? Relationship? He could deal with the firm on that later. Besides, Nelson Gilles had encouraged him. Okay, so one problem put aside for now.

What other problems could he think of? Would she feel obligated to see him, just because he stopped the bleeding with the Philbrick case? That would be awkward. But so what if she did? He'd have to sell himself on his personal manly merits sooner or later no matter what happened. He could do that. He wasn't going to apologize for his flashy performance just because it turned out to be a tool to get his foot in her door. A second issue dismissed.

His thoughts wandered to Kira Ono, that aggressive little sexy dynamo from last evening who had fibbed about not stalking him. Jon felt for his wallet and found the card she had pressed on him before he left her at her building to find a municipal trashcan for the dogs' poop bags. The card had her picture on it. Senior Recruiter, I-Tech Executive Search. He was amused that the little headshot managed to hint at her impressive bustline – in a tasteful, tech-exec-utive-attracting sort of way. She was a beauty for sure, but Jon had felt guilty in thinking of their conversation, even as it was happening, as kind of a rehearsal for the kind of real date-talk he hadn't practiced in years. He had given her his card, too, and he'd already had a text exchange with her that morning. But his recollection of their walk dissolved as Chloe strode forcefully back into his mind.

Ticking off his list of obstacles to a lifetime of indescribable ecstatic bliss with Chloe Manning, it occurred to Jon that he did not know how to contact her.

He did not recognize the number that appeared on his ringing phone.

᛫

"Jon. This is Chloe Manning from yesterday's meeting. Is this a good time?"

Holy . . . . Her. Pull it together. Breathe. "Sure, hi, of course I remember. I usually remember meeting world-famous CEOs for at least three, four days. Yeah, now is fine, dogs working on their mid-morning nap, just finished loading the dishwasher with my weekly plate and fork. How may I help you, Ms. Manning?"

"The first thing you may do," Chloe said, "is to call me Chloe. The second thing is to accept my thanks again for your incredible help yesterday on that case. I didn't expect to walk out of there free and clear."

"Oh, no problem, you're welcome," Jon said. Lame. "You know, finding the odd angle is kind of what I do at that firm these days. I'm glad they thought to call me in. Pure good fortune that the bad guys' own filings tipped us off to the bankruptcy and from there to their attempt to pull a fast one on their creditors."

Lame! Lame the minute the words left his lips. Lawyer talk. It dawned on him this was it – their first real conversation, and he didn't even have to risk rejection. It excited him that she was reaching out. But this was his chance; he had to say something nice to her now, right? "Of course, it was also a very great pleasure and honor to meet you." Christ, that was lame, too. But he couldn't be too familiar, could he? Couldn't say *so, babe, hows about a date?*

"Well, thank you," she said, "but the fact of the matter is that I was very dissatisfied with my failure to express my gratitude to you personally at the time. I mean, all that justice for a dollar!" She took a breath. "I'm wondering if you could meet me for a drink after work on Monday at the Chicago Chop House so I can thank you properly."

Holy . . . . There was nothing to say but:

"Yes. I would like that."

Lame.

"Thank you."

So lame.

"I would like that a lot, Chloe."

Still lame. Sixteen-year-old-getting-unexpectedly-asked-out-by-a-hot-JV-cheerleader lame.

"I was also sorry I had to jet out of there and we didn't get to chat more on Friday. So maybe we can exchange apologies. Long way of saying yeah, I can absolutely do Monday and I'll look forward to it."

Better.

Chloe farking Manning just called me for a date.

CHAPTER 8

CHLOE CHOSE THE CHICAGO CHOP HOUSE BAR FOR A REASON

CHLOE CHOSE THE Chicago Chop House bar for a reason: She liked the light in there. With her bright flashing hair and fair skin, she thought that sometimes her look might come across as a bit . . . icy. Which was a good thing when staring down freight forwarders trying to raise her rates, but not when you are hoping a man won't be too intimidated by all the other intimidating things about you. The Chop House was not too bright, not too dim; with the legacy tungsten illumination, it warmed her up, modeling the swells and slopes of her face, and took the edge off her coolish makeup in a pleasing way.

And she liked that it was a little away from the office towers downtown, so an early after-work drink there usually meant plenty of places to sit and not so many gawkers.

And she liked the way Jim the pianist set up in the front window and played the jazz standards with enough improvisation thrown in to challenge the ear.

And she liked that Irving, the young bartender there for the early shift, knew her and her drink, didn't blab to local gossips, and used the name Irving.

She had tried on five different outfits before leaving for work that morning. First decision: Casual or CEO-dressy? Gotta be CEO-dressy, she'd advertised this as just an after-work thing, so she'd better look worky. And Jon Rider – as he said, he was business, not casual. She was seeing him in a suit.

So she had put on a little show for herself. The Luisa Spagnoli – beautiful, but too red, too Christmassy, too Kate Middleton. And they'd freak at the office. She looked great in the Jay Godfrey jumpsuit, but today was a day to show some leg, more. Something brighter? The Donna Karan semi-floral one-piece, so fun, not too long. Maybe a little casual, a little too stylishy housewifey? Wouldn't look good on a bar seat. St. John today? Ooo, whoever St. John was, he or she was a saint for sure, amazing perfect stuff for tall slim power babes – damn! What's that stain?

Got it: A black Escada, skirt tightish through the thighs and featuring her comely nates to excellent effect, but drapey around the knees, good for leg-crossing on a bar stool, maybe pulling it up an inch or two. Knees are sexy. Hers were, anyway. But the blazer – whoa, that's a sale. It plunged pretty dangerously, especially for a woman with her high large breasts, which she would be elevating further with an adorable Lise Charmel bra suitable for all kinds of scenes; but with a soft and sheer grey-blue scarf to circle the neck and tuck in down there between those globes that all men wanted to circumnavigate – a nice blend of the modest but suggestive, with just a hint of shape. That scarf would match his eyes.

She put herself together and went to the office.

She couldn't get interested in the to-do list and files Amy had laid out for her review and decisions.

She had a floor-length mirror in her office for occasions requiring her to prepare for an impromptu media appearance or other public showing. She stood before it and struck a pose.

Something just . . . off.

She headed to Jimmy Choo.

❧

Jon Rider pulled a grey Hugo Boss from its hanger. A light lavender Zegna shirt with standard collar would look sharp with that. He pulled out a couple of ties with some pink in them and picked one. A pocket square too much just for cocktails? Nah, she would appreciate the detail. His favorite old soft Ferragamo loafers were looking a little too loved, but a spot of wax and a buff sharpened them right up. He dug out some Bullwinkle Moose socks for fun – he didn't want to come across as a complete stiff. Then he put them back and put on some well-traveled Brooks Brothers hose. He put it all on and went to the office.

❧

Chloe's first thought when Jon Rider walked in the door was *it is too soon to think about sex.*

Her second thought was *no, it is not.*

So, as he walked up to join her at the bar, she thought about the man's raw physical appeal, and her own raw physical reaction to it.

Look at him, she thought. Who does he look like, what star, what model? No one, just like himself; a man, not a boy, but with a boy's secret energy and danger. He was tall and slim, but there was that instinctive muscular restlessness throbbing under those yummy fabrics, like that body under there was ready for anything. Even his shirt – disappears right into his waistband, not a hint of an officeman's roll. The way he wears clothes, the way he moves, the casual theatricality of his gait, his gestures, wow – he could make a fortune with Calvin or Tom or Vera. She knew some photographers she could call. Clean-shaven, his full head of sandy hair not too shaggy, not too buzzed, just brushed down and across with a hint of a part. None of that spiky beardy look for him. And that face: Smooth and even, soft and friendly but with just the faintest threat of menace if provoked. It was a face with some living behind and beneath it.

And there they were: Friday's eyes, he'd brought them along this afternoon. They didn't stray from her from the moment he'd spotted her as he spoke briefly to the hostess and descended the short stairs from the street into the bar. Still arctic blue; still seeing, still reaching even from across the room.

Maybe Lisa was right, she thought. My hormones are

screaming at me to seduce this classy sack of premium genetic material and screw him early and often and with maximum violence to whatever nerve endings blow your brains out the top of your skull when it hits, it *hits, it hits, it . . . .*

"Hello," she said.

"Good evening," he said. "My *Elle* mag arrived in yesterday's mail so I recognized you right away."

"Ah, your first fib. That was last month's cover. And I figure you for more of a *Vogue* kind of guy."

He laughed and looked around at the mostly empty bar. A couple of men were pretending not to look her way. A couple of women weren't even pretending, they just stared and one took a picture, a nuisance Chloe had learned to tolerate; maybe the woman would buy a hedge trimmer someday. "I spotted you from the street," Jon said, "and when I walked in – hey, I just looked for the *chaussures élégantes.*" He hadn't done that, but now he took the opportunity of calling attention to her shoes to admire her slim ankles merging seamlessly into the smooth even rise of her calves.

"What? Oh, these things?" She'd dropped off about $1100 with Jimmy a couple of hours earlier for some sleek but season-friendly stilettos with muted sparklies at the toe and along the sole. "A little spiky, but I liked them with the necklace."

"You're not wearing a necklace," he said.

"Exactly," she said.

This is going to go great, he thought. *That's precisely the kind of oblique, catch-'em-off-guard thing I would say.* "Yes," he said, "I see, you're quite right."

"So, you check out the feet first?" she said.

Okay, she's making reference to me reacting to her ini-tially as an attractive woman whose physical person men will evaluate before anything else happens, but she's doing it in a non-hostile, cute, flirty way, which is good. And I brought up the shoes. And I'm already overthinking this.

"Gotta start someplace," he said.

"Thank you for making time," she said.

"The pleasure is entirely mine. The social calendar is not overloaded on Monday nights, or any other nights."

"Irving, this is Jon. Irving will serve you up right."

"At least until I'm no longer upright," Jon said. "Splendid, hello, Irving. Hendricks martini super cold, hold the vermouth but can you spare a couple-three drops of orange bitters? Regular olives but not dirty, straight up. May I ask you to put that in a rocks glass, please? Sorry for all the specifications."

"Got it all," Irving said. "And next time, all you have to say is 'another.'" He had already poured her Sonoma pinot grigio.

When his drink arrived, she raised her glass. "You're the talk of Barbiron, thanks to Amy," she said. They clinked.

✧

My lord, Jon thought, she's unbelievable. One of the most celebrated businesswomen in America, and incredibly gor-geous, and she is giving me her time and full attention. At her invitation. And she's already teased me a couple of times. On Friday, most of her had been covered up by the Rockwell Morton conference tabletop, a distinctly uninformative presentation of her body. He savored the words *her body*. He scanned her from top to bottom when she would turn to look away, which he sensed she was doing on purpose to give him the opportunity to take it all in. Tasteful, elegant, but Jesus! scorching, although Jesus had little to do with his reactions. Wait, was that why she wanted to meet at the bar, to lay out the whole picture from a stool?

Legs. Legs good. Good for propelling a woman from place to place, good for crossing and dangling from a bar stool, good for wrestling in the dark.

He liked that plungy thing she had going on with the scarf and that jacket, too. Guess that's why the big designers get the big bucks, they can make an outfit look classy and naughty at the same time. Helps if they're dressing someone classy and naughty, or at least put together that way.

Wait, he thought. This isn't the way we treat women these days, and this isn't why she grabbed me in the first place. She'll always be beautiful, and okay, there she is, and that body and face aren't going anywhere. She'll look great tomorrow too, and the day after that. But what's inside? The women in his life who meant the most to him – Amelia shot across his consciousness – were smart, intriguing, creative, believing. He resolved to factor out her appearance for the next couple of hours to take the measure of their shared humanity.

Right.

"Well," he said, "here we are."

"Yes," she said, "we do seem to be here."

"Now that that we know that we're here," he said with a conspiratorial smile, "where do you come here from?"

᳁

She told him. Her father Henry was a steelworker in the years when steel was declining in Ohio and Pennsylvania. They moved around a lot; he didn't wait to get laid off, he was always checking where the mills were running. She remembered her father very fondly as a smart, funny man. He had an artistic bent and when he wasn't working he was puttering in a workshop he'd set up in their garage. He made things for the house, he made things for friends, and sometimes, he made things because he liked the way they looked, things that were pretty. She didn't think of them as sculptures, but when she grew up and thought back on it, that's how she thought they should be remembered. She particularly recalled a birdbath she would fill from a hose every few days in the summer. He made her a dollhouse out of steel scraps he brought home but the dollhouse itself was wooden, the steel was just the bones of the place. It was beautiful; he painted it several different shades of pink. She loved that he made it for her but she never told him, and he never quite saw, that she did not play with dollhouse dolls very much, just Barbies who were too tall for the house, and anyway Barbies were always out at the beach or displaying fashions to other Barbies and not hanging around in a house. She had two older brothers. One went into zoo science – his name was Andrew, Andy — and he was a senior administrator at a wildlife park in Utah. The other, Roger, went into the army and was a full-bird colonel stationed at Fort Campbell in Kentucky, but the word was that if he would accept a transfer to Germany he'd be promoted to brigadier general. Chloe wasn't her real first name, she really hated her real first name and had managed to make sure most of her official records never used it. She warned Jon not to go looking for it. Warned him twice. She had a great relationship with her brothers. She still does. She loves being Aunt Chloe to the three nieces and two nephews, and a couple of the nieces are getting old enough to get it that Aunt Chloe is in fashion magazines and is a big deal. Her father died a long time ago of some kind of unusual cancer they didn't catch early on in the smaller hospitals near their home in eastern Ohio at the time. When they figured it out it was too late. Her mother, Iris, was still alive and Chloe was in touch with her a lot. Her mother pretty much stayed home and raised Andy and Roger and Chloe but as they got older, she put some office skills and smarts to good use and did all the admin for a firm of small firm of investment advisors and affiliated lawyers and CPAs. But going back to her father: She was more into Barbies when he made the dollhouse, but what she really liked to do was hang around when he was banging stuff around in the garage, except she could see that although it could be noisy, he wasn't really banging stuff around. A lot of what he was doing was really fine work, cutting and shaping and fastening that took gentleness and skill to do correctly, and that took extra special care to make it look effortless, so that the joints and the sunk screws and the seams didn't show. It was like the things he put together were what their materials always intended them to be. Andy and Roger weren't that interested in the shop but she bugged him to let her help. When she was old enough, he sat her down one day and took her through all the tools in the shop, the ones you grip and the ones you twist and the ones you plug in, and all they talked about was safety. She would bounce up and down *please let me do something* and the second time he sat her down it was all about safety again. And the third time. The fourth time, he gave her a piece of mahogany and a jack plane and a try square, sat her up at a vise for the board, and told her to plane the long edge of the board and then sight down that length and run the square up and down to see if it was even or if you could still see light through parts of it. Do it until you couldn't see any light under the blade of the square. She planed and she sighted and by the time she took the board back to her father it had lost half its width, but it was perfect. And she hadn't hurt herself, not even a splinter. She was thrilled when her father smiled and handed it back to her and told her to sand it down and he'd burn her name into it to put on her desk some day when she was President, and she still has it and it's on her desk at Barbiron. But even that small plane had been heavy and awkward and she was certain that experience had planted the seed. There were all kinds of women out there doing craft work and even some bang-it-together building work, and she thought with some proper engineering and advanced materials – and attention to color and shape and things that women appreciated – she could make lighter-weight, sturdy tools aimed at that market, which, incidentally, would work great with kids, too, and she was thinking of starting a line aimed at the disabled. She had always been good at math, fair at science but okay, so she studied materials engineering at Carnegie Mellon on a scholarship and after that, hell, B-school was a snap and she got her MBA in a year at Wharton she paid off herself. From there on it was getting some designs and prototypes together with some men and women who were still with her today, and banging on doors to raise money, which she managed to do with some wealthy individual investors so she didn't have to go the venture capital route. Nothing against VCs, they're valuable and create a lot of wealth and support innovation, but god, the fees and the impossible cap structure and the unreasonable timetables for profitability and the loss of control, no thanks. So that's how she got started with Barbiron. Oh yeah, Barbiron: She came up with the name when she was kicking around names with some of her engineers. She wanted to suggest femininity and toughness, and she thought about her Barbies – people told her she even looked a lot like Barbie, with the long legs and impossible figure and yellow hair, not the meanface fashion-model Barbie but the happyface teenish Barbie – and combined that word with the hard elemental mineral behind her father's work. Barbie + iron, and the name wasn't already taken, so Barbiron it was. And from there it was more banging on doors to get some sales interest, and figuring out the best way to get these items made, and to make enough different things so that she'd have a decent catalogue. She started out dealing with established toolmakers who did private branding deals with her but she had to dump some who started to steal some of her design ideas, so she buttoned that loophole up with some better lawyers and better deals and, when she could, brought the manufacturing in-house. High-wire act to keep enough sales revenue coming in on time to pay vendors, build up credit and credibility with buyers and sellers. And then one day Oprah spoke to the Northern Illinois Business Council at the Drake about women's initiatives. Oprah was hardly in Chicago anymore but she was there that day and Chloe about fell over when she held up one of Barbiron's lightweight power drills and said *you'll be seeing this in next month's issue on "Tools for Living"* and Chloe introduced herself and she guessed Oprah liked what she saw but in any event they hit it off because next thing that happened was she had a two-page spread in the *O* magazine and Barbiron sales blew up, then she was on the show, then some of the other mags and designers called, and she had to be careful to keep her eyes on the prize which was Barbiron and not a bunch of clothes-horse stuff, that's really not a great message for women in the long run, she guessed, and —

Chloe stopped. Her eyes got big.

She was horrified. *I've blown it. I've totally blown it. How could I have so totally blown it?*

Jon's eyes had not left hers since she began to speak. His brow now conveyed a question: *Why are you stopping? Please go on.*

"Oh my god," she said. "I've been talking for forty minutes. I am so, so sorry. You must think I'm a total . . . self-centered . . . something."

He was smiling. It was a sincere smile, the crinkle around the eyes, a silent, breathy chuckle. My god, Chloe thought, that face. It needs to belong to me. I need to see that beautiful picture every day.

He held out his hands, inviting her to place hers in his.

She did so. He lowered them to her lap. Their first touch outside the conference room.

Is this man made of electricity? she thought. The tingle . . . .

His eyes were soft.

"This is the best date I've ever had," he said.

᰾

"You felt the same way Friday that I did," Chloe said.

"Yes," he said. "I think so. I hoped so. And now, as we both observed a bit ago, here we are.

"Listen to me, Chloe.

"First, I loved all of what you had to say. I could have kept listening all night. More. To me, the best thing human beings can do is learn about their world, and the world is people, and you learn about people and your world by listening and watching and smelling and tasting and touching and not by talking.

"And what did I learn? All of the things you said, of course, but also the way you said them. The look in your eye. You misted up when you talked about your father and also your mother. The excitement in your voice when you talked about founding Barbiron, and the steel in your sound when you talked about banging on doors and shutting down the guys stealing your designs and avoiding the venture capital traps.

"I learned you are a woman of high feeling and through-the-roof intelligence. You are a great teacher; everything followed; everything was clear.

"So I have been just fine with your talking, and, as long as we're both admitting that we're not exactly doing this entirely as a thank-you for Friday, I'll also say that I am thoroughly stunned by your beauty as well as your brains so sitting here listening to you is not exactly what I would call a hardship."

She started to say something, but he held up a finger.

"Second, we are both nervous. We both sort of knew that we might be a thing, but neither of us quite knew how to approach it. I still don't. So you are probably a little nervous because we might be this thing. And on top of that, you took the chance. You called me. You put your ego on the line. I just sat there and said yes.

"On top of that, you are a woman who faces a lot of pressure every day. I doubt today was any different. This is your winddown time. So maybe you need to talk a little to work out the stress of the day and the nerves of maybe us possibly being a thing. That's okay. Men need to listen to women. I'm a man. I'm listening. I'm learning. Don't worry about it."

He's as sweet and kind as I had hoped, Chloe thought. With just the right amount of BS for seasoning, so you know he cares.

And very handsome and smart, of course. Lisa's genetic hormone magnet. Her eyes flicked at his wide, full mouth.

"Third, I think this counts as a first date. We finish our drinks, let's get a table. Agreed?"

"Yes," she said. This was going even better than she expected. This man!

"Fourth –" He leaned in and reached toward her bosom.

"Hold still." *What, he's going to feel me up, what is this, what is THIS? Oh my god, I hope he's not weird.* He picked at the right lapel of her blazer, teasing something from the fabric, then pinched lightly at a couple of other places on the left lapel on the roll down by the button. He leaned back and held up four or five white-grey strands between his fingers, giving them a twirl.

"Fourth," he said, "I like cats."

∽

Jim played "You and the Night and the Music" as they made their way to their table.

At dinner, Jon told Chloe his story. He never felt he had much to tell and his account was brief. Grew up near Kansas City on the Kansas side of the Missouri. Mother worked for AT&T, industrial sales. Father was an actuary for a succession of life insurance companies. One brother, older, software. Everyone still alive, not super close but close enough to suit everyone on holidays. Princeton, then Stanford Law School, but decided he was a Midwest guy at heart. Whole legal career at Rockwell Morton. He mentioned his marriage to Amelia, who worked in particle physics at the Illinois Institute of Technology with an investigational interest in quantum gravity and intranuclear forces. He wasn't any more specific than that. She was, he said, one of those women who died of an unexpected heart attack.

"You know how they say heart attacks are a leading cause of death in women but you don't seem to know any who've had one?" he said. "Well."

Chloe felt his voice drop a notch when he mentioned Amelia, and he looked away as he spoke, but did not display any other emotion or describe their marriage with any color at all; he just said it was happy – no, he said it was very happy, Chloe recalled later – and he smiled a little when he said it. He didn't say any more about her and Chloe did not press.

"No kids" was all he said about that.

⚮

The evening proceeded with some self-consciousness on both their parts. Each wanted to learn about the other without prying too much; each wanted to give a good impression without overdoing it – and, if they were being honest with themselves, without revealing too much, either. But the feeling at the table was good. Chloe, having the more interesting and varied life, continued to do most of the talking, but now Jon would interrupt with questions, a couple of supportive illustrations from his own life, and an assortment of gags, puns, and amusing observations that were actually funny and made her laugh.

It was a fun evening.

It was a successful date.

That's what they were each thinking when they left the Chop House. And they were each thinking that a date with the right person could actually be good for people like them, contrary to their recent experiences.

And, being the kind of woman and man they were, they were also each thinking ahead about that most awkward and sensitive of subjects, the end-of-first-date strategy, invariably played out at the woman's door.

That door happened to be located in one of the top floors of a luxury condo building on East Superior Street, an easy walk from the Chop House. Jim played "The Very Thought of You" as Jon tipped him a twenty, and they walked out of the Chop House into the cool May evening where a following Chicago breeze urged them to her home.

Actually, Jon had been thinking about it almost all evening. What would be best, what would top everything off just right? Not to stammer around in front of the doorman, but to know in advance how it was all going to go and get buy-in from Chloe who, he had determined, was not without a touch of her own brand of squared-awayedness.

"With your permission," he said, "I would like to walk you to your door, not your building's door, but your door-door. I'll say goodnight and Uber on home. Would that be an okay way to wrap this?"

"It would," she said.

Perfect, Chloe thought. A little romance, no pressure. She didn't expect him to expect sex and it pleased her that her reading was sound and pleased her more that this was the kind of man he was. She was less certain about the kind of woman she was, because a little devil on her shoulder, who looked a lot like Lisa Blazier, was saying *if you're wrong and he wants it, surrender the tulip, baby.* But Chloe's earlier Lisa-inspired visions of Darwinian seduction had cooled with the sheer normality and pleasure of their evening, and the little shoulder-devil vanished with Jon's civilized suggestion.

A gentlemanly way to proceed, and gentlemanly to cover it with her in advance of arrival at her building where they would be greeted by George, the evening doorman. George, the discreet evening doorman. She thought about George's overseeing all the ins and outs of those revolving doors. He saw it all: the lovers, the cheaters, the married-for-life, the drunks, the closeted, the violent, and the virtuous. He had his reward in fat Christmas envelopes.

"Good evening, Ms. Manning," George said as they entered the lobby.

"Hi, George," Chloe said. "This is Mr. Rider."

"Good evening, sir," George said.

"Good evening to you," Jon said. "Your building is gorgeous."

"Wish it was my building," he said, "but thanks. Elevator is fixed, Ms. Manning, should zip you right up."

Jon suppressed thoughts of zipping up and zipping down.

At her door, Jon said: "Thank you for calling, thank you for the thank-you, and thank you for everything that came along after the thank-you."

"It's been a lovely evening," she said. "That's a lot of thank-yous, but I thank you again. You know, now that you mention it, I don't think we even talked about the Philbrick thing, the thing I was supposed to be thanking you for as – well, as an excuse to see you again. Thanks for that, too."

A pause, a very short one, but in that pause the pulses began to race and the blood to flow.

"May I kiss you?" Jon said.

Chloe nodded. She could not remember the last time

a man had asked if he could kiss her goodnight. She liked that he did. Men should, even if the answer is almost always positive even with bad dates and you'll never go out with them again if they were like some kind of Twilight Zone Burgess Meredith last man on earth.

But tonight, she started to say "uh-huh" under her breath but Jon's mouth was already over hers and his hand was lightly pushing her hair over her ear and cupping her neck and in the next moment his lips were brushing hers so, so lightly, but only for a moment until he pressed into a real damned kiss, their lips agreeing to part just a little, and when he nibbled gently at her upper lip Chloe felt the heat rising in her face, that first-time burn, that sensation that you wanted to *mean* something, that you hoped *meant* something, and it was perfect because just when their coming together like this at her door threatened to turn into something neither of them quite expected from their evening, he moved softly from her.

"Good night," he said.

"Good night," she said.

§

"Good night, Mr. Rider," George said.

"That it was, sir," Jon said. "And good night to you."

CHAPTER 9

BANDIT AND GLORIA HAD THEIR NOSES AT THE DOOR

BANDIT AND GLORIA had their noses at the door and the moment it opened they ran to the kitchen. Chloe had her phone out and immediately began texting Lisa and Lily and Jordan about her night. Their exchanges featured "awesome" and "amazing" and "sweet" and "next" and, in Lisa's case, various conjugations of the verb "do" and its Urban Dictionary synonyms. Then she fed the cats and asked them how the hell they'd managed to get fur on her Escada blazer that had been covered by a dry cleaner's bag until the very moment she put it on that morning.

She told herself not to think about what was next, but just to enjoy the memory of this great night with a great guy. Could he be *the* guy? There she was, thinking ahead again. Were there problems? She couldn't think of any.

But there were always problems, always things men and women needed to overcome. What would they be with Jon

Rider? She didn't want to wait. She wanted to know now. She wanted to start working on them, get them out of the way, and get that man into her life and into the bed she'd just turned.

Or . . . did she? Was the whole thing just too, too . . . meet cute, too Hallmarky, too impossible? Too not-Chloe? No, no. But how could she know without knowing whether there were going to be serious problems? Some problems can't just be dreamed away.

When her head hit the pillow, she knew she had to see him again soon, and knew as well that until she could she would not be able to shake this new and unaccountable unease. First date, she thought, everything's light and happy and *wow*, like tonight. Second, third dates, then we're a couple and . . . couple stuff emerges. Always something, always some difference to overcome or to compromise or to blow the whole thing up.

Then she thought about the cat hair and the kiss and felt better. Romance! It's here and now! Problems, maybe later. Maybe never!

With a final recall of the serial delights of her evening, she laughed a little laugh into the dark of her bedroom, encouraged the cats to get off her legs so she could roll over, and was gone.

The One, different now, Gloria said.
Maybe, Bandit said.

⁓

Jon hooked up Bridey and Teeko without changing out of his Hugo Boss and took them out for their nighttime relief.

Huh, he thought. Chloe Manning.

That date actually happened.

She was actually beautiful and tall and blond and sexy; her photographs in the fashion and business press did not lie. Neither did they capture all her beauty. Neither did they nod one time to her brains.

I actually kissed her. Chloe Manning. The Chloe Manning. The Oprah *Vogue* Chloe Manning.

Almost up to mouth level in those heels, she was. He smiled at the thought.

She enjoyed it. We enjoyed it.

We could have wanted more, I could feel it in her – hell, I could feel it in me – but we were too cool, too this-isn't-just-sex-is-it.

I actually leaned into her, took her hands, picked puddercat hair from her chestal area.

Am I star-struck?

Why shouldn't a Chloe Manning be interested in me? And why shouldn't I treat her like any other woman?

He snorted. *Any other woman*. There hadn't been so many.

And the reason that he shouldn't treat Chloe Manning like any other woman, he determined upon very brief further reflection, is that she was not like any other woman.

Of course . . . is any woman like any other woman?

I'm overthinking this.

He looked at Teeko and Bridey snuffling around the curbs and landscaping and stairsteps they snuffled around every night.

"I don't impress you, do I?" he said. "Why am I talking to you?"

Now what? Jon thought. I should call her? Do I need to figure out some kind of event to take her to, or another dinner, or what? And like right away, like for next weekend? Like we're assuming it's already a thing? Is it?

"Come on, pups, it's late," he said. "Get busy."

Dogs don't overthink things, he thought. Boy dog, girl dog, heat, boom, puppies. Yet they seem happy enough, and pretty much all the time.

But romance! All the condiments we spread over the male-female bond that add savor and color and laughter and joy to the coming sexual thrill. That, Jon thought, was what he should focus on.

Fun.

He'd have to remember that when things got difficult. Which they would.

But not right now.

Gonna bask, gonna remember, gonna be excited until I have to figure out what to do next. Then I'll be excited to see her again. Then we'll have another great evening. Then maybe complications, but until then, fun.

"I'm overthinking this, pups," he said. "But I'd rather overthink this than think unpleasant things. I've been talking to you a lot lately, haven't I? Why am I doing that? She's made me a little crazy."

Man is happy, Goodgirl said.

Poops, then Treat, Goodboy said.

CHAPTER 10

CHLOE ARRIVED AT BARBIRON THE NEXT MORNING READY TO CONQUER THE WORLD

CHLOE ARRIVED AT Barbiron the next morning ready to conquer the world, starting with that portion of it occupied by Jon Rider.

But before commencing Jon Rider-conquering activities, she made the rounds of Barbiron headquarters, which she did at least every two or three days to get a feel for the flow of the company, learn the new faces, and let employees feel and absorb her commitment and enthusiasm. She would invite random groups of employees into one of Barbiron's several small conference rooms to request feedback, give pep talks, find out more about them and their views on how things were going. She sometimes sensed a more delicate problem with an employee and would gently suggest a private conference, where some friendly chitchat might reveal a personal struggle; she would offer to assist with time off, an advance, or even a gift of money or her time. She regularly toured Barbiron's off-campus facilities as well.

While Chloe was on her good will tour, Amy cleaned up the endless list of emails Chloe had skipped on the weekend and ignored on Monday when Jimmy Choo beckoned. Amy marked as urgent those absolutely-without-any-question-whatsoever requiring Chloe's personal attention and forwarded others to company personnel who should have received them instead of her. She deleted the ads that escaped the spam filter and similarly ashcanned emails attaching pundit columns from Chloe's friends on the left and right who incorrectly believed she agreed with them, or cared. Finally, she deleted all emails except the last in those endless chains of replies and forwards where Chloe was only copied because the principal communicants were covering their asses by keeping the boss in the loop on their turf battles and decisions they feared Chloe might second-guess. Chloe might read those; she might not.

This left only a dozen or so Barbiron and personal emails, some notes from board members, the usual interview and photo requests, and reports from the finance department. And that unopened personal-and-confidential envelope delivered on Friday. Nothing passing through Chloe's office was off-limits to Amy, but the anonymity of that particular item told her she'd best let the boss lay first eyes on it.

Amy had long thought Chloe needed to let go a little; delegate, empower those who had earned her trust to manage their areas so she wasn't inundated with irrelevant crap like this every single day. Take some time to enjoy her success and the attention the world was directing her way. But it was not easy to tell a woman who had arrived where she was going by holding tight to all the reins that the horses would keep going if you relaxed your fists a little.

∽

Chloe noted no messages from Jon Rider in the eight hours since she'd seen him, so she attacked phone messages and the hard-copy mail. She spied the oddly blank personal/ confidential envelope delivered by messenger Amy had texted her about on Friday. It bore only her name, hand-printed; there was something ominous about it. She left it until all the other hard-copy mail had either been pitched or prioritized for ignoring at a later time, until such time as what the sender wanted no longer mattered even to the sender and the pile of paper could be disposed of in an ecologically responsible manner.

She pulled the tab to open the cardboard envelope and removed the letter inside. She began to read it but didn't finish.

Looked like she was going to see Jon Rider sooner than she thought.

She punched up Nelson Gilles's cell. He said they'd see her Thursday morning.

∽

Chloe had considered whether to invite Jon to the Cook County Animal Rescue Ball scheduled for that Wednesday night at the Four Seasons, one of the only formal charity functions held mid-year in the city. All the local shelters benefited from the money raised, and the dozens of dogs and cats in attendance – rescue animals waiting for adoption and some pets of the guests – were an adorable draw in their own party attire, which most of them hated, especially the cats.

But she thought it was too-short notice, too soon after their date, and too much her doing all the asking. And it was a very visible society event; couples would show up in photo spreads in the Sunday *Tribune* and *Chicago* magazine and she thought maybe Jon was not quite ready to be identified to the world, if only by implication, as Chloe Manning's date/escort/boyfriend/man.

She went for the Jay Godfrey jumpsuit and the new Jimmy Choos. Had thought about a springy Roland Mouret off-the-shoulder thing, but decided to stick with black. She was going alone; no need to shout about it.

She walked around a bit, complimenting the animal outfits and offering the occasional scratch and stroke. She put in a few bids on some silent auction items she didn't want. Checked the bids on a Barbiron "Women's Essential Home Tools for Living" combination screwdriver/wrench kit the company had donated, saw they were a little slow, and tracked down a felt-tip to sign the cool-blue metal carrier "Get ~~Screwing~~ Busy WOMEN!! – Chloe Manning."

She felt good. The Jon Rider thing was off to a promising start; she looked forward to basking in the warmth of that feeling for a few days. It was one of the best things about the beginning of a new relationship, just letting it simmer until it was time to turn up the heat. Relationship! She marveled at the word when it came to mind. It used to be "affair" and other things that everyone understood to mean sex outside of marriage, but *relationship* was so much more, so much warmer and more inclusive of the whole range of man-woman stuff but definitely, at a minimum, inclusive of sex.

But all that other great stuff, too, Chloe was careful to remind herself. Companionship, support, the pleasure of giving as well as taking. She promised herself she would do that, give as well as take, although a little voice – maybe that Lisa Blazier shoulder-devil again – warned her that might be a challenge after the years of being the boss lady who wouldn't give an inch, and the only thing she wouldn't take was *no* for an answer. She told herself she would not let the anticipation of the relationship overshadow her experience of it when it all happened. She would savor it, appreciate it, *value* it and him. Him. The Him. The Big He. Brilliant, handsome. And nice. Classy. Understood money. Understood power. Understood women's needs, or at least seemed to understand hers. But he was gentle, and respectful without showing any celebrity-sniffing tendencies, a definite relationship hazard for her.

She ran into some old dates who chatted her up while they were on their way to or from fetching drinks for their dates for the night. And she fielded some hits from a few unattached men who figured *what the hell, no downside to taking a run at Chloe Manning*. She said something nice and unencouraging to each. She was relieved to run into some married friends who invited her to sit at their table with some other marrieds.

She relaxed, picked at her salmon. A few Chicago notables stopped by the table to say hello. Nine-thirty, which she judged to be decent-departure time, could not come soon enough.

She was considering whether to sample the chocolate caramel cheesecakey thing they'd plopped down in front of her after the salmon departed when something bright and noisy sparked in the corner of her awareness. It flashed from a group several tables away, bending over laughing, scream-laughing.

In the first half-second, she saw a small Asian woman in a bright yellow thing that opened dangerously into her creamy décolletage, and saw as well that she was adorable.

In the balance of that second, she saw Jon Rider.

She looked away. Her thought was to get up and move away quickly, move quickly out of the building and move quickly to her home to – do what? Cry? Pound the pillow? Text curses on him to her girlfriends?

No. Be cool. Think. They'd had one date which was only kind of accidentally a date. Let's not overreact, Chloe. Maybe they're not together. Maybe they're not dating. They can't be fu – can –? No. No! I am not overreacting! This is not the story! This is not our story, it is not our romance that two days after he about melts me at my door like one of the Wicked Witches, I forget which direction the melting one was from, he shows up at this big deal public thing with this little trick with big tits and having fun, having laughs with these, these people! Who are these people? This is not *my* story. This is *not* my story. This is not my, my *narrative*! This is not –

Her thoughts were interrupted by an even louder explosion of mirth from that table. The men were heaving with laughter. The women were shrieking and wiping their eyes. Surrounding tables were laughing at their laughing. Then, almost as one, all the women got up from the table and ran to the ladies' room past Chloe's table. She observed that the Asian woman's dress was a cheongsam style with the skirt side-split up to here. And that her legs were short, but really good.

Shoes: Damn, cute too. Valentinos? Sh – who was this woman?

Chloe followed the women into the restroom. A couple were in the stalls; a couple, including the Asian woman, were at the mirror, wiping off tears, fixing the damage caused by all the hilarity.

"Excuse me," she said to the Asian woman.

She glanced at Chloe in the mirror. "Oh, wow," she said, displaying a delighted smile, "you're . . . I'm sorry, the name . . . ."

"Chloe."

"Chloe – Manning!" the Asian woman said. All the women looked at Chloe.

"I'm Kira Ono," she said and held out her hand. Chloe had no choice but to take it and hold it briefly in acknowledgement. "Did you need to speak with me about something? Excuse me while I fix a few things here."

"No, I just . . . your dress is beautiful."

"Oh! Thank you!" She smoothed her skirt and swished it a little. "It's Chinese, I'm Japanese, big deal. So is yours."

"Thanks. I – I thought I recognized the man sitting next to you and I wanted to know – is that Jon Rider?"

"Yes, it is!" she said. "Do you know him?"

"He's – done some legal work for me."

"Oh," she said, "please come over and say hello, I'm sure he would be delighted to see you."

"No no," Chloe said, "I was just curious. I didn't know" – might as well just ask – "when I saw you over there I wondered if you were dating."

"First time out," Kira said. "I met him walking his dogs last week, thought I might snag him as a date to this thing and he was really cool about it on short notice, and I'm glad I did. He's incredible, so quick and funny, and, *and*, he had his own tux! Fate!"

Of course he had his own tux, Chloe thought, but you are not part of any Jon Rider fate, dollface. "The place is dying to know what was so funny," Chloe said. "Can you tell me?"

"I can, but I'm afraid if I do, I'll crack up again. Although I don't know, maybe you had to be there, maybe a little wined up. Also, it's a little off-color." A couple of the women at the mirror shook their heads and one of them said *oh god* and the other said *go ahead, I want to hear it again, I couldn't believe he said it.*

"Okay, well," Kira said. "My boss" – one of the women mumbled *my husband* – "well, let's face it, we'd all had a few cocktails, but Dale — Carrie, I hope you don't mind this" and Carrie mumbled *no, you can say it* "had definitely been overserved. And he was kind of carrying on and getting a little dirty like I said and thinking he was being funny, and he was, kind of, but it was getting a little loud and – "

"And embarrassing," wife Carrie said.

"– and he said 'evolution can't be true, because if

evolution was true, men's dicks would vibrate.' And the table kind of got quiet, no one quite knew what to say to that, and then Jon said, in kind of this sad, quiet voice –"

The women began to snigger and giggle and snuffle quietly and began pulling out their tissues again.

"'Yours doesn't vibrate?'"

The women began to return to repair mode as the tearful laughs began again.

"And we were all just howling, and even Dale was laughing, and it was the way Jon said it and after he said it he didn't smile, he just kind of shook his head as though Dale had just confessed to some horrible male problem, and he looked at Dale and jiggled his index figure real fast and kind of shook his head at him as though to ask 'doesn't vibrate?' with this so sad look and Dale started to play along and shaking his head with this sad look and Jon keeps mumbling stuff like "oscillatory dysfunction" and said he knew an electrician who did a little urology on the side, and he just kept riffing on this and we're all laughing even harder."

"And then," one of the women said.

"And then, as soon as we'd stopped to catch our breath there was this slight pause, perfect timing: Jon turns to Carrie and says very quietly, as though this was supposed to be confidential but just loud enough for us all to hear and of course we were all listening to him at this point, he says –"

"Oh my god," one of the women said, and ducked into a toilet stall.

"— he says, in this sincere voice, as though he wasn't saying anything out of the ordinary, he says to Carrie 'you know, next time you guys are in the throes of passion, take a half-dozen Duracells and shove 'em up his ass.' And that was it for me. I'd started to take a sip of wine and I spit it all over my desert and I thought I'd better get in here quick." And all the women were laughing again, and Chloe found herself laughing too, although she caught herself and swallowed it back some, trying to find the right pitch of amusement for the room.

"Jon Rider said all that?" Chloe said, although she'd heard Kira's story perfectly well. Kira handed her a tissue she didn't need but she patted her cheeks anyway. "Wow, that is amazing," Chloe said, "so hilarious. Yeah, he's definitely a witty guy. Listen, Kira, Carrie, everyone – a favor, please? Don't tell Jon you ran into me here, okay? You know, I don't want him thinking he needs to go looking to chat up his client when he should just be enjoying his evening. I've got an appointment at his office pretty soon, I'll see him then. Please?"

Kira looked at Chloe and began to understand the cloud she was seeing in her eyes. "Yeah, okay, sure," she said. The other women nodded. "I'll ask one in return," Kira said. "Take my card and call me if you need anyone in tech management."

Chloe made her way quickly out of the banquet hall. She was so glad she had picked something to wear that didn't pop.

She had been afraid one of the bathroom ladies was going to ask for a selfie, but no one had.

CHAPTER 11

ONE WEEK, TWO
LAWYER MEETINGS; TOO
MANY, TOO SOON

ONE WEEK, TWO lawyer meetings; too many, too soon.

Chloe put a smile on her face and asked the Rockwell Morton receptionist to announce her to Nelson Gilles.

∽

She had calmed down from her hurt and fury of the night before. Kira Ono had asked him to the animal ball before Chloe had called him over the weekend for their Monday Chop House date. He was under no obligation to turn Kira down, and no obligation not to keep the date with her even after their magic Monday evening. The Chop House and the walk home and the goodnight added up to a wonderful evening, but they did not sum to a commitment.

Still, it burned. All kinds of horribles crossed her mind.

Did he give her a wonderful goodnight kiss? Surely not more. More? Did either of them say anything about getting together again? What was the answer? Was his performance at the charity table so fun for him that he associated that good feeling with Kira? Does he like Asian women? Was his wife Asian? Kira was really, really cute; okay, she was beautiful, if short. Does he like short chicks? Does he like brunettes? Kira seemed nice, too; does he like nice chicks as opposed to pushy broads like herself? Does he like short, nice, beautiful brunettes with big boobs and a nice ass and not so much tall, pushy, beautiful blonds with big boobs and a nice ass? Is he a guy who will try to keep a couple of women on the line? He said he was nervous with her at the Chop House; he didn't seem nervous last night, he was the star of the show and working blue. Does he still think they are on the way to being a thing? Did she even still want that?

And as the horribles mounted, the pain regrew.

She tamped it down.

The date had been innocent.

Everything was going to work out.

She was Chloe Manning.

Nelson Gilles hung around just long enough to greet her and deliver her into the capable hands of Brian Accardo and Oona Karras. Jon Rider was sitting at the conference room table. This time, he had his own laptop set up. He was in a yellow button-down with a brilliant red tie. Its dimple was deep and dark.

Chloe wondered who knew what. Brian probably knew

she'd seen Jon. Maybe Nelson, maybe Oona. She decided it didn't matter and she didn't care. Enough high school bullshit. Focus on the meeting.

Of course, she couldn't do that, not entirely. She had wondered how she would react to seeing Jon again after the promise of Friday, the thrills of Monday, and the crash of the night before. He rose to shake her hand and smiled that Jon Rider smile just south of those Jon Rider eyes. What she felt was his calm and his care aimed her way. She felt no manipulation; she felt no betrayal. She felt like a woman who had some work to do but the goal was there as it always had been. Maybe an unexpected linebacker or two to juke, but if she, Chloe Manning, couldn't do that, then . . . well, that was not a possibility.

She was ready for the meeting. She sat down and pulled some folded pages out of her purse, distributing a page to each of the three lawyers. It was a letter on homemade letterhead dated a few days previously:

Blake Bondurant
4218 DuSable Circle
Unit 413
North Riverside, IL 60546

Dear Ms. Manning,

As you know, I am claiming that you terminated me because of sexual harassment and wrongful termination. You did not have any reason to fire me other than sexual harassment and also because of the hostile sexual environment at Barbiron. Also my job performance was good. The numbers were because of Myra Altobelli did not like me and you know she had trouble with other men who reported to her and also the numbers were faked up to make me look bad.

I know you do not want me to file a lawsuit against you because there would be VERY bad publicity for Barbiron that could cause you and the company a lot of trouble for a long time and you know how that can go when things like this get into the papers with ALL the "dirty laundry" which you know I have.

You may think I'm just blowing smoke well I'm not. I went through all the EEOC complaint and investigation and they turn everyone down so now I have a deadline to file a lawsuit in court. I can file the lawsuit in federal court, not just the state court judges who would kiss your sweet ass. I wanted to give you a chance to make things right with me before I file a suit with lawyers who will get all of the facts into the newspapers. I demand 2 million dollars.

Sincerely,

Blake Bondurant

Brian noted that it was unusual to have this kind of claim come in from the complaining employee rather than a lawyer. It was also unusual, although by no means unheard-of, to have a male complainant in a harassment or hostile sexual environment case. He began by asking what Barbiron had done when it got the complaint notice from the Equal Employment Opportunity Commission.

"We regarded the claim as BS, which it was and is," Chloe said. "Like most companies, we'd had harassment complaints before. None of them went anywhere. My god, the company was built on respect for women and that's the way I demand we treat everyone, men and women. The EEOC only takes the low-hanging fruit or big flashy civil rights claims and this one obviously didn't qualify. We had good records on his performance, or lack of it. I could have involved counsel, but I let HR handle our response, as we do with most EEOC letters. As he says, the EEOC closed the file and did so pretty quickly, as I recall."

"Obviously he hasn't hired a lawyer," Oona said. "Probably hopes you'll cave and pay so he won't have to pay a contingent fee."

"Yeah," Brian said, "but looks like he's at least done his internet homework, got the right buzzwords in there. Followed the rules on filing with the EEOC first. Knows he has a deadline. So what's the story here?"

Chloe told them that at the time of his termination Blake Bondurant was the Director of Quality Assurance/Quality Control. His department checked the quality of Barbiron's processes and products at all of their fabrication and assembly facilities, most of which were in the Chicago area, but some of which were third-party suppliers from other locations across the country. It was a highly responsible position and exposed him to Barbiron's entire manufacturing and distribution process. He had joined

Barbiron as a product inspector who had a background in construction – and thus, tool use – and had shown initiative and honesty in flagging products, including entire product lines, that weren't manufactured to the standards Chloe had set for the company from the beginning. He was promoted to manager after six months and to Director of QA/QC after another six months.

"Don't tell me," Brian said. "Ladies' man around the office, the plant. Big chaser of skirts, if women even wear skirts to work anymore."

"Big time," Chloe said. "God's gift, you know?" It was ridiculous he was making this claim because after he was promoted to QA/QC Director he'd been rumored to have made unwanted advances in his department and elsewhere in the company, although nothing that resulted in a complaint to Human Resources. Of course, Chloe conceded, some of his advances had not been unwanted; some had been very much wanted. There had been suggestions of affairs and sightings of meetups with female colleagues at after-work joints. It was a known worry to management; but in the absence of complaints, and with growing public concerns over employee privacy, Barbiron had taken no action.

Jon was quiet. He was looking at his computer screen.

As to why Blake Bondurant was terminated, Chloe said that they had begun receiving a number of complaints from retailers about product quality, and the accuracy of those complaints had been confirmed by the product returns Barbiron was seeing. While these were manufacturing problems in the first instance, QA/QC was supposed to catch issues with the manufacturing process as well as with the products headed out the door. This was where Myra Altobelli came in. She was Vice President/Manufacturing and Blake's immediate supervisor.

"Was there any thought on your part that Myra had treated Bondurant unfairly?" Brian asked. "Did she have any particular animus towards the guy?"

"No," Chloe said. "The numbers told the tale. Weak and faulty merchandise was getting through. The percentages were tiny, but even a very small number of sub-par items is too many. And when you're talking about tools, it's not just whether the item is defective for what you need it for, there's also the safety concern. The drill falls apart in your hand, you've got a gigantic lawsuit, unhappy insurance carriers, increased premiums, not to mention reputational problems for the brand. Myra might not have liked Blake for other reasons – she wasn't exactly Ms. Amiable with anybody – but she didn't make up the numbers we were seeing."

"Did Myra have a problem with other men?" Oona asked.

"Myra is a tough boss," Chloe said, "but she holds her male and female reports to the same impossible standards. She's been with me since we ramped up our own manufacturing. Blake just thought he was special since he'd been a fair-haired boy at the outset and – that's just the way he was. She put him on a performance improvement program as required by our employee handbook and HR approved. He pouted about that. Then Lowe's rejected a shipment of hammers – hammers, can you believe it, the simplest thing you can imagine – where a bunch of the heads were loose on the handles – and that was it. We terminated him, every step was by the employee handbook and I'm thinking we may even have had this vetted by some outside counsel since he was senior."

"What about his harassment claim?" Brian asked. "Is it just some kind of hostile environment thing with Myra, or is there some evidence that someone harassed him, stalked him, wouldn't leave him alone?"

"I think it's that hostile environment thing," Chloe said, "Myra on his case maybe more than on others because he sucked. The women under her didn't have the performance issues he had developed. Did he get hit on by women at the company? Probably, but he invited it and probably initiated it often as not." This was not territory Chloe wanted to explore in detail. "The point is, his discipline and termination had nothing to do with his – with his behavior with women. And I should add that he himself never made a claim with HR about any kind of harassment or hostile environment, so he can't even claim we retaliated against him for complaining. And, of course, he himself didn't follow our procedures for reporting harassment or hostile environment and giving the company a chance to investigate and discipline if the complaint appears justified. We do training every year and every employee absolutely knows to report things like this."

"So far this looks pretty straightforward," Brian said. "Performance-based grounds for termination. Failure to follow internal procedures. No known evidence, at least not known to Chloe or HR, of harassment or hostility. No retaliation. His own harassing activity which we can prove with our own witnesses. Not worth two cents, much less two million. Oona, let's brainstorm later on whether to take some kind of preemptive action on this to forestall a suit, maybe, shall we say, a strongly-worded letter to Mr. Bondurant."

He turned to Jon. "You've been pretty quiet over there," he said. "You got anything?"

Jon was quiet some more. He continued to look at the screen. It all sounded like a garden variety claim from a disgruntled employee. But he was troubled by the tone of the letter. And he was doubly troubled that there was a hidden problem that might fall on the shoulders of a woman who had snagged his emotions like no woman since Amelia. He didn't know whether he should probe, or just assure her that Brian and Oona knocked stuff like this out of the park all the time, which was quite true. But his duty was to the client Barbiron.

Duty – passion's cold shower.

Jon shook his head slowly. "Brian summed it up to a tee. Several killer defenses. No evidence to support his claims described in the letter other than his claim of dummying up the books, which I assume is nonsense."

"It is," Chloe said.

Jon thought again about whether to go on. Too late.

"What's pulling on my sleeve," he said, "is that Bondurant has got to know, even if with nothing more than the internet research he's obviously done, all of the weaknesses in his case that Brian laid out. I think he may know he doesn't have a sex case, much less one worth two million." He paused. "So I'm asking myself, is there something else going on here?"

Chloe did not react.

He said, "This letter looks personal. He didn't want a lawyer to write it. He wanted you to be personally afraid of his lawsuit. He wanted to be threatening in a way that a lawyer wouldn't be, or couldn't be. This is not a model of English composition, but I'm thinking he's not stupid. He's done some homework. He's got to know that companies like Barbiron get sued on stuff like this all the time and the public yawns."

"He could be stupid," Chloe said. "He is stupid."

That rang oddly in Jon's ears. "Did you have much contact with him?" Jon asked.

"No, although – no. I know all of our employees, certainly down to the director and manager levels."

"I'm going to take a little flyer here," Jon said. "This is going to come out of left field, but let me ask you this: Has Barbiron got something big in the works, maybe planning to go public, or to go to the market to do some big capital raise, or merge, get bought out, something really big?"

Jesus, Chloe thought. *HTF in God's name did he know that from this bonehead letter?*

"How is that relevant?" she asked.

"Maybe not at all," Jon said, noting that she ducked the question. "I'm just trying to figure out why he's emphasizing bad news for the company, and 'all the dirty laundry' and whatnot since the public and the markets are not going to care anything about a fairly standard employment dispute, especially one involving a private company."

Chloe was quiet. This was not going as simply as she had assumed it would. A tiny star of fear sparkled in her gut.

"It just looks like a ransom note, that's all," Jon said. "It looks like he's trying to say that he's got some dirt that would hurt the company in some way other than just dealing with his harassment lawsuit, trying to say it without saying it. But that raises more questions: What does he know, how does he know it, and how would it – how does he phrase it? – 'cause the company a lot of trouble for a long time'? And the personal hostility directed towards you, the 'sweet ass' reference. Nasty, entirely gratuitous. And the huge demand, two million. He has to know that's ridiculous for this kind of claim, even without advice of counsel. I'm repeating myself, but it looks like he thinks he has some really bad information that will screw up some really important thing for Barbiron."

He looked down at his screen again at the smirking, model-handsome face in the headshot Blake Bondurant had selected for his LinkedIn thumbnail. Google Images had found a few more photos of a tall, well-built man with fashionably brushed-up hair and facial stubble. Terrific teeth; too white to be entirely natural, but really phenomenal choppers nonetheless.

"Are you thinking some kind of whistleblower thing, some kind of company wrongdoing?" Oona said.

"Maybe," Jon said. "I'm not sure what I'm thinking, if I'm thinking anything. Yeah, maybe a whistleblower thing, as Oona says," but he did not think that was what Blake Bondurant was insinuating.

"I don't know," Brian said. "If he thought he had some kind of smoking gun about company skullduggery that wasn't related to his weak harassment claim, you would think he would be more explicit about the threat if he wanted Barbiron to take it seriously. I see what you're saying but the letter is also just consistent with the guy being kind of a thug."

"Yeah," Jon said, "It is. It is. I may be overanalyzing this guy's prose that barely merits analysis at all. But I can't help but feel that something's missing here." He looked up at Chloe. "Can you think of anything else, any other unusual circumstances surrounding his employment or termination?"

She shook her head and paused two beats. "I don't know what that would be," she said, looking at Brian. "His numbers were in the toilet. He knew it."

Jon left it there. He did not know what else to do. This extraordinary woman who might be his future was lying to the room, and he was in that room.

"Well, if there is anything, and probably there isn't, I can tell you that Brian and Oona will dig it out and deal with it. If the records on his performance are as you have described, this should not be a very difficult case no matter what he claims to know. Despite what the public may think, employment cases are difficult for fired employees to win if they were demonstrably poor performers, and I'm sure this one will be no exception, especially in the hands of these two burners," nodding to Brian and Oona.

There was a hint of sadness in the smile Jon gave Chloe as he rose to leave the meeting.

"But I've got no miracles for you today," he said. "Sorry."

CHAPTER 12

CHLOE FELT LIKE SHE WAS SLEEPWALKING

CHLOE FELT LIKE she was sleepwalking as she felt herself drawn to Jon Rider's office.

She stood in his doorway. The star of fear had gone nova into panic as the meeting had progressed, but now, as she looked at him, it had begun to cool into resignation.

"Hello," she said.

"Well, hi," he said, standing. "Please come in. It's lovely to see you again so soon. I wish the circumstances weren't so worrisome for you."

"This is your office?" she said. She closed the door behind her and looked around. A laptop sat on a small wheeled table. An old beat-up Samsung was the only visible phone. Other than the Aeron chair he was sitting in, there was only one other chair, a simple mesh work chair with wheels. A file caddy held a few papers, but the Pendaflex folders were mostly empty. There was no other furniture. There was nothing on the walls.

"I stare into space a lot," he said. "I don't like distractions. Please sit."

There would be no getting-to-know-you talk today, and no more small talk.

"Are you a wizard?" Chloe said. "Are you a sorcerer?"

Jon did not seem surprised. "No," he said. "Neither."

"How did you know?" she asked.

"How did I know what?"

"Everything."

"Obviously, I didn't and don't."

"You guessed."

"I guessed. I'm still guessing."

"What are you guessing? Take me through it. One lousy letter that says nothing – it says nothing! – and you figured it all out. I want to know how you got there."

"Are you going to tell me?" Jon said.

"Yes," she said, sighing, "I am. I have to. If you and I have any chance of doing something here after last Monday, I can't keep things from you. And, I can see now, from Brian or Oona. But I thought –"

"You thought maybe this could go away like the Philbrick case did."

"Maybe," she said. "Yes. Yes. Maybe you could make it go poof. Instead, you saw right through that piece of crap letter to the real problem, but I just don't see how –"

"First, you're here. Barbiron typically has the CFO supervising routine cases with outside counsel. Employment litigation for a company like yours is the definition of routine. And Brian nailed the summary of its obvious and fatal weaknesses. So what brought the CEO to her feet on this particular threat? Something about this one was bothering you on a more personal level. And it was important enough that you wanted it dealt with somehow before a lawsuit was filed, like most companies would do if they got a garbage letter like that, not even from a lawyer, no details, nothing. And I note Amy was not invited.

"Second, as I said at the meeting, it looked to me like he was suggesting he had some secret negative information that would be especially meaningful to you and harmful to Barbiron beyond his stupid harassment claim.

"Third, so what if he did, unless Barbiron had something at stake like a public financing or merger of some kind and they couldn't afford some big crisis or scandal? Or, if not some big deal for the company, something damaging about you?

"Fourth, how would a jamoke like Bondurant know about a big-time confidential company initiative like that unless somebody high up in the company who knew about it told him?

"Fifth, Bondurant looks like a younger, bigger Richard Gere with even better teeth and bedroomier eyes.

"And sixth, not to treat this unseriously, understand me, but he seemed to have an opinion on the sweetness of your ass, a reference I thought was extremely menacing, almost threatening. It wasn't just a rude vulgarity like it appeared, it was a sly shot at you personally, something you would understand. So . . . ."

"Unbelievable," Chloe said. "You got most of it."

"This letter is blackmail, isn't it?"

"Yes."

"How long?"

"How long what?"

"How long was your affair?"

"How dare —! We were *not* having an affair! How dare you think that?" She felt like she might start crying, he was so close. In that moment, she hated him for his gift of insight that had drawn her to him less than a week earlier.

"Is Barbiron going public?"

She flared at him, stood up. She'd drifted to his office knowing she was going to confess it all, but hearing him nail it again reminded her that she was not the boss of this process, and that angered her. Her instinct was to use her height to look down on difficult men.

Jon did not move and did not raise his head. He looked her in the eye from under his brow. "You said you were going to tell me," he said. "You are going to tell me. You are going to tell a lot of people before too long. Please don't go; sit down. I'm sorry for the cross-examination but we've got to know what we're dealing with here."

Chloe stood there breathing hard, glaring at him, feeling all of the romance of the past few days drain out of her, putting her emotional life back where it started – nowhere.

Jon let her stand there. He watched her. Took a chance and smiled a tiny smile as he raised his head to face her. "May I get you a glass of water, something else to drink?"

The fire left her eyes and her breath returned. "No, thank you," she said. She sat down and gathered herself. "Yes, Barbiron is considering going public. It has been in the works for a while. The board and I have been interviewing investment banks. It looks like it is going to happen. How the goddam hell did you —?"

"So," Jon bent closer to her and dropped his voice. His tone was almost kindly, gently searching. "No affair. I'm sorry I jumped there, that guess was a stretch I should have kept to myself. Not all my inferential leaps end with me on my feet. Come on. Please forgive me, Chloe."

She looked at him through reddened eyes. She nodded. His guess wasn't that much of a stretch.

"But Blake knows about it," Jon said. "Interfering with the public offering is his threat here."

Chloe nodded.

"That leaves two more questions: How does Blake Bondurant come to know about Barbiron going public? And what does he know that could endanger an IPO if he went public with it? Something that could completely tank your IPO if everyone knew what you're about to tell me, something he thinks might be worth a couple million."

The tears began to appear, just a few. "I've been so stupid. Stupid to think I could get rid of this without – without anyone knowing what I am going to tell you, which was the original main stupid thing. I guess I imagined you as the man who knew how to make all my troubles go away."

"I wish I were that special, Chloe," Jon said. "I can't make problems go away if I don't know what they are."

They both sat there quietly. Jon had pushed her far and hard enough. He knew she was going to tell him what had happened. She had to do it in her own way at her own speed.

"Nobody knows this. Not Amy, not anyone."

"Not the board," Jon said.

"Hell no, not the board."

"Not Lisa?"

"Not Lisa. No one."

Jon whispered. "All right. All right."

And then it all came out.

"This happened about a year ago. About six months before we terminated Blake. We had had an amazing Q1, a record-setting quarter for us. The preliminary numbers had just come in and I was on top of the world. The board had been kicking around an initial public offering, and this was the kind of quarter that made us all want to go for it.

"It was the end of the day. I didn't want to go home, I wanted to go out and celebrate. But the numbers were confidential, it was a Friday, people had snuck out early – they thought they were sneaking but I knew who was there and who wasn't but I usually wasn't a hardass about Fridays.

"So, it was just me. No one I really wanted to call, no one I could really tell what was going on, anyway. I decided I was just going to go somewhere out of the way, somewhere I might not be recognized, maybe try to find some live music, have a couple of drinks, maybe read a Don Winslow on my Kindle, just get lost for a couple of hours. We were having a jeans Friday; I pulled my hair back, pulled my shirttail out, changed into some flats I had at the office. I even had some black eyeglass frames with plain glass. Put on a White Sox hat. I was about as incognito as I could get.

"There was this new little jazz hangout on Hubbard near Ogden, not far from the office, Lloyd's I think it's called. Lloyd's Jazz something. Kind of a new hot spot then. Don't know now. Neighborhood okay, felt safe with Uber. Found a small hightop along the wall away from the front door and windows. And I was reading *The Winter of Frankie Machine* and it was great and I felt rich and sexy and like I could do anything and the place was loud and cool and I started to drink. I think it was a Russian River pinot grigio, doesn't matter, but it just went down smooth and fast and I kept 'em coming and I'm not that big a drinker. I should have ordered some bar food but I didn't.

"There was a quartet that was really loud and I hadn't eaten lunch and the wine and the music and the noise of the crowd was really pounding into me and I thought about Robert DeNiro playing Frankie Machine in the movie and how cool that would be when of course, there he was. Blake, not DeNiro. Standing at the bar, talking to some men and women. I only focused on him but I've wondered since then if there were any other employees there. Hope not, no one ever said anything, but I couldn't swear. He was the only one who came over to talk after he saw me. Probably noticed me because I was drunk-staring at him.

"Blake was QA/QC Director, a pretty senior position so yeah, I knew him some. He could be flirty at the office and I wasn't interested and I didn't encourage him but I didn't tell him to f off, you know? So he came over to try his luck. I knew it, he knew it. I was drunk, really drunk, and he obviously could see that, too. We had at least one more there. I don't remember exactly what his line was, but I know he had one. Some insinuating BS about 'quality,' I think. I only remember it was so loud with the music and the crowd, he would bring his face close to mine when we were trying to hear each other and then we were kissing."

"And somewhere along the line," Jon said, "you mentioned that the company was going to go public. You may have been a little more certain about that happening with all that pinot grigio going through your veins than was actually the case at the time."

"I probably did," she said. "I did. I had all the great news from the day bouncing around up here." She tapped her head. "Bragging about this IPO I was pretty sure we were going to do."

She paused, thinking.

"I have a feeling that's not the end of the story," Jon said.

"No," she said. "It's not the end of my stupid story." Jon waited.

"Some of this is not so clear," she went on. "I was so drunk. So drunk. I remember the next day wondering if I'd paid my tab. But I must have paid because I got my credit card back from the waitress. Anyway." She paused to take a breath.

"Anyway, we ended up at the FOUND Hotel over on Wells. It kind of has an upscale hostel vibe to it, very inexpensive but kind of a cool place, and it has a bar off the lobby downstairs so we had another drink. Just one, because we were still pretty much all over each other and they kind of scowled us out of there."

She paused again. "And then we checked in. And then it just got weird. I was so drunk."

"Was he?"

"A very good question," Chloe said. "I think probably

not so much, not nearly as drunk as I was. But me being incredibly drunk may have ended up being a kind of half-assed good thing because of what happened next. Ready?

"I took off all my clothes. Every stitch. Soon as I got in the room."

"Chloe," Jon said gently, "you don't need to go into a lot of detail with me right now. You can just tell me generally –"

"Oh yes," she said, "yes, I do need to tell you all of what happened because it was so weird and awful and important to the story and because – because I want you to know.

"So, I'm standing there totally nude, my clothes thrown all over the place, staggering some to try to stay upright and I think I was demanding that he get going, you know, raving like a drunk. Not like a drunk, an actual drunk. He starts to undress.

"And right then, I started feeling sick. That last glass of wine was too much on top of already too much. I thought I was going to pass out. I stumbled into the bathroom and felt like I was going to throw up so I was bent over the toilet, naked, bent over the goddam toilet! And holding my hair back so I wouldn't fucking vomit on myself! And retching, but nothing was coming up because I had nothing in my stomach, but I kept retching until I could spit a little something out – I'm sorry this is so gross – but when I stood up I thought I saw a vision of myself, you know, like when you die? But it was just the mirror and I'm standing there with retching tears running down my face and still wearing those stupid black frames I forgot to take off looking like goddam Sarah Palin but not nearly so good and fucking naked and shitfaced! I'm sorry for the pottymouth but the whole thing was just a f—a nightmare. And it hit me with that kind of fake insight that drunks experience, I guess, but whatever it was I realized I was completely nude in a hotel room with an almost nude Blake Bondurant who was expecting to have sex with me in about thirty seconds."

"Did he – ?"

"He never touched me in the room. I have to say that. I ran out of the bathroom and I think I was saying over and over *I have to get out of here, I have to get out of here* and gathering up my clothes and trying to put them back on at the same time, putting on whatever I could find and grab. I couldn't look at him. He approached me saying stuff like *come on baby, let's just do it, no one's going to find out*, you know, really comforting and persuasive stuff, but I threatened to scream. And I was still drunk, of course, but trying, trying so hard to concentrate on getting away.

"And I got my jeans and shirt on and grabbed my jacket and purse and Sox hat and got out of there. It wasn't super late and it was walking distance to my building and I didn't want to throw up in an Uber so I walked home. I should have worried more about the lone-woman-walking-around-at-night thing but, you know, totally drunk and not being smart. I took a long route, walked around some blocks trying to sober up a little before I had to face George. Thank god I had the flats on. It was chilly, late March, so that helped wake me up a little. George nodded at me as I kind of poured myself into the building, but I think he just said to let him know if I needed anything, and I think he reached in the elevator and punched my floor."

Jon waited, but she was done. She was looking at the floor.

"So, intoxication aside, and maybe the making out in public, the absolute worst thing that happened was that you were in a hotel room with a Barbiron employee and you were both nude, or at least you were. And you told him some company secrets. You refused to have sex with him and you left. He did not assault you and you did not assault him."

She nodded.

"No one died," Jon said, "and no one broke any laws. In the context of Barbiron planning to go public, the blackmail story is about your judgment with an employee, maybe even about your alcohol use, your comportment in public. He'll either claim you had a sexual relationship, or claim you attempted to initiate one and he refused. And that as a result either of an affair gone bad, or him refusing you, eventually you fired him. Bad CEO judgment in the 'me too' era with a gender reversal, a river of pinot grigio, and some other colorful aspects. And in the course of all of this, it will come out that you disclosed highly confidential board information to this supposed lover, more questionable judgment. But even that isn't illegal. You're not a public company. He was a somewhat senior employee. He wasn't buying or selling your stock."

"Are you trying to say this isn't so bad?"

"I don't know how an underwriter would feel about an offering with something like this in the papers, or threatened," Jon said. Actually, he did know – with Barbiron being so closely associated with her leadership and celebrity, they'd run like hell until she was long gone from the company.

"There's Barbiron," she said, "and then there's me."

"Yep," Jon said. "There are multiple issues here, for sure. Barbiron could suffer in the financial and even retail markets, and your personal reputation is also in play, and I don't want to downplay that. Let me ask a couple of things, okay? I know that was rough, Chloe, I know you hated pretty much every syllable of that, but just a couple of details, if you remember. First, did you pay for the room?"

"Yes," she said.

"Use a Barbiron credit card?"

"Yes. The statements on company cards come to the employees and they seek reimbursement for all business expenses. I never submitted that one for reimbursement. Amy kept reminding me to turn it in but I told her I only had a few personal items on it for that month."

"Did anyone at the hotel recognize you or your name on the card?"

"The staff was real young. They didn't seem to, weren't the type to be up on business or fashion. Same with the waitress at Lloyd's."

"Is it possible he took any pictures?"

Chloe blanched. "I swear to God I didn't consider that until this moment. I don't know. Damn, that snake could have snuck some while I was standing there and he was handling his own pants with the phone in the pocket. Or while I was bent over the toilet trying not to puke on my hair. I don't think I closed the door. Hell, he could have video or audio!" She put her head in her hands. "Oh my god."

"His letter doesn't hint about having anything like that," Jon said.

"I'll tell you what he does have," she said. "Remember I said I threw on my jeans and top and jacket? Well, that's all I threw on. That creep probably still has my bra and panties."

Jon thought back to the letter's remark about *dirty laundry*, which Blake had put in quotes, and which said *which you know I have*, not *which you know I know*. "There's a fair chance," he said. "So even though no laws were broken, this can be painted in rather lurid colors if it's being threatened to muck up your offering or your life."

"Stupid," she said. "So stupid."

Not so stupid, Jon thought.

She's a superwoman.

But a woman.

And a human being.

"What happened at Barbiron after that?" Jon said. "He didn't get fired until months later. I notice his letter starts out 'as you know,' like this was not the first time he'd threatened you. When did he start making noise about this?"

"Several months after we let him go, he sent me an email that looked the same as the letter I brought today except for the stuff about the EEOC. That was a while back, several months ago. It was just an email, no lawyers involved, he only sent it to me. He hadn't been threatening around the office before we fired him, so I figured I'd ignore it until I heard from a lawyer." Jon agreed that was a reasonable strategy at the time and asked her to forward that email to him. She said she would.

"What about things around the office?"

"I kept my distance and I was a little surprised that he kind of did the same. He never approached me, never mentioned it, and as far as I know, he didn't gossip about it. No one ever brought it up to me or hinted around about it, ever. If there had been even the slightest whisper, Amy would have heard it and come to me. For a while there, I thought hmm, maybe he's being a gentleman about this, not taking an advantage of an impaired woman. Now I see he was just saving it up for a payday."

"There's your silver lining," Jon said. "He's got to keep saving it up if he's hoping to extort you. As soon as it gets out, the secret will do whatever damage it is going to do, and it no longer has any value to him. Assuming we don't pay the blackmail and he files his suit, I'm guessing this encounter won't be mentioned in the complaint or any public filing. It's not beyond imagining that he won't tell his lawyer, at least at first. Waiting to see if Barbiron blinks and eventually caves if it wants to go to the market for financing or an IPO. If Barbiron goes to trial on the sex harassment and hostile sexual environment claims, the blackmail will have failed but they'll use it before the jury and try to get their payday from them. So we have some time to decide what to do about this.

"Now, the cloud that surrounds that silver lining," he continued. "We're going to get Brian and Oona back in that conference room and tell them about this. And I'm going to try to round up Nelson; we'll need him. They absolutely have to know. It may not need to go any further outside the company, it will all depend on what happens when the case is filed. But for now, yes, they have to know."

"I know," Chloe said.

"And then . . ." Jon said.

"The board!" she said. "I can't –!"

"You can," Jon said. "Nelson Gilles is a master with directors. He will be there with you when you disclose this to the board. Perhaps an informal meeting where there aren't minutes; Nelson will know what to do and will guide you through the whole thing. And the board will have to decide how to respond to this. They will need all of the information, and they will need your input and they will need Rockwell Morton's input."

"And your input?" she said. "What is your input, Jon Rider?"

Jon was afraid this was going to come up. The question of his position in all this had been nagging at him since he read Blake Bondurant's demand letter. "My input is figuring out what that letter was really all about. My input was you trusting me enough to come to my office after the meeting when I was going to let you off the hook today. My input was you knowing that I knew, because, babe, like Cher, you got me the minute we saw each other last Friday. You came to my office because you knew I knew and you wanted to tell me, but at the same time hated me for knowing, or, if I'm going to be honest about it, guessing. But your little good angel told you you had to do it."

She thought about a tiny Lisa Blazier in angel garb telling her to be good but that image popped and dissolved as soon as it appeared. She was tired of sitting. Standing was too dramatic. So she sat, composed herself in Jon's lonely wheeled chair, and said:

"I lied to you."

"Perhaps . . ."

"I lied to you and then I was furious when you found me out, it was like I felt a dark side to your brilliance even though I was in the wrong and my feelings went all sideways because I didn't think I was whoever that lying person was."

Jon hated that she was going through this. Even though it was entirely her poor judgment that had given rise to this impossible situation. Hated it. And suddenly he understood why he hated it so much.

"I have something to say, Chloe. And the first thing I have to say is, shut up."

She opened her mouth, then closed it.

"You are Chloe Manning," he said.

"You were lonely. Loneliness is the queen of sadness.

"On that day you had reached a kind of pinnacle, a real pivot point in your life with the great numbers and the prospect of heading up an IPO that was going to make you millions and one of the most famous executives in the country. Of either gender.

"It was a day to celebrate.

"It was a day for your lover to take you in his arms and tell you how proud he was of you and take you out for a wonderful dinner where you would split a bottle of Russian River pinot grigio, and you would toast and talk about your future together while the quartet played 'Unforgettable.' Played it softly.

"And then you would go back to your place and make love with visions of this amazing future bouncing around in your fevered brains like Christmas sugarplums. So good, the best ever.

"But there was no lover that night. You had no lover in your life. Maybe a lover would have distracted you, kept you from whipping Barbiron to achieve those numbers. No room for a lover, so no lover when Q1 closed.

"There was only Blake Bondurant, who, if I might be so bold to observe from his online presence, is one of the handsomest men I have ever seen in my life.

"We have all done and said shameful, dishonorable, absurdly ridiculous things with the opposite sex when we've had too much to drink. Yes, I have.

"Most female humans in your position and your condition would have plopped themselves down on that hotel bed and, please excuse the graphic imagery, spread their magnificent stems and let Blake Bondurant fuck *completely* out whatever brains she had left after all that alcohol. And awakened next morning with middle-management Adonis snoring next to her and a much worse problem than you have now.

"You did not do that.

"Something, through that Russian River haze, told you that this, that that scene, was *all wrong*."

"Yes," she said.

"And that is why," he said, "you are Chloe Manning."

"So I try to tell myself," she said.

"And that is why," he said — was he ready to say it? Was it too soon? Less than a week since the day they'd met? He had a fleeting vision of himself as a protective bubble that would surround and move with her always, in which she could move through life free from threats, free to bless the world with her gifts.

But he was Jon Rider. He stepped back. Because that is what Jon Rider did. He didn't say it, couldn't get his mouth around that simple word.

He said instead: "And that is why nothing you said here today changes anything about my feelings about you and what we started on Monday."

"What about the lie?" she said.

"Every lover gets a mulligan," he said

"But we're not lov –"

"I believe I instructed you to shut up," he said, smiling. He stood over her. "I'm renewing that order now."

She stood. He put his hands on her waist. "You want to know my input?" he said. "My input is that until further notice I am your man and you will not have to be alone."

He kissed her so hard that she fell back into her chair and he didn't break the kiss but bent over and pressed his mouth into hers and rolled the chair into a wall and he put his hand behind her head to cushion it and deepened the kiss and she started to spread her legs to hook his but at the same instant they each realized it was 11:40 a.m. on Thursday in the offices of Rockwell Morton & Gilles LLP, and Jon stood up and as he rose played with a few strands of her hair and then went to his phone to call Brian Accardo.

CHAPTER 13

A LOT HAD TO BE DONE QUICKLY AND QUIETLY

A LOT HAD to be done quickly and quietly.

Jon initiated a low-key response to Blake Bondurant's demand letter.

The Rockwell Morton team established protocols for communicating among themselves and with Chloe to keep the matter out of digital files available to anyone at the firm or at Barbiron.

Jon and Nelson developed a careful plan for presenting this information to the Barbiron board of directors. The account would have to come from Chloe's own mouth. This was going to be shocking information to the four men and two women on the board, who were her major original investors. But she could have had a worse audience for her revelations. She had raised her seed money from these investors in their role as wealthy individuals and not as representatives of funds or investment banks or syndicates.

They were themselves mavericks who had been excited by Chloe's vision – and her energy and brains, and in the cases of a couple of the men, her beauty and charisma – and signed on without a lot of the folderol and rights and backstops that institutional and venture investors required. These men and women were used to risk and used to crisis. She had not let them down in the years since they took a chance on her. Around the board table was oil money, car parts money, gaming software money, and even some actual gambling money. Tough money.

Jon had corporate governance and securities experience from the cases he had handled, and one thing that was clear to him, and needed to be made clear to the board, was that information about Chloe's indiscretion was potentially of critical legal significance to the company. Blake's threat was real.

He explained it to Nelson to translate for the board:

One way to look at it was that it was an almost comical, one-off drunken episode that had no implications for the management and success of Barbiron, the kind of childish sexual misadventure everyone has had and everyone has buried as live-and-learn.

Which was true.

Another way to view it was that the founder, CEO, and extremely public face of a near-billion dollar company had gotten sloppy drunk in public at a down-low jazz joint, stripped nude for a non-executive employee with the intention to have sex with him at a local low-cost hotel, and blurted out the very most sensitive kind of corporate information, leaving her undergarments behind in the process.

Which was also true; but, for purposes of determining its effect on Barbiron's public corporate strategy, more true than the first version.

That is, Jon explained, her behavior and Blake's resulting extortion attempt would be considered significant – to an unknown degree, but significant – to someone deciding whether to purchase stock in Barbiron. Someone, for example, who would consider buying stock as part of an initial public offering – underwriters who bought the initial issuance of shares, and their customers to whom they resold them. Which meant, in turn, that unless Barbiron were willing to disclose this to underwriters investigating the company before deciding whether to participate in the IPO, and also willing to disclose it in the public filings that accompany IPOs – there could be no public offering of Barbiron stock.

Nelson arranged an informal cocktail hour for the board in a meeting room at III Forks Steakhouse advertised as an off-the-record discussion of Barbiron's next steps. After Chloe delivered a forthright and even graphic account of that long-ago evening's sorry activities, each of the board members expressed deep disappointment in Chloe's behavior, which she acknowledged with humility and regret. Although their disapproval was sincere, Nelson later reported that a couple of the men and one of the women, herself a beauty from the eighties who had busted through a couple of glass ceilings in her time, had to fight back smiles as they imagined their lovely celebrity founder and CEO drunk and nude with a movie-star-handsome subordinate.

Nelson and Brian laid out the board's choices. None was attractive:

They could reach out to Blake Bondurant's lawyers – he would have to be hiring some soon – and negotiate a settlement, paying the blackmail at some negotiated but very substantial amount pursuant to an agreement that would include confidentiality terms (and return of photographic and lingerie evidence, if any). There was some sentiment among the directors that Barbiron should make the best early deal it could with Blake and be done with it, even at a high price. But Nelson pointed out that even if Barbiron settled on those terms, the unusually large cash outlay to settle a routine case by a provably poor employee would draw the attention of the underwriters during their due diligence for the public offering; they would question why Barbiron overpaid so drastically and so quickly. They would want to know what company circumstance could possibly have justified a seven-figure payment on something usually settled for nuisance value or resisted until the case was dismissed. And Barbiron would have to tell them. Terms of the settlement might even have to be disclosed in the public filings with the Securities and Exchange Commission and in the documents given to potential investors. In the end, a quick settlement at a high price would not have accomplished anything. Even if Blake couldn't blab, Barbiron might have to.

Or they could terminate Chloe and proceed with the IPO in the hope that her termination would cure the terrible-drunken-CEO-judgment issue, even if the event had to be disclosed. That discussion lasted about eleven seconds.

As appalled as the board was at Chloe's indiscreet naked celebration of the healthy Q1 numbers, no one wanted her out. And everyone in the room knew that her share position, plus that of just a couple of other investors, elected most of the directors; if she didn't want to go, she could stay right where she was. But it was not going to come to that. She was not going to play hardball with these long-time supporters, and they appreciated her brilliance and leadership and the asset of her being Barbiron's dynamic public face. There was even some question whether an IPO could succeed without her, at least at a share price that reflected Barbiron's true value. Forgiveness was a foregone conclusion, even though any kind of capital raise was going to have to wait until this unfortunate drama had reached a final act.

In the end, the board made the only rational choice: Continue to conduct Barbiron's business as usual, postpone the IPO and any other major financing, and let the Rockwell Morton team resist the case with sensitivity, but with an aggressiveness that would not spill over into provocation. Nelson assured the board he and Brian would be able to secure a protective order that would keep all discovery in the case confidential. He would also seek an expedited discovery and trial schedule to try to force a resolution at the earliest possible date – for better or worse.

Nelson promised reports no less frequently than monthly. He cautioned that there was a lot that could go wrong. The situation, as he put it, would be like the guy who tightroped between the Twin Towers all those years ago: The guy was walking that tightrope real good, but you can never see the wind coming and it was a long way down.

And, he added:

You all know how unpredictable the Chicago wind can be.

∾

Jon considered where matters stood in the few days following Blake Bondurant's threatening letter.

Confidentiality protocols in place. Board advised and hanging in there with Chloe. Litigation strategy would have to abide whatever complaint Blake Bondurant filed, but the general outlines were clear enough: The evidence that he was fired for cause was right there in black and white – his job performance had measurably deteriorated. There was no harassment or hostile sexual environment of which Blake could credibly claim to have been a victim. All evidence would be kept confidential at least until trial, and they would try to push the case to a conclusion as quickly as possible.

But there was a loose thread, and Jon knew he was going to have to pull on it very soon.

∾

One date. One office meeting that ended in a kiss and a promise. And one towering crisis in the life and career of Chloe Manning.

"I think I owe you another thank-you," she said

over her pinot grigio – from Monterey, having sworn off Russian River.

"Not at all," Jon said.

"You were strong. You were calm during my tantrum. You treated me with respect even while you were making me stop lying. And at the end, very sweet," she said.

"None of that was hard, with you," he said.

"And you whipped the team into shape and nailed down the secrecy and you and Nelson and Brian handled the board beautifully. All within a few days."

"The board trusts and, frankly, loves you."

"What's next?" she said.

"Between us, I'm thinking that we keep exploring our feelings if that is what you want. It is what I want. The thing with Blake – I've already told you how I feel. It actually deepens my respect for your fundamental goodness and also reveals the vulnerability that awakens a man's – that would be my – protective feelings towards a woman no matter how strong or smart she is. Oh, you'll feel my weaknesses and needs, too. I got a bunch. So while we can't act like it never happened, in the long run it'll end up being just a crazy milestone in your life – in our lives."

"Oo, you do speak with such honeyed tongue, *kemo sabe*," she said. "Do you ever say the wrong thing to women?"

I'm about to, he thought.

"What's next in the case? Wait for the complaint?"

"Good news there," he said. He knew this was not going to deflect the coming bad news, but he pressed on. "Brian and Oona are absolutely excellent, none better in the city, and – this is almost unheard of – Nelson is going to stay actively involved with the case. I don't know how he and Brian will divvy things up, but when decisions need to be made and the company needs guidance Barbiron has the A-plus team."

"I didn't hear your name mentioned on that team," Chloe said.

"No," Jon said. "I'm not going to be working on the case from this point."

"You're kidding."

"No. Chloe, I can't."

"Of course you – why not? You've saved me twice with your smarts and I need those smarts now more than ever."

"Because if we're going to be a thing, I have to be completely there for you emotionally, and that is a very different thing than being completely there for you in the case. They can't exist together and I want the first thing, not the second thing."

"That's ridiculous," she said. "Sounds like a bunch of technical gobbledygook to me."

"It's a formal ethical rule with good reason behind it," he said. "All firms, at least all firms that are any good, have a rule against attorneys getting romantically involved with clients. Rockwell Morton has that rule, and it's also in the rules that govern the legal profession here in Illinois. Sure, sometimes they're winked at, you hear about lawyers marrying clients from time to time, but you more often hear about those relationships interfering with legal representation to the detriment of both the representation and the relationship. Sometimes a case goes bad, sometimes the evidence doesn't go the way the client expected it to, and the lawyer has to be completely free to deliver bad news and deal with it as he or she sees fit."

"I don't see why that has to be a problem for a relationship."

"I'll give you an example that's about to come up. In fact, it's come up in this very conversation. When we talk about this case, we, you and the lawyers, casually talk about representing 'you,' Chloe Manning. You just said 'you saved me twice' and 'I need you now more than ever.' In fact, we do not represent you, we represent the company entity Barbiron. Do you remember when you were in my office and you said something like 'there are Barbiron's issues, and then there are my issues'? Well, you were exactly right. They're two different things.

"Now, I fully expect when this complaint is filed it will name you personally as a defendant alongside the company. Question: Who will represent you? Answer: the company is allowed to pay for your defense and damages as long as the claimed activities were performed while you were acting as an officer of Barbiron. And we will be allowed to represent you as long as your interests are perfectly aligned with Barbiron's.

"But you can see where this is going: When you were shouting at Blake to strip and drunkenly disclosing company secrets, were you acting as the CEO of Barbiron? Or were you off on a personal toot to get laid –"

"Shut up!" she said. "I can't believe those words are coming out of your mouth."

"You're going to hear a lot worse from the witness stand. This is what I'm talking about, Chloe. I'm not even entirely your boyfriend and look at us! Fighting about this godforsaken case. Now listen to me and use your formidable brain. The board could say sorry, Ms. Manning, you were acting for your own interest on your own time that night at the FOUND Hotel in your jeans and White Sox hat and fake glasses, so your defense and any damages assessed against you personally are out of your pocket. This is only one of the issues where you could have a conflict with the board, which means a conflict with your own company, and we would only be able to represent the company and not you.

"Now before you blow your stack – I can see the steam coming out of your ears, but hold on – this board is not going to cut you loose. We know that. But it may hire separate counsel for you. Rockwell Morton might not even represent you. And by the way, that's something that Nelson will advise them on, whether Barbiron should defend you or not, and that analysis changes as the case progresses. The board will constantly be considering it, and the firm will be constantly advising it on the conflict issue as the case evolves.

"But even aside from a conflict between you and the corporation, your lawyer may have to give you some unpleasant advice and insist that you do things you don't want to do.

"Maybe he's going to say Chloe, settle this damned thing.

"Maybe he's going to say Chloe, we're not going to get out of this without some of this stuff leaking.

"Maybe he's going to say Chloe, the time has come to get you separate representation.

"Maybe he's going to say Chloe, if you don't schedule prep time for your deposition like your life depended on it, or if you smart off to opposing counsel, you're going to get it shoved down your throat at trial.

"And maybe he's going to say Chloe, let's cool it with the fashionista stuff until this is over.

"And there's another side to that coin: You wouldn't want a lawyer whose feelings for you would bias his own judgment on what was best for you, who would pull punches that needed to be punched because he didn't want to upset you.

"I don't want that for *us*, my sweet and lovely woman. I am for *you*, the *woman*, and not for you, the client who may have to hear unpleasant advice and criticism. And who, frankly, will frequently be told what she must do for her own good after balancing a whole bunch of, yes, technical gobbledygook but it is technical gobbledygook that may well determine how this case comes out.

"The Ramones said it best, they always do: 'I wanna be your boyfriend.' I don't wanna be your boss lawyer telling you what to do. My ethical duty is to provide clients with advice based on the law unclouded by emotional considerations or a phys – a romantic relationship. So, do you see why I can't work on the case?"

"No!" she said. "You're quoting the *Ramones* to me?"

Jon sighed. "Just trying to keep things light after all that law stuff. I didn't think 'I Don't Wanna Go Down to the Basement' would have hit quite the right tone."

"This isn't funny!" she said. "You are always walking away! You walked out of the conference room the day we

met! And I came after you. You walked out of the conference room the day I brought the letter in, when you knew
something was wrong! And I came after you. And now
you're walking away again because of some old-fashioned
lawyer rule about not getting involved with clients! You
expect to date me while your buddies are stumbling around
with this howitzer pointed at me and the company and
we're just going to act like nothing's happening?"

"Yes," Jon said, "I do expect to do just that, but that's
not fair. At this point, they actually know more about the
case than I do and they're going to take exquisite care of
you. Brian is a beast, Oona's got brains to spare, and Nelson
is an operator who is undoubtedly going to know the judge
and has your board eating out of his hand."

"No!" she said. "Not good enough! I need your lawyer
side and your man side! You're not them! You realized the
problem almost immediately. How come no one else saw
what you saw?"

"That's a fair question," Jon said. "The answer is because
they are *better* lawyers than I am. Their first instinct, and
it is the right instinct for an advocate, is to be one hundred percent on their client's side from the very first sign
of trouble, to form the fighting mindset right away – not
to look for holes until the holes actually appear. That's what
clients want. That's what makes Brian great and you can
see Oona developing into that same kind of champion for
clients. Nelson – forget about it, he never heard a client's
story that he didn't believe with all his heart until all appeals
were exhausted, and even then. With me, you get a skeptic
who goes looking for holes, or for shadows on the page

that might be hiding them. Don't get me wrong, Brian and Oona would have figured this out eventually, and probably pretty soon. But my job is to find the problems first so right decisions are made from the outset. Sometimes the problems are the other guy's; sometimes they're my client's.

"And the value you get with Brian, Oona and Nelson too, raises another point," Jon said. "I haven't had case responsibility since – for several years now. What I've done for you so far in Philbrick and with this Bondurant thing I've done in twenty minutes of looking at some papers, not preparing a case for trial. I just flat don't do that anymore."

"You say you want to be my man, you say I won't be alone, but I feel like you want to keep your distance."

"No," Jon said. "I don't want anything to get in the way of reducing that distance, reducing it a lot."

"Oh, you are quick," she said. "Well, I'm not buying."

"I'm sorry to hear that," Jon said. "I think we should give it a try. I think you would find yourself happy with the arrangement. The case isn't going to last forever, and I've already told you I don't care about the Blake thing. And I don't care about what may or may not happen in this case. And I'll tell you something else, Chloe Manning. I don't care about you being *the* Chloe Manning. I'd be your man no matter who you were."

"Well," she said, "too bad, because I am *the* Chloe Manning and I don't intend ever to be anything else. I didn't think you were the kind of man who couldn't handle that."

"Whoa," Jon said. "Now you're twisting my words."

"Isn't that what lawyers do?" she said.

There was nothing further to say. She was going to

have her tantrum one way or the other, and the tantrum was going to be on her terms no matter what he said, so he said nothing.

"I'm just overwhelmed with the ups and downs of the last couple of weeks," she said, "and now this. Why can't you be there for me for everything I need?"

"I'm sorry if I haven't been clear on the answer to that," he said. "Maybe I'm not such a hot lawyer after all."

"Maybe not," she said. "Oh! I'm sorry, I didn't mean that."

"I know," he said.

"I'm just confused about what you want," she said. "There's you, there's me, there's my problems, men and women work through each other's problems, they support each other, right? It's not all fun and games, right? For better or worse, right? Although we're not there yet, maybe we never will be. Maybe that's not what you want? Maybe just the better, not the worse?"

He thought of a lot of responses and thought he would keep them to himself. No point until the storm blew over.

"You don't want to jump in with both feet, is that it?" she said. "You want to date that little Chinese thing with the big tits?"

"What?" Now it was Jon's turn to raise his voice. "You were stalking me?"

"No," she said. "I was at that animal affair, you just didn't see me. But everyone saw you yukking it up with that China doll and your dick jokes."

"Wha — WHAT?"

"I ran into her in the bathroom," Chloe said. "All right, no lies. I followed her in there."

"Chloe, she invited me to that function –"

"I know, I know, before we set the Chop House date. I know."

"And she's Japanese," he said.

"I know," she said. "Sorry."

"And she's not a candidate," he said. "Only you."

"Only me," Chloe said, "but only part of you."

Not the right time for a joke about parts. He called for the tab.

"Our first fight," he said. "I hope not our last."

Or do I? he thought.

As Jon had predicted, Blake did not go public with an account of the hotel encounter. His complaint, filed a few weeks later in the United States District Court for the Northern District of Illinois by a well-known employment plaintiff's firm, was similarly silent. It relied on generalized allegations of harassment and a hostile sexual environment at Barbiron without mentioning his relationship with Chloe, instead assigning to Manufacturing VP Myra Altobelli the role of Blake's chief antagonist. It was impossible to tell if Blake had told his lawyers about the naked goings-on. The team would have to wait until they served and responded to discovery in the case to know how Blake's lawyers would play out the threat of exposure.

Blake's lawyers had done one unexpected thing: They asked the federal court for permission to file the complaint under seal, so it would not be visible to the public. Not even reporters who routinely checked all new court filings for newsworthy disputes would be able to see it.

This seemed odd to Jon.

The complaint named Barbiron, Myra Altobelli, and Chloe Manning as co-defendants.

The case was assigned to U.S. District Judge Cleon Achebe.

CHAPTER 14

LISA. CHLOE.

"LISA. CHLOE."

"Hey! How are you? How are things with Rider?"

"I'll get to that. Do you have a few minutes? Maybe more than a few."

"Always. Hold on." Lisa said something to someone in her office about too many typos, can't file it like that, get Jessica to proof it, pain of death. "Okay, all yours."

"This is on the clock," Chloe said. "I'm consulting you in your professional capacity, so this is all privileged. You can start earning down that Philbrick fee."

"Understood. Shoot."

"First," Chloe said, "I'm dying to know: How was your conversation with the Dad back at the bar a few weeks ago?"

"Dad? Oh, the guy with the daughter, Whitney. Dad — name Jason, can you believe it, gosh, you hardly ever run into a Jason these days — Dad was pretty okay. We had a perfectly decent conversation in front of young

Whitney. Talked about school and careers and keep your knees together."

"Lisa, you didn't!"

"Not in those terms. Just told her to keep her self-respect. At least until she's fifteen."

"Lisa!"

"Kidding, kidding," Lisa said. "You'd have agreed with my advice about boys, it was dignified and I told her to be strong and not just do what the other girls did and not be afraid to talk to her mom about stuff. That kind of thing."

"I still can't believe he brought a twelve-year-old to a bar."

"You know what she said about that? When he went to the men's room she told me that this was his weekend with her and he wanted to take her to some young-adult movie he thought she would like but she told him he really, really needed a girlfriend so she wanted to go where he hung out if they would let her in, and they ended up there."

"So contrary to my assumption, the pimping was her idea," Chloe said.

"Yeah, pretty much. She said he'd had his eye on some skanks, as she called them, but she directed his attention our way."

"The dear."

"Yeah. You know," Lisa said, "I must have left a card somewhere on the table because he's called me a couple of times. I may add him to my Jason collection sometime. So, what's up?"

"Oh, man, what isn't?" Chloe said. "I've had a wild ride the past few weeks but things have settled down, which is to say I have settled down, and I just need to talk some things out."

"I'm all ears and boobs."

"First, you already know I took your advice and asked Jon out for a thank-you cocktail after work and it went great. It turned into dinner. I jabbered my head off but he was a hundred percent sweet and he walked me home and –"

"Oo, getting to the good stuff early. You were pretty sketchy and coy when we were texting that night when you got home."

"Just a kiss. A lovely, romantic kiss, but just a kiss. The whole evening – just a great first date. But then, a few days later, I see him at a charity function, that animal shelter thing I support, with a beautiful Asian woman. She was really a dollbaby. I swear, her last name was Ono. He was having the time of his life doing stand-up at his table. He didn't see me. I find out that it was really pretty innocent, she'd snagged him for the date before I called him, but at the time it upset me a lot."

"You sure this is billable?" Lisa said. "It sounds like girlfriend."

"Getting there. Okay: A long time ago, maybe a year, I did something really, really stupid. I don't want to go into it on this call but I'll give you the details when I see you. You just need to know that it was terrible judgment on my part and related to Barbiron."

"Oh my god," Lisa said, "you were fucking the help."

"No. No. But it did involve an employee who we terminated months later for reasons having nothing to do with my terrible judgment. And this terrible-judgment thing was so terrible that it could affect the company if it got out."

"When you say 'terminated,' did you kill this guy? What could have been so bad?"

"Just take my word for now," Chloe said. "Anyway, this employee who knows about the bad-judgment thing sends this threatening letter to me complaining about his termination, saying he was going to sue if we didn't pay him two million dollars."

The Flamethrower low-whistled.

"So," Chloe said, "who you gonna call when someone's got a gun to your head, legally? Ghost Rider! Hey, that kinda fits. I was thinking maybe there was a quick fix here and he could make it go away like he did with the Philbrick case without me having to tell anyone about my bad-judgment thing."

"Hard to fix extortion," Lisa said.

"Yeah, well, my judgment wasn't too good there, either," Chloe said, "because that damned Rider saw through the letter and saw through all my hemming and hawing and before I knew it I had confessed the whole thing to him."

"Don't you hate it when guys are right?" Lisa said.

"And he was sweet about it again and gave me a big understanding speech about how he was going to be there for me so I wouldn't be alone and we kinda made out in his office, he kinda mashed me a little to show he didn't care about this bad-judgment thing. Which was nice. He really is sweet."

"Don't you hate it when guys are sweet?" Lisa said.

"Man, I should have made a bigger play for that hunk of genome."

"Pretty soon the suit got filed and I got named along with Barbiron."

"I'm seeing it," Lisa said. "This causes a problem with the Rider relationship."

Wow, Chloe thought, she's picked up on Jon's issue. *I'm not going to win this one.* "Yeah. He tried to tell me –"

"He tried to tell you he couldn't screw you and represent you at the same time, so he – no, he didn't dump you. He dumped the case."

"He didn't say anything about screwing, exactly. But you're saying there's some rule about this? He wasn't just jerking me around?"

"Oh no," Lisa said, "not jerking. Very hot topic right now too, with MeToo and male lawyers said to be in an inherently coercive position with respect to vulnerable female clients who are in trouble of some kind."

"I'm not vulnerable. I kind of blew my stack. Not just kind of."

"So you need me to step in?"

"Uh . . . ."

"I'm kidding, no idea what your case is about or if it's even my meat. Although I'm hoping I'll hear the whole story someday soon. Cocktails Friday?"

"Sure, somewhere noisy," Chloe said. "Of all people, I should have been more thoughtful about mixing business and pleasure. The number of times I got propositioned in my business life when I was coming up and I was glad I never succumbed, and now here I am trying to get this guy

I care about to mix my pleasure with my business and his pleasure with his business."

"I only had a relationship with a client a couple of times," Lisa said. "Regretted it both times. One time was a divorce; had trouble collecting from the son of a bitch and he threatened to turn me in to the bar. The other time was a guy with a so-so injury case but the relationship was, you know, oo-la-la, I was invested. I should have assigned that case to a junior when he walked in the door, but he was, you know, hair and eyes and smile and ripped and not too badly injured, not badly enough for the oo-la-la, anyway. We needed to settle but his expectations were way out of line and we had a big fight about it. He said I should be giving him 'emotional support' in our relationship by trying his worthless case instead of explaining to him that the intersection camera clearly showed him walking against the don't-walk sign and the red light. Never again. I'm sticking to divorced dads with needy pubescent daughters."

"So, you're saying he had a point."

"Yeah," Lisa said. "Sorry. Even though you're not a classic pathetic female client. I don't know what your legal problem is, but it sounds pretty serious, which means somewhere along the line you're going to have a come-to-Nelson meeting where he's going to lay some stuff on the line that you will not want to have heard from a guy you're sleeping with. And sleeping-with man won't want to have to say it to you, no matter how much you need to hear it, because he loves you and doesn't want to hurt you or scold you or bring you bad news. Nelson or Brian OK; Jon, no. And sleeping-with man himself needs to be able to work the case independently of his feelings for you, and that's a problem, too."

"It gets worse. I was a jerk to him about the Asian girl."

"Never possible to be a jerk about other women," the Flamethrower said. "It turns men on to think you're jealous, even if you're wrong. Jealousy sex good. So where did you leave things with him?"

"We just kind of – left. He wouldn't fight with me, he just let me be a brat and accuse him of stuff. I really kind of slammed him but he kept trying to tell me everything was going to be all right, let's try it, blah blah. But he did the old rope-a-dope; I just kept swinging and he covered up and let me beat him up and eventually I talked myself out. He got quiet and eventually he walked away. This was a few weeks ago. We haven't spoken since."

"So, are you saying he's available?"

"No! Well, he is, but no. No! Lisa!"

"Hm. How do you feel now?"

"I miss him," Chloe said. "I want him. I think about him all the time. You're telling me he was right and he tried to be nice about it, but why couldn't he have fought with me a little, shown a little fire? Maybe he could have gotten it through my hairspray if he'd raised his voice a little instead of just trying to calm me down and be reasonable with me. I'm not used to men not sticking up for themselves in some way other than walking away. But I guess if he was right about the conflict of interest we should have kept working the relationship. What should I do? There's nothing going on in the case right now and he's right, Brian and Nelson and even Oona are as good as anyone in the city in a case like this. No offense."

"None taken," Lisa said. "I'm still hearing reluctance in your voice about this, but you have got to get past it if you're going to jump back in his game. Look, I understand your position that your man should be there for every issue in your life. That position sounds perfectly reasonable. But here it puts Rider in an impossible position – he cannot date you seriously and represent you in the case at the same time. You want both things but you can only have one."

"I guess," Chloe said.

"Look, girl," Lisa continued, "I don't know who you murdered or slept with or defrauded or what you did that was so horrible, but there are thousands of cases filed in Chicago every year. Not a single one of them has Jon Rider working on them, and every single one of them is going to get resolved. So will yours. But Jon Rider is the only man you want in your arms and vice versa, and the conditions may not be entirely to your liking, but them's the conditions that prevail, dear. And, like I said to you before, that is one gorgeous vessel of choice reproductive material and he's finally back on the market. So don't mess this up by being impossible. The Asians are at your shores!"

"My god, Lisa!" Chloe finally laughed; she was surrendering to Lisa's common sense, not exactly what she had expected from The Flamethrower. "All right, all right, uncle. But you and all your talk about his good genes. Really, you talk like he's just a sperm donor."

"Oh, there's the fun and the romance and the being together and don't I know it, but girl, come on, babies is it. He is for you. You know it. You felt it. He felt it. Two gametes both stuffed full of brains and beauty. You will have amazing babies with that man. Your girls will be the first Faces of Calvin Klein to cure cancer. Your boys will announce their reconciliation of quantum mechanics and general relativity when they accept their Grammy."

"Gametes – quantum – what? Lisa, have you been holding out on me? Are you a secret science and math girl?"

"I hope to marry smart myself. Sometimes, you want to intrigue a tech guy. They'll always have a job. I want my own smart babies someday. You read a few books, learn a few smart words. And get some boobs."

"It's a little premature to be talking about babies," Chloe said, "since we're not actually speaking at the moment."

"Oh, no, I can see it. It's fate. The universe wants it. Little cute buttoned-down Rider babies are in your future."

"One thing at a time," Chloe said. "I do want him back, although I guess I never really had him. The truth is – even though I've only known him for a few weeks, my mind had been picturing us together. Is that love? All right, it's love. All the issues, the Ono girl, my old bad behavior coming back to haunt, the legal issues about dating clients – it was just a weird bunch of stuff to all hit at the same time after we had such a good start. We didn't even have time to build anything that might have gotten us through these problems slamming into us within the space of just a few days. But god, I hate to call him again. Seems like I'm always the one coming to him."

"Let me think for a minute," Lisa said.

Lisa the Flamethrower thought.

"I may have been the spoiled princess but I don't want to go back on hands and knees," Chloe said.

"You won't. Just the opposite. You can deal from strength. I've got the play. Listen. I want you to put together an outfit. We're going to combine style and sleaze. A super-tight sweater worn with some kind of push-up thing underneath, not that you need support with your magnificent natural boobs. Doesn't have to plunge, just needs to feature those tasty boobalas. By the way, I hate you for those natural girls of yours, have I ever told you that?"

"Why do we call them boobs?" Chloe said. "It makes them sound stupid."

"Good point. For what mine cost, they should be supporting themselves. Anyway, light wool or blend, something soft-looking, begging to be felt. Red, I'm thinking ambulance-flasher red. But tight on the boobsters and tight around that Barbie waist of yours.

"Then some kind of short skirt, not a pencil but something a little sheer and flouncy and clingy. Something a breeze would catch. Plenty of leg. Maybe a short jacket. Something dangly on the ears. Something fun with your hair. The highest spikes you can stand. I'm not talking hooker stuff, I know you'll have the best pieces. Just think grown-up frat party for rich chicks looking for kicks.

"Have the outfit ready; in fact, you'll need to have it at the office. And maybe some extra makeup, maybe a little vampy, a little flashy. Deep and dramatic around those big green kittycat eyes of yours. Bright red lips, for sure. They'll go with the boobsy top."

"This doesn't sound like me," Chloe said. "Where is this going, Lisa?"

"It isn't you. I know a guy. Just have this stuff handy and make sure you can take my call whenever. I'll give you further instructions."

CHAPTER 15

JON WAS SPENDING TOO MUCH TIME IN BARS

JON WAS SPENDING too much time in bars, he thought. He wasn't a big drinker, but he was still feeling blue over the early collapse of the Chloe Manning romance a few weeks earlier. When Wednesdays rolled around – why do they have to call it hump day? – he felt the empty weekend looming and he didn't feel like going home to mope. Teeko and Bridey could wait a couple of hours. He left a little early and went to mope at the giant horseshoe bar at the flash hotel a couple of blocks from the office.

Earlier in the day, Brian Accardo had caught him moping in his office.

"Just call her," he said.

"I should," Jon said. "I'm not afraid to go back to her, take the initiative to hit the restart button. But I don't know what I'd say any different. The issue is still there."

"But is it really?" Brian said. "You wouldn't be trying

the case. Maybe things get dicey, maybe we have to press her on something tough. Nelson and I will be handling that, even if you're providing some guidance behind the scenes. She's smart; she'd understand that it had nothing to do with your feelings for her or hers for you."

"Hey, speaking of the case: Did you find it odd that they filed it under seal?"

"It was a little surprising," Brian said, "but not really. Part of their strategy to keep the nude drunk hotel info out of the papers to preserve a high settlement value."

"But the complaint doesn't have that information in it. It's a very plain vanilla wrongful termination complaint, completely unnewsworthy, so why file it under seal? Eh, you may be right, it's belt and suspenders; maybe they're being extra careful not to let this get out. Anyway, I really cannot be involved if we're going to be a thing."

"I love things," Brian said. "Especially things with gorgeous famous CEOs. Come on, there's got to be a work-around, Jon. We can figure something out."

"Remember Marv Hendricks in Corporate Finance a few years back?" Jon said. "Remember how he got involved with that sharp young Hillfarm Energy CFO in that rollup merger where all the minority stockholders started waving their shareholder agreements and complaining about getting squeezed out? And he went in and gave the executive committee and board a big technical PowerPoint presentation on how they needed to recalculate what the minority was going to receive if they wanted to meet the timetable for closing without a lawsuit. A big chunk of cash they hadn't counted on having to spend. And she started to cry. Said

Marv had told her there weren't going to be any problems. Said she was pregnant. Remember what happened to him?"

"No."

"Neither does anyone else."

"Well," Brian said, "I don't think this would be like that. Chloe is strong."

"Strong, and emotional, and stubborn. I'll tell you something else," Jon said, "I was willing to try it with me not working on the case, but as I think about this, or maybe overthink about it, I don't think it works even if I'm only working at the firm but not on the case. Think about it: She comes to me with some big complaint about the case. What do I do? Come to you and complain about how you're handling it? Or tell her I can't do a thing about it? I'm right back in it and nobody's happy. I'd love to make a new pitch to her, and I think she'd pick up the phone. But there are no good answers."

"She's too special," Brian said. "One of the most desirable women in the country. You're first in line, at least for now. There's got to be a way to step up."

"Yeah," Jon said. "You would think so. Thinking. It's what I'm good at, right? But women, jeez. Problems. I feel like an insurance salesman knocking on the door at Area 51."

"I don't think Area 51 has a door," Brian said, "or needs insurance."

"See?" Jon said. "Problems."

∽

Jon sat at the bar reading a Joe Gores novel on his phone

and sipping a local microbrew. He always picked a seat at the far end of the bar that was a little darker, a little quieter. He liked to read his book and he liked to observe, to look and listen to the people who were there because that was the place they wanted to be for some reason you could discern – or invent – if you let yourself really see them. The place was beginning to fill up with the local Wednesday happy-hour crowd and business travelers staying at the hotel.

A couple who had been sitting next to him paid their tab and got up to leave. The moment they vacated, a big man in sharp casual clothes took the chair next to Jon. Jon started to scoot a bit but the man said "no, you're fine, I have plenty of room, but thanks." The big guy ordered a bourbon and water and began texting on his phone. Every so often he would raise his head and look around the bar. Took his time with his drink.

Jon liked the noise. He liked to watch people come and go. We all get by, he thought. We all find someplace to go, contrive something to do. And we run into someone and we make copies of ourselves to go someplace and do something and reproduce all over again. He'd have to give that more thought.

Chloe, yes; special. Incredibly special. If going, doing, and reproducing is what we do, it should at least be special.

Like this big guy, he thought. I hope he has a good friend or girlfriend meeting him here. He turned back to Joe Gores.

The big guy finished one drink but only killed about half his second when he called for his check. When the barkeep delivered it, he turned to Jon. "Sir," he said, "I'm sorry to interrupt your reading there, but I need to tell you something: Play along." He signed his tab.

"Excuse me?" Jon said.

"Just play along, go with what's coming," he said, and as he stood to leave he said "you'll thank me" and was gone.

From behind Jon a hand reached out and claimed the empty chair, and Chloe Manning slid into it before the leather had a chance to cool.

Jon was stunned. He was delighted to see her, ecstatic, really, but she – what had she done? She was always sexy enough in her CEO duds, but this look was deliberately, dramatically, smokin' hot. It took him a few seconds to take it all in. Breasts straining at a lightweight maroon sweater, a springy light floral wraparound skirt that had never seen her knees and that rose fetchingly up her thighs as she arranged herself on the elevated bar chair, and a kicky cropped cream jacket that did nothing but call attention to her magnificent bust. And her makeup was – different, more of it, a little darker around the eyes, a little more color in the cheeks. Her hair was down and loose and she'd arranged it to fall over half her right eye. She shook her head to move it aside a little. Jon wondered if anyone these days had heard of Veronica Lake.

Lips: engorged, blood red.

"Hi!" he said. "It is really, really great to see you. I'm so glad you – I guess you found me."

She looked at him blankly. "Excuse me," she said. "I don't believe we know one another."

He took a sip of his beer and thought about the big

guy's instruction to *play along*. She looked away ostentatiously. He took that as an invitation to take it all in.

Do-me sweater.

Apparently with some do-me foundational undergarment presenting her breasts to a grateful world.

Do-me skirt.

No stockings over endless slim do-me legs.

Do-me makeup.

Do-me hair. *Oh man*, Jon thought, *she's wearing it over her eye that way to give her a reason to toss her head*, which she proceeded to do, diamond-tipped ear wires swinging out dangerously as she did so.

And – holy Mother – fatal, terrifying, do-me stilettos.

Amazing. Oh yeah, this woman is special. Crazy, out there, but special. She is for me. It is not possible, but it is happening. He stifled a chuckle.

"Yes," he said, "I see I am mistaken. I do beg your pardon. You bear a resemblance –"

"Yeah, yeah, I've heard it," she said.

"Again, sorry."

"I'm waiting for a friend," she said.

"Got it," he said. "When he gets here, you can have my seat."

"Won't need it," she said. "We're just meeting here. And who said it was a he?"

"Excuse my presumption," he said.

She got the barkeep's attention. "Johnny Walker Double Black, if you have it, Black if you don't, lots of rocks. And an ice water, please."

"Do people order Johnny Walker Red anymore?" Jon said.

"I wouldn't know," she said unsmilingly.

She scooted her chair to face into the bar. Jon swung back around to face the bar himself and pretended to read his phone. Now what? Whose move? They sat there for a good minute-and-a-half. Jon considered calling for his check to see what she'd do, but this was her play.

A stocky man with close-cropped hair and a good-natured way about him sat down next to Chloe on the other side. "Is this seat taken?" he asked.

"Uh, no," Chloe said.

"Great," he said. He sat down and placed what looked like a computer bag on the floor between his chair and Chloe's. He ordered an IPA.

"Great city you have here," he said. "Gets a bad rap because of all the killing, but, you know. This part of town, can't beat it. Is it always this cool in June? I'm up from Houston, you can cut the air with a knife down there."

It was all Jon could do to keep from laughing. This could not have been in her script.

"My name's Hal," he said.

"Welcome to Chicago," she said noncommittally, and without looking his way.

"Thanks, I actually get here pretty often. A lot of conferences up here. Software sales and development for military. Are you from the Chicago area?"

"Uh . . . no. I'm actually leaving later tonight. Omaha."

Jon caught her eyes flashing angrily his way. The

amusement in his own could not have assuaged her growing irritation.

"Omaha!" Hal said. "Great city. USSTRATCOM south of there, Strategic Command, you know. Used to be called Strategic Air Command. Dr. Strangelove, all that. I'm there all the time. Hey, did you ever see that George Clooney movie 'Flying in the Air'? It's all about flying into and out of Omaha. Could have been me! Ha!"

Jon could not let her suffer any longer, or he might lose her again.

"Hey, babe," he said. "I just got a text from the hostess. They're saying our table won't be ready for another 45 minutes or so but they've alerted the bar to buy us a round for our trouble."

She turned to face Jon. "Well, that sucks," she said, "I'm getting hungry."

"Yeah," Jon said, "I was doing okay but in the last few minutes my hunger seems to have sharpened."

Hal returned somewhat sadly to his drink. Jon thought he saw Chloe break character for a tiny half-second smile.

"I'll text Warren's pilot and tell him we'll be a little late," Jon said. "We should still be able to get to Omaha tonight. Only about two hours by private jet to Eppley, if I remember. Warren's sent Greg before. Great pilot, nice guy. He'll probably have some champagne chilling, although Warren himself, not a drinker." Over Chloe's shoulder Jon noticed Hal pretending not to listen.

He wondered if this was the ice-breaker or whether Chloe would return to character. He was amused to see her let her features settle and return to looking into the bar, away from him. Glanced briefly at him as she swooped her hair off her eye.

❦

Chloe did not know exactly how she was going to play it. She had imagined little scenes in her mind, but none of them seemed likely to light the fire that would bring them back together.

Lisa had given her the situation and strongly suggested that she aim at seduction. Of course, Lisa always thought that the indicated strategy was to aim at seduction no matter what the actual goal was supposed to be, but the more Chloe thought about it, the better idea it seemed. She wanted him. She wanted him in every way. She'd seen enough of his kindness and calm to be satisfied that he was a good man, and enough of his brains to be satisfied that he was a special one.

She wanted his eyes over her eyes.

She wanted the rest of him.

She wanted him to take her the rest of the way.

Nothing to do but jump in with both stilettos.

She wasn't taking any chances that Hal might take another stab at it, so she did not wait to speak. "May I ask you a personal question?" she said.

"You may always ask," Jon said.

"I noticed you looking at those two women across the bar," she said.

He had not been looking at any women anywhere, it being hardly possible to do so with this parallel-universe version of Chloe sucking all of the sexual energy out of the rest of the place. He looked now. Two attractive, stylishly-dressed women were having a discussion over wine and finger food. One maybe forty, one maybe thirty.

"Do you find them attractive?" Chloe asked.

"I don't know," Jon said. "I'd have to talk to them some. Need to make sure somebody's home. Looks aren't everything, you know, inner beauty, book by its cover, et cetera."

"Come on," Chloe said, "don't BS me now. I saw you looking over there. Do you find them physically attractive? Maybe I should put it this way: Based on their looks, would it be worth your while to find out if anyone was home, to find their inner beauty, as you say?"

Jon looked again. One, the younger one, looked like she might be a Latina. Long, shiny dark hair. The other woman was fair; softer lines and some miles but actually rather sexy from bar-level up.

"Yeah, sure." Jon said.

"Which?"

"Both."

"You don't have a 'type'?"

"Ah, you know us guys," he said. "When a guy says he has a 'type' it turns out to be whatever type is giving him the time of day at that particular moment."

She sipped her drink. "Is it true what they say about men?"

"Probably," Jon said. "Most things about us are true. It's why men are so excellent. We're so true."

She ignored his yammering. "When men look at women do they, you know, undress them with their eyes? Picture them naked?"

"Oh, yeah."

"All men?"

"Oh, yeah, all straight men for sure. Others, can't say."

"You?"

"Oh, yeah."

"All women, or just women they find –"

"All."

"Even out in places where there are groups of –"

"Studies have shown that under that kind of stress men can visualize up to seven women naked over a three-second interval."

"Even unattractive women?"

"Eleven to seventeen."

"Are you picturing those two women naked?"

"Oh, yeah." He was now, anyway. "Bar's in the way, but yeah. Bar actually makes it better. You know, in case they're bronto-assed or something. You can fantasize the model of ass you prefer on them, you know?"

"That is disgusting!"

"Not to us men. It's a constant delight."

She almost broke.

"You just said you wanted to know what was inside, you hypocrite."

"Not at all," he said with a hint of indignation. He leaned in and lowered his voice. "That's why I try to get inside as quickly as possible."

"That's disgusting!" she said, but she was having trouble keeping it together.

"You're the one with all the dirty questions," Jon said.

"Wait!" she almost shrieked. "Are you picturing *me* naked?"

"Oh, yeah. Totally nude. Way starkers. From the moment you sat down." And for some weeks previously, and especially during her Blake Bondurant story featuring extensive full-frontal Chloe Manning nudity.

For the first time, she smiled.

Jon shivered a little. She was a genius. They were going to reconcile for the best of reasons, in the best of ways, and without having to go through all that ethical crap that wasn't crap but was way too legal and really had very little to do with extensive thrilling nudity featuring Chloe Manning.

She leaned toward him a little. Her warmth was returning.

"How do I look?" she said.

Jon sat back and surveyed her as suggestively as he could without attracting excessive attention from the bar crowd, some of whom had been staring at Chloe for a while. The two women across the bar had even looked over once or twice. He moved his gaze from the pencil-sharp tip of her shoes, up her languid bare legs to her thighs, more of which had begun to appear beneath the hem of her filmy skirt as her fake indignation had progressed, to her breasts straining against that poor abused fabric, to the new colors in her cheeks and around her eyes, to the golden waves cascading over the side of her face. When his eyes got there, she gave those waves a shake until her vision was clear and their eyes met again.

"Blond," he answered.

"I see," she said. "Anything else?"

"Everything else."

"I'm thinking," she said, "that if we left for Omaha now, we could eat there."

"I was thinking the same thing," Jon said. "Your Omaha or my Omaha?"

"Oh, mine this time, I think," she said.

Jon called for his tab and hers and briefly excused himself to call Chelsea, the teenager who looked after Teeko and Bridey when Jon was away and asked her to walk and feed them. He was, he told her, working very late.

Chloe took Jon's hand and led him from the bar.

On their way out, they wished Hal a safe trip.

Waiting for their Uber, Chloe reached down with both hands to secure her skirt against the mischievous Windy City wind.

CHAPTER 16

CHLOE SHOVED JON INTO THE UBER WITH SOME IMPATIENCE

CHLOE SHOVED JON into the Uber with some impatience and sat with her hip pressed against his. She took his head in her hands and kissed him.

"Jon Rider," she said, "are you ever going to stop rescuing me?"

"Not unless you stop getting yourself in situations where you require rescuing," he said, "and I hope you never do."

"I had to pick Omaha," she said.

"Hal was pretty harmless, not a dangerous rescue operation. Besides," Jon said, moving a wave off her eye with his finger, "I think I'm the one who got rescued tonight."

On the way home, Chloe explained the big guy at the bar. He was a private investigator Lisa used on some of her cases. His assignment was to observe Jon's after-work habits, which turned out to include going alone to a nearby bar for his moping drink on Wednesdays before returning home. He was to alert Chloe when he had secured a seat next to Jon, which he was to hold until she arrived to begin her dramatic presentation.

"Quite a production," Jon said, "and not cheap."

"Lisa owes me," Chloe said, "and besides, it's expensive to be as cheap as I was tonight."

Jon kissed her forehead. "Sometimes," he said, "you just can't put a value on cheapness."

Doorman George appeared nonplussed at Chloe's look of strategic allure for the evening.

"You remember Mr. Rider," she said. The two men nodded to one another.

As he and Chloe waited for the elevator, Jon noticed that George was still nodding, his stare slightly glazed.

❦

"This is Bandit here underfoot," Chloe said as they entered her unit to a chorus of meeows, "and over there is Glor –"

Jon took her arm and spun her toward him. He pressed her gently but firmly into the wall of the entryway and kissed her hard.

"Jon," she said.

"Kick off those damned spikes," he said. She did and dropped half a foot. He pressed the kiss now from above, firmly in control. She thrilled at his mastery in this shocking dance.

He reached into her skirt-top and found the snap,

unwrapping it and tossing it aside. She was, as he thought she would be, innocent of panties. He stood back. She put her legs together in the classic feminine one-knee-bent pose and smiled. She made no effort to cover herself.

"Who is this Jon of whom you speak?" he said. "Who is this Mr. Rider?"

"We never did get introduced, did we?" she said.

"I am Rodrigo," he said. "Many call me Rod." He'd thrown his jacket and tie on the floor and had started to unbutton his shirt.

She'd taken her jacket off in the elevator, thinking she might be giving George an eyeful on one of his security screens. Jon took it from her and threw it in the clothes pile. "Stay right where you are," he said.

He dropped his pants and boxers.

"Well, hi there, Rod," she smiled as she looked him over. "I'm most pleased to make your acquaintance."

"The pleasure is increasingly mine," he said. He kicked off his shoes and tore his socks off. He spun her again, gently this time, to face away from him. "Hands up."

She lifted her arms over her head. Jon took the hem of her top and peeled it up off of her. He almost felt bad about the tremendous strain that garment must have been under as he worked it over her breasts. He briefly wondered if maybe this was something you wore once then had to take to Goodwill, its tensile potential completely exhausted. When it was gone she shook her hair back into place.

He cupped his hands over her evanescent Sarrieri bra and gently pushed it up off her breasts. He caressed her as he nosed through her hair to kiss the back of her neck.

"It undoes in front," she said.

Chloe was startled at how easily Jon released the not-entirely-intuitive clasp. The bra fell from her and she shrugged it off. He continued to caress her and kiss her neck. Her nipples stiffened under his touch.

He picked up her stilettos and handed them to her. "Put these back on," he said. "Now."

He took her hand and they walked nude in the direction he guessed the bedroom to be. He briefly considered tossing her on the couch and finishing her there as a can't-wait finale to their crescendo of starved desire.

His eye caught a small collection of magazines she'd set out with her picture on the cover and he thought again, as he had in the days when he fantasized about their love-making to come, that with this woman there would be an added voyeur's thrill in the act. He would be driving into the languid let-go body of the totally together woman on those very magazines, a woman looked up-and-down by millions of men and women, and now wholly known only to him. A tug of shame at this feeling was overwhelmed by the frisson of fucking the famous.

"Wait," she said. "I don't want to break the mood but I need to feed the cats before we get going."

Jon pulled her along. "Rodrigo says: Some pussies can wait to be fed," he said, "other pussies cannot."

"But they'll be howling all over us if I don't feed them."

"I see your bedroom has a cat-excluding device known as a door," he said. "They can howl all they want out here in the hall, and if we do this right our howling will drown out theirs." He closed the door.

She dove onto the bed and posed on her side for him. He was astonished and delighted that her reality matched his imaginings and, he was suddenly energized to see, his preferences. Not that his preferences were unusual – long smooth legs, large full and firm breasts with distinct, round pink aureoles and – had she groomed her ash-blond muff for him? That blessed triangle could have been trimmed by Pythagoras.

He was aware he was staring, and he thought it would be gentlemanly to let her stare for a few moments, too. He was not self-conscious; he was just who he was, and he stood there in no particular pose and let her see him.

Chloe saw that his body was straight up and down. No fat, but no bulging muscles, except one, which may not have qualified as a muscle at all, but she wasn't going to quibble about its taxonomy. His flesh, like his build, was smooth and featureless. She considered that there's not that much to see on any man, so she looked at what there was to see.

Her own experience, while not vast, and what she'd heard from other women in the occasional wine-fueled confessional, suggested to her that size mattered, but that most men operated within a range that, all else being equal, would not disqualify a man as a lover. Within that range it was the "all else" that mattered, and as she looked at Jon Rider, and thought about the things he had done for her and said to her and let her say to him, all without judgment, the way he looked into her and seemed to know her from the moment they met, his kindness, the sexy, funny way he had improvised his part at the bar. The romance in her head segued into a physical hunger, a longing in her belly that could only be satisfied by taking him into her and doing him to within an inch of both their lives.

As he stood by the bed she reached out and took his penis in her hand. She moved toward him.

"No," he said. "Another time for that. I need to feel all of you now."

He paused. "You want to pull the comforter back, do it on the sheets?"

Goddam practical Rider. "Stop worrying about the damned linens and fuck me, Rodrigo," she said. "Fasten your seat belts for Omaha. I can see you're already in an upright and locked position."

"I didn't know Nebraska was so beautiful this time of year," Jon said as he climbed in next to her.

She reached to his cock and lightly squeezed the head.

"Go Big Red," she said.

ॐ

And he was on her.

Their life as lovers began with fun. Their first act was to laugh at their wordless memory of the whole crazy chain of events that had brought them to the moment, to hold and stroke each other and roll to feel each other's weight and flesh and heat.

"One date and an office kiss and one fight," she said, "and a sleazy bar pickup with my big red boobs raised to the sky and ready to fire. Am I easy, or what?"

"We're mutually easy," he said. "It's the essence of true romance. Enough talking."

Jon felt himself beginning to soften during these pre-
liminaries, but his erection returned as though angry at
the delay. He kissed her ankles and licked up the inside of
her thighs. He brushed his face into her silky thatch and
hummed deeply into the pubic knoll above it. He continued to run his hands lightly up and down her body,
moving his touch to her back when she would writhe as he
slow-danced up her legs and belly. He brought his mouth
quickly up her stomach to her breasts. Her nipples were
hard and full. He kissed her breasts all over, licking and
nibbling gently as he went and bringing his hands up to
stroke and play.

He was at her mouth. He kissed her and spread her legs
with his and moved to enter. She had reacted fully to his
journey up her body and was ready to accept him. But he
penetrated with excruciating, breathtaking slowness.

He was in and Chloe thrilled at the intimacy, so foreign
that it felt they had invented it on the spot. She raised her
thighs and crossed her ankles and squeezed to urge him in
deeper. She heard a foreign sound and realized it was her,
moaning and gasping.

Their lovemaking took on a music of its own, sometimes hurried and hard, other times long and slow with that
illusion of a new act with every push.

It was the oldest human act and not unknown to Chloe
but it felt new to her with this man. She was used to sup-
pressing her feelings as a woman. She was used to all eyes
being on her, looking for imperfection, waiting for her to
show some kind of female vulnerability, some time-of-the-
month irritability, some questionable fashion choice, some

disharmonious color scheme, a couple of extra pounds. But here, now, with him – release, no one to see, no one to judge. It was like something was coming unknotted within her. She dissolved into her womanhood and felt a new kind of strength, the strength of invisibility to all but one.

She caught his timing and rocked with him, each slight shift in rhythm and attack a new movement in this symphony of carnality. She scraped her Prada spikes across the small of his back and stuck him. He gave a clipped gasp and she said *sorry* but he said *no, okay, do it, goddam it.* She held him tight but fought the urge to grip his flesh until she heard him say *you can mark me* and she dug her nails into his back, scratching him from shoulder blades down and back. She envisioned men in a locker room admiring the stripes she delivered and she dug in even more. *Let it all go,* he whispered, *don't hold out, lady. Everything is allowed to you, to you, to you, it's all for you, nothing is forbidden.*

～

Jon called up the voyeur's images, letting the small secret shame of it stoke his rising fury:

> *She's addressing the Barbiron board,*
> *She's speaking to a business luncheon,*
> *Men are looking at her on the street,*
> *She's being interviewed by Rita Braver on CBS*
> *Sunday Morning,*
> *She's crossing her bare legs in the bar, those legs that*
> *secretly rose to her secretly nude sex,*

And she had all her clothes on all those times but
none on now, for him, only for him.

He reached behind her raised thighs to her ass and lifted her to the beat of this final chorus.

"Jon," she breathed.

"My rod and my staff, they comfort you," he said.

They both knew this was stupid but Chloe bucked with a short explosive laugh, and that new pressure on the best place, her emotions sparking, their wet bodies banging the headboard into the wall, and the cats' rising wail outside the door crested in a cascade of sight and sound and touch as she began to detonate. Jon sensed the change; he slowed and comforted her as she shivered and groaned and suddenly she was there, she was here, now, she was fully present in the universe, all of its pleasures gathered and pouring over her and delivering a new memory of joy, her sex convulsed and she reached for breath and found it and it was good.

This man! Mine. A good man, and he does it fine and straight and cool.

As he let go, Jon felt that indescribable burn in his shaft and through to the base of his spine and beyond. Tens of millions of sex acts on earth each day, thousands of miles of flesh traversed, but the flush that came to his face as he finished and he looked into Chloe's now-opened and watering eyes felt like the final touches of color to the portrait of his life. He was utterly and completely for her.

Jon buried his face in her neck and breathed in hard as though to take into himself her entire essence.

"I love your fragrance," he said

"I'm not wearing any," she said.

"Exactly," he said.

∽

They lay with their legs intertwined, her head on his shoulder.

"You're incredible," he said.

"You're incredible," she said.

"It's not the same," he said.

"I know," she said.

"This probably isn't the right time to say this," he said.

"Were you going to tell me you love me?" she said.

"Well, I was going to tell you –"

"I love you," Chloe said. "There, now you don't have to worry about thinking that if you told me I would think it was because I let you make love to me and it was – I don't know what to call it. Heaven. Galaxies moved. The words don't matter. Because now I've said it after great sex so it's okay if you say it, and we both know that's not really it. It's something, but it's not the whole thing of it, you know?"

"I appreciate what I think you just said," Jon said, "but what I was going to say was that I realized during our time apart that I had fallen in love with you. I was miserable thinking it was over before it had a chance to start. And I was going to tell you if we ever had the chance to try to talk things out. So my feeling had nothing – nothing much – to do with sex. And tonight, your little cocktease drama at the bar didn't seem like quite the right venue for me to confess. Seemed wrong to say it to a total stranger, even a pretend total stranger. So, Chloe Manning – I love you. I know we haven't known each other long, but I feel it, and you've now told me you feel it, so there has got to be something there and I'm just giving myself up to it – it's love. But there's something else you must know."

"Uh-oh."

"I'm going to hold you for ten more minutes, then I'm going to get up and feed the cats, and then I'm going to come back and hold you again, and I'm not going to stop holding you until a time of my choosing, which I expect to be sometime tomorrow morning, unless you have a very compelling reason to avoid George imagining graphic visions of your social life and make me leave."

"Sex and cuddling and cat-feeding and doorman-titillating," she said. "Exactly what I put on my Match.com profile. You're perfect."

And Jon did all those things, and when they woke before sunrise he was ready and she was ready and they made love and slept again and when they woke a second time he fed the cats again.

CHAPTER 17

THE NEXT DAY, JON WALKED INTO NELSON GILLES'S OFFICE

THE NEXT DAY, Jon walked into Nelson Gilles's office and resigned.

Nelson objected vigorously, as Jon knew he would, and he even called Brian Accardo in to try to dissuade him from what they both considered an extreme interpretation of the firm's rules, which forbade exactly the behavior in which Jon was planning on engaging and, indeed, in which he had already engaged.

"Hell, Rider," Nelson said, "you're discreet. You won't knock her up like – what was his name? – Hendricks with that Hillfarm woman."

"I might," Jon said. "Maybe already."

"Oh, man," Brian groaned, "please stop, I won't be

able to get that image of your ass banging away at Chloe Manning out of my head all day or forever."

"We're doing more and more work for Barbiron," Jon said. "You've got Corporate Transactions doing their contract work, we have two new cases and one transferred case in addition to the Bondurant case, and you will definitely be able to get Finance's foot in the door to pitch their IPO when we – you – get Bondurant cleaned up. You just can't have a partner having a relationship, as we so coyly put it these days, with the CEO. The firm handbook is pretty clear about that, and it actually makes sense."

"Damned firm rules," Nelson said.

"It's not just the firm," Jon said. "I refreshed my recollection on the bar rules. Illinois Supreme Court Rule 1.8(j) provides that a lawyer may not have sex with a client unless the sexual relationship existed when the lawyer-client relationship began."

"There you go," Nelson said. "You're not having sex with Barbiron."

"There you go," Brian said. "More sex-with-Manning imagery that's killing me." He made unhappy moaning noises.

"I remind you that Chloe is a defendant and thus a client in the Bondurant case," Jon said, "and in any event the rule forbids sex with the officer of the corporate client who oversees the legal representation."

"Shit," Nelson said, "I could have half the firms in Chicago up on charges."

"Uh, are we that sure about our own house?" Brian said.

"No," Nelson said.

"What are you going to do?" Brian said.

Jon told them that he was financially secure for the foreseeable future ("you could be a kept man," Nelson said), and proposed a compromise: He would work from home as an independent contractor on limited firm litigation and transactional matters, but no Barbiron matters, at an agreed hourly rate. He would not have online access to firm files, but would continue to use his firm email account to communicate on matters where the firm engaged him. He could develop his own clients; he could work for other firms.

"So, this is real," Brian said. "Chloe Manning and my pal Jon Rider."

"Part real, part I-can't-believe-it-it's-not-remotely-possible," Jon said.

"You can come back," Brian said.

"Not if I don't screw this up," Jon said.

❧

"You did WHAT?"

"I removed the only barrier to you and me doing this thing," Jon said.

"Are you crazy, or the most wonderful lover a woman could possibly have?"

"I hope to be both."

Jon assured her that while he would miss going to the office, it beat missing her by a very large delta.

He explained more carefully the formal ethical problem their relationship presented. Same thing Lisa had told her. He assured her he was okay financially. He told her he was going to do some limited projects for Rockwell Morton and would be able to pick up work elsewhere. He told her he wasn't worried.

He told her he was ecstatic.

She believed him.

❧

— *What is smell? Goodboy said.*

— *I remember it from shelter. I think cat, Goodgirl said.*

— *Yes, Goodboy said, I remember now, I smelled it too in shelter. Cat.*

— *Girl came to feed us and walkies while Man was with cats and did not come to us until sun. Man came to Pups happy with cat smell.*

— *Man slept in shelter? Goodboy said.*

— *I do not know.*

— *Other smells I smell.*

— *Yes, Goodgirl said. Some sweet smell on his clothes.*

— *I smell a salty sour smell before he showered.*

— *I do not like new smells, Goodgirl said.*

— *I do not like new anything, Goodboy said.*

— *I do like Man happy, Goodgirl said. It is my favorite thing.*

— *It is my favorite thing, too, Goodboy said.*

CHAPTER 18

AMY COULDN'T HELP HERSELF

AMY COULDN'T HELP herself when Chloe rolled into the office around 11.

"Oh, Chloe!" she said.

"What?"

"You are really, truly, GLOWING!"

Chloe put her hands to her cheeks and looked at herself in her office mirror. "So I am," she said, laughing, "so I am."

"So, things . . . ?"

"Let's just say – better."

"Wow," Amy said, "if that's better, I think the best would probably kill you."

"Amy, really!"

Chloe was very fond of Amy and would liked to have helped her a bit in her love life. Amy had assets, a great large-featured shining smooth face and a soft hourglassy build that was starting to come back in style. Both needed more appropriate adornment and a bit of firming here and there, but both packed lethal potential. A little advice, maybe a makeover referral. Amy already had the sunny and generous personality that would make her a great girlfriend. And she was making good money at Barbiron and set to make a lot more. Chloe asked if she had lunch plans.

"If we have lunch you have to tell me."

"If I tell you, then I will respectfully invite you to listen to a few affectionate recommendations," Chloe said.

❦

Amy was transported the rest of the day.

She had listened to Chloe's story and her advice and had a salad for lunch.

And in between bouts of fighting with Excel to display the last month's inventory results correctly, she conjured up low-res images of fun boyfriends.

CHAPTER 19

BOYFRIEND

BOYFRIEND.

Chloe liked that word. She liked the way it felt in her mouth and sounded in her ear when she said it.

"I was telling my boyfriend the other day how much I missed being able to go to Dairy Queen whenever I felt like it."

"My boyfriend likes that kind of top on me. Where did you get it?"

"I think we can make it but I'll have to check with the boyfriend."

"The boyfriend was telling me that the Village of Carol Spring was named after a girl named Carol Spring."

"This is my boyfriend. Jon Rider."

She used it so often that her circle started referring to Jon as "The Boif."

The first thing they decided was that there was no rush to live together. Partly for the usual reason – it was prudent to see how things were going to go, which was going to take some time – and partly because they each had a lot of stuff. Not only did each have a lot of stuff, but they selected a lot of that stuff to match their own tastes and design preferences. Which they did not share. Chloe liked luxuriously-upholstered overstuffed chairs and sofas with carved wooden arms and many pillows. Many pillows. Jon was more of a Prairie Style guy, his spaces resembling a prairie much like his office. Few items of furniture, all straight lines and square angles and monochrome earthtone fabrics, and no pillows. No pillows on the prairie. His bed was barely more than an elevated mattress, but, as Chloe observed, it didn't need to be.

One thing that neither of them knew about the other was that neither gave a damn about furniture as long as they could be together.

There was one other reason they didn't move in: Sleeping over still felt a little naughty. Whoever slept over was invading the domain of the other, leaving a little more of themselves behind each time. The later-arrival/earlier-departure sleepover pretended to the world that they weren't boffing like demented peccaries, and that felt naughty, too. And feeling naughty was part of the fun.

There was, of course, the question of the pets. Neither species had ever been exposed with regularity to a specimen of the other. There was, of course, no question of either Chloe or Jon giving up their beloved companions. Bandit and Gloria quickly got used to Jon, since he made it a point to be involved in their feeding and brushing and scooping when he visited or stayed over. Or, being cats, perhaps they didn't; getting used to something suggested that the cat considered itself in relation to that non-cat something, which would require the cat to think that it was not the center of all existence or existence itself, a cat capability science had failed to detect after years of study. In any case, he hadn't lied on their first date – he did like cats. And Bandit and Gloria both made immediate peace with the Feeline Feeder automatic food-and-water dispensing device she bought to make sure they were well provisioned when she was going to be away more than a night.

Teeko and Bridey were typically doggy about this new visitor and walkies companion, always waggy and welcoming, always ready for petting and scratchies, although they could smell the cats on her and wondered about that. They were won over after a particularly vigorous and lengthy session of double-tuggies-and-fetch, and their doggy affection deepened into doggy love when they realized that with this tall soft golden one a whole lot more doggy bags came through the door for them. Unlike the cats when Jon slept over, they didn't complain those nights she took their place in his bed. Also, unlike the cats, they didn't sneak back onto the bed later. Chloe asked Jon about their names.

"I read somewhere that it is easier for dogs to hear hard-edged, more explosive consonant sounds like *k*, *d*, *b*, and *t*, and bright long vowel sounds. I made up names I thought they'd like to hear, that they'd respond to."

"You named your dogs based on dog research," Chloe said. "No favorite names, no actor or musician, no family names. You gave them *logical* names."

"That's right."

"Of all the Jon Riders in the world, you have got to be the Jon Riderest."

"You got a problem with that?"

"None whatsoever."

They tabled the topic of the meeting of the pets until the time somewhere down the road when they figured out their living thing, which would be when their loving thing demanded it.

Jon privately tabled mentioning his observation that naming a cat is about as useful as naming a stone.

⁓

Chloe loved Jon and she loved having a boyfriend.

She loved doing things with him that she would be reluctant to do alone, or that would be too pathetic to do all the time with just girlfriends. Dinner, movies, theater, concerts. Jon liked public lectures being given at local schools, or by traveling authors, and Chloe found herself getting interested in topics she never had time for (or thought she didn't) and, in some cases, had never thought about. Sometimes in the evening they would stay home and read. She loved those evenings just as much, being together quietly, just the tiniest bit married.

And it gave her great pleasure to be out in public with him. In his profession he moved in circles of money and influence; he knew how to act and not act, what to say and not say, when encountering the rich and powerful in her circle of friends and fellow business leaders at society and professional functions.

He was perfectly content, actually amused, on those

occasions when he was called upon to be arm candy for the celebrated Chloe Manning. He never did anything to dilute her spotlight, and she was solicitous of not ignoring him. She was proud to introduce him. They even ran into Kira Ono at a function one night. She laughed and said, "I knew it."

He was surprised to learn that despite her obvious ability to take care of herself, the older men in her circle displayed an almost paternal concern for her welfare and just the slightest hint of what was supposed to sound like teasing but felt like provisional disapproval:

"So, you're the boyfriend who's stolen the heart of our Chloe."

"You better treat her like a queen or we'll be coming for you."

"I was talking to Nelson Gilles about you the other day. Said you were some kind of guru."

"What have you got that Jon Hamm doesn't?"

"Every man in this room has checked you out on Google. I think Benson over there might have ordered a background check."

Jon had developed a collection of self-effacing comebacks, but the mostly good-natured jabbing was a small price to pay for her company.

"They're afraid I'll just fall for some vapid stud who only wants me for my money," Chloe told him.

"They're one-third right," Jon said.

Girlfriends were their usual mixed bag. They were all happy for Chloe, or said they were. But some were jealous of her having a cool smart cute boyfriend, and some were jealous that the cool smart cute boyfriend was occupying their rare Chloe Manning time. She got the usual *does he have any friends* and *does he have a brother* and *can we clone him* and even *is his father still alive*. And once in a while, *is he always quiet?*

Jon liked most of her friends and professional colleagues, and liked most of the boyfriends or husbands, including the couple of instances where there was a boyfriend and a husband. There were exceptions; he wondered that Chloe tolerated a couple of the more shallow and ill-read women in her circle, and a few of the men were poseurs or dumb or both. Later he would ask her about them.

"Nobody much likes her," she would say, "but she's always been in the group and we're girls – we don't kick people out." And she would always conclude: "She's OK, I guess. I could do without the boyfriend."

Chloe also very much liked the sex.

To his surprise, Jon eased into this new domesticity much more comfortably than he expected. He not only loved Chloe, he liked her. He liked to hang out with her. In public, alone at home, even when she was the center of attention he never felt – she never made him feel – spare or waiting in the wings or a decoration for the evening. She was always interesting; when she spoke she usually said something worth hearing, and she decorated even the most mundane observation with something offbeat, unexpected, unseen. Even when they disagreed – which was seldom and usually mild – they never elevated it to a fight; their talking things out struck notes that created chords and not cacophony. In any event, Jon went along with her on most things because whether they did her thing or his thing was an almost invisible consideration to him compared to the whole of doing a thing, any thing, with her.

He never grew accustomed to her beauty and her charisma. When she entered a room, he felt his body react as though he were seeing her for the first time. And it struck him that to keep this woman he had to earn her every day, inspire that same jolt of discovery in her whenever he would appear. He had to be a good man, a good companion, a good lover. And she deserved a man who cared about looking as good as his gifts would allow. He was in good shape to begin with but he started hitting the East Bank Club with greater regularity, lifting and swimming.

And if he was going to be seen with a fashion leader . . . . He took a roll call of his closet and realized that his casual collection needed some freshening up, a task in which he enlisted Chloe's enthusiastic counsel.

"I told you I wasn't casual," he said.

"The question is," she said on a visit to his closet, "whether you're living in the second half of the second decade of the twenty-first century."

She had some advice about his hair – he'd look cute a little shaggier – but when it came to issues of being squared away, he drew the line.

When they rose in their mornings, the bed would be made before she figured out which K-cup she would use for her coffee.

Jon noticed a change in the way men and women

reacted to him. His male friends were happy for him, and perhaps even a little surprised that this mostly-quiet man was dating a capitalist bombshell. He heard the word "congratulations" more than once, but their reactions did not have about them the feel of a sniggering locker-room insinuation that he stood in their midst as the sexual conqueror of Chloe Manning. In the locker room itself, though, he got some looks; he wasn't sure why.

At first, he had no awareness of any difference in women's reactions to him. Then, on a few occasions, it was beyond ignoring that one of Chloe's girlfriends, or the wife of a business associate, or a colleague on one of Chloe's charitable boards, was tossing some light flirtation his way – once, where the wine got refreshed too frequently, not so light.

"Babe, you're not going to believe this," Jon said, "but someone put a phone number in my coat pocket. Who is – can you read this? – Malesia?"

"I don't have to read it. Melissa. And I believe it."

"Which one was she?"

"The slutty one."

"Um . . . ."

"The slutty one who pretended to lose an earring so she could bend over, give all the gentlemen a good look at her big tits and her big ass in that wretched plunging tight green thing she had on."

"Was I out of line with her?"

"Not at all. You are always charming to all the ladies in a non-insinuating kind of aw-shucks way and I like it because you always leave with me trailing a bunch of sighing women in our wake."

"Sweetie, I never, ever even want to hint . . . ."

"This is not an issue, honey. Not the first time Melissa's been over-chardonnayed at one of these vendor functions. Or the first time she's misbehaved with someone's date. She's a regional sales manager for our former drill-bit supplier."

"Former? Then what was she doing at . . . ?"

"Starting tomorrow."

He was sometimes astonished at her take on women's reactions to him. He first experienced it when they dined one evening at a neighborhood Italian restaurant. The young, pretty waitress took their order. She was chatty; Jon chatted back. He was always gracious to service personnel, working at tough gigs for not much dough. She took their drink order and returned with it, said she'd be back in a bit for their food order.

After the waitress had returned to take their dinner order, Chloe asked: "Did you notice that?"

"What?"

"Our waitress."

"What about her?" Jon said. "Seems OK."

"Did you see what she had done?"

"I guess I didn't."

"When she first came to the table," Chloe said, "her hair was pulled back and knotted. When she came back to take our order, she'd been to the ladies' room. Her hair was down and brushed out. She had put on fresh lipstick and added some blush. She'd tucked her blouse in so her boobs would be tight against it, and I think she might have unbuttoned a button. Did you catch the fragrance she'd spritzed? And her focus was entirely on you. She was flirting."

"Good lord, babe. I'm supposed to be a noticing kind of guy but that went right past me. Are you sure?"

"Very sure. And do you know why she did all that?"

"Well, I'm obviously not going to make any connection with her with a date sitting here, especially a date like you. I don't know, maybe she thinks I'm attractive or something."

"Oh, you are attractive, dear," Chloe said, "very amazingly cute, but in the world of women's reactions to women's men, I'm cuter."

"Lost me."

"She is interested in you because I'm with you," she said. "I don't know if she knows who I am, but she knows I'm hot and I have my pick and I picked you, so you must be something." She said this unselfconsciously, not intending to brag on herself, and certainly not to offend him. "I've been out with trolls when something like this happened."

"You were out with trolls?"

"Business."

"She may have prettied up," Jon said, "but I think it's more likely she thought I'd be making the tip decision."

None of it mattered. There was not the slightest chance that he would be unfaithful.

For many reasons.

But, among them: Jon also very much liked the sex.

⌁

They stayed over at one another's home three, maybe four nights a week.

The dogs and cats were unhappy on those nights, and at first that was a consideration for Jon and Chloe. The couple got over it, and so did the animals.

The on-off rhythm of nights together and, on many such nights, intimacy, worked well for Chloe and Jon. Their feelings for one another were intense and true; but each came to the romance from lives of solitude in which there were unique riches, and they agreed they should honor that in one another until their feelings told them it was time to reevaluate the geography of their lives.

The electrifying joy of discovery that marked their earliest sexual encounters dimmed some with time, but it was replaced by something just as good, better on some nights, some mornings, too, and the odd afternoon: the warmth of security and trust and the courage to explore each other's preferences and dislikes, and from time to time, something fresh.

Chloe loved the closeness. She sensed its value would grow and last in their lives much longer than the sexual thrill. In the mornings she would lay barely awake, feeling the stroke of Jon's deep breathing next to her, this love of her life right there and soon to stir in a prelude to waking and drape an arm and a leg over her, an exquisite gesture of possession and need of which she never tired. Bandit on her chest, Gloria on the pillow above her head, both purring and occasionally changing position to let her know, gently, that at this time of day it was all about Breakfast. This, she thought, this you cannot put in a bank account.

Unchanged was their mutual excitement at stoking the emotional furnace beneath the snaps and buttons and zippers of their fine wardrobes, the raw animal cravings under the rich fabrics that crept to the edge of violence between the sheets and left them heaving side by side as their sweat cooled them, and when their breath returned they talked about how what they just did to each other was the foundation of absolutely everything.

∽

"Hey, boyfriend, you ready to go?"

"All ready."

"You put on sunblock? Where's your windbreaker?"

"Don't need 'em," Jon said. "Because wherever I stand, my lovely snakehips earthangel, I am in your shadow, where I'm always protected from the bright Chicago sun and the blowing Chicago wind."

"My my, Lord Byron," Chloe said, turning to him with a surprised smile, "aren't you just the totally friskiest sugar-voiced sexy thing today?" She dropped to her knees, pulled his pants-snap open with her teeth, and hooked her fingers in his belt loops. "But you're only half right."

CHAPTER 20

NEW LOVE AND GOOD SEX HAD NO EFFECT ON THE BONDURANT CASE

NEW LOVE AND good sex had no effect on the Bondurant case.

The matter proceeded more quickly than most cases in the Northern District of Illinois. Nelson Gilles knew Judge Cleon Achebe from when they had cases against each other in the years before the judge's appointment to the federal bench. He secured an order imposing an expedited discovery schedule and early dates for pre-trial proceedings. Blake Bondurant's lawyers had not opposed it – they and their client were as anxious to get their money as Barbiron was to get this case behind it, whatever might happen. The trial was scheduled for early the following year.

Discovery in the case was confidential pursuant to the terms of the protective order Brian Accardo had negotiated. Since information the parties exchanged would be protected from public disclosure at least until trial, it was not long into discovery before Blake's lawyers revealed how they planned to use their volatile information: Blake was going to claim that the romp in the hotel was entirely Chloe's idea; that she pressured him into it as his direct-line superior at the company; that he was the one with the attack of conscience and sober good sense at the hotel and turned her down; and that from that point on, Barbiron contrived to find fault with his performance and eventually terminated him.

As long as Blake was going to lie about this, at first it seemed odd to the Rockwell Morton team that he was not going go ahead and make the even more lurid and dramatic claim before the jury that they had sex, and maybe more than once – a real, if brief, affair that had ended badly, followed by his retaliatory firing. Oona Karras suggested the answers: If he claimed an actual sexual affair that she was coercing, then it would logically follow that Chloe was the one who ended it, dumping him somewhere along the line, impliedly for lousy sex or some other female need he was failing to satisfy. A guy like Blake Bondurant would not want his studly brand tarnished in that manner. More significantly for a trial strategy, Oona observed, his current story also made him look at least a little noble in his refusal to mount his boss on her demand, a very attractive story to a public newly aware of quid-pro-quo sexual politics in the officeplace. In any event, a longer-term affair would require evidence of comings-and-goings that did not exist and would require even more extensive lying, so the story stayed at Lloyd's Jazz Depot and the FOUND Hotel. His version of the encounter was entirely consistent with the circumstances that would become known to the jury: Blake Bondurant, having succumbed initially to the drunken demands of his CEO Chloe Manning to get a room, realized his error and turned her down, and from there it was all downhill for him at Barbiron until the day he was fired.

༈

Blake's lawyers had been careful. They had filed the case under seal, so its allegations would remain hidden from the public. In the complaint and all their filings to the docket, they did not mention any of the most embarrassing facts. Even if someone had hacked the electronic filing system, no one reviewing the court file would have seen the evidence of Chloe's poor judgment and distinctly non-CEO-like behavior, including the drunken prelude at Lloyd's and the naked denouement at the FOUND Hotel.

Chloe's secret, in the form of Blake's distorted version of it, was his property to trade for what he hoped and expected would be a huge settlement before trial in return for dropping the lawsuit and securing Blake's silence thereafter. But even if the case did not settle, Brian and Nelson advised Chloe, Blake's lawyers would then use his tale of drunken seduction, rejection, and termination by a spoiled and powerful executive to try to shock the jury into an even more gigantic verdict at trial.

So far, Blake's pretrial settlement strategy had not worked. Chloe would not pay that creep Blake Bondurant a large amount of company money for the selfish purpose of avoiding embarrassment for actions she alone had taken.

It wasn't just petulance; that was shareholders' money, money whose presence on Barbiron's bottom line was going to attract the investors in the initial public offering, and money she and the men and women she had selected to stand with her had wrestled out of a difficult economy and one that had greeted her venture with ridicule. It wasn't going to be used to make Blake Bondurant rich unless the very last appeals court commanded it.

And, as Nelson had told the board, a big early settlement would pique the interest of underwriters and require disclosure anyway. There was no reason to pay Blake and his lawyers for nothing.

So the Bondurant case continued its steady movement toward trial.

꿍

There was something else moving Chloe Manning, something she kept to herself. She did not believe in destiny; she did not believe in fate. But she did believe that whatever caused things to happen in the universe would not come together for her destruction now. She was not a dreamy fool. She knew that in refusing to settle, she had preserved the chance that she could lose control of Barbiron's operations, and the near certainty that she'd be the subject of mortifying news coverage and the ridicule of late-night talk hosts. She did not know how her escape was going to come about, but she believed she and Barbiron were eventually going to emerge into daylight and leave these shadows behind. Maybe it was not destiny or fate that would save her; but maybe, somewhere along the line, she would stumble across a little luck. It had happened to her before.

But, her premonitions aside, the fact was that Chloe thought they would win the case. It was true that win or lose, a trial would mean exposure of her bad judgment, but if the jury found her actions in firing Blake Bondurant's handsome ass were not improper from a legal standpoint, it would go a long way toward marginalizing her mistake and preventing its characterization as something that affected the operation of Barbiron or her management of it. She had been stupid, but Blake was a liar and an incompetent manager. She had fired him for good reasons other than his being an asshole, which in her judgment would have been reason enough. Her human resources director had persuaded her that the Barbiron employee handbook could not be read to cover a termination solely for being an asshole or a jerk or a useless sack, so she was glad she had pretty good – not perfect, but pretty good – evidence of his unsatisfactory performance even when fully clothed and on the job.

⚜

Chloe and Jon found it easier than they had expected to avoid discussing the case when they were together. Other than routine discovery, there was seldom much happening. The defense had been formulated at an early date and was well-known to them both: Blake's performance had deteriorated, and that deterioration had been quantified; the company had given him every opportunity to improve; he didn't; adios, BB.

Also, Chloe would be able to tell her own version of

the hotel encounter on the stand. That version itself wasn't pretty, but it was true – if hard to believe beginning at the point where two beautiful naked adults are facing each other in a hotel room – and the trial team had crafted the story for her in a way to make her actions if not sympathetic, at least understandable.

Chloe got along well with the Rockwell Morton team: Nelson, who handled some of the preliminary motions and was always available for a board consult; Brian, who would be primarily responsible for all other court proceedings, including the trial; and Oona, who coordinated all the discovery and researched and wrote all the motions. Still, as the trial date grew closer, Chloe secretly wished Jon could do his Rider thing, gazing at the whole record and identifying what rocks to turn over to find the hidden key to resolution.

The lead attorney for Blake's team was Jolene Marovitz. She was a name partner with one of the leading Chicago plaintiffs' employment and civil rights firms. The firm had assigned the case to her to avoid any appearance of some manly-man lawyer bullying the defenseless pretty ladygirl Chloe before the jury. If a woman was asking the tough questions, if a woman was advocating that Chloe's behavior had been reprehensible – that was worth something to those twelve men and women good and true.

Jolene Marovitz did not cut Chloe any slack when she took her deposition. Chloe's patience extended only so far; even though Brian Accardo had warned her that her attitude would not play well if her videotaped testimony were replayed before the jury, she couldn't help herself:

Q   Ms. Manning, you removed your own clothing in the hotel room, did you not?

A   Removed it from what?

MR. ACCARDO: Chloe.

Q   Removed it from your body. You completely undressed yourself, did you not?

A   You know I did. Your own client has said it.

Q   You need to answer the question. You removed your own clothes.

A   Yes.

Q   Mr. Bondurant did not remove or attempt to remove any item of your clothing, correct?

A   Yes.

Q   He didn't touch you, did he?

A   Not in the hotel room.

Q   You ordered him to "get your fucking clothes off and I mean yesterday," didn't you?

A   I wouldn't call it an order and I don't recall what words I used but I doubt I said "fucking." I might have said something to hurry things along, at first, but I changed my mind. Women are allowed to do that these days, you know, Ms. Marovitz?

MR. ACCARDO: Chloe.

Q   In fact, you removed your clothes with great enthusiasm, tossing them around the room, didn't you?

> MR. ACCARDO: Objection. That is completely irrelevant and also vague as to what is meant by enthusiasm and what would constitute tossing. Also prejudicial. You can answer if you can.

A   I didn't fold them up and put them on hangers, if that's what you mean.

Q   Are you aware that you left your bra and panties in the room?

A   Wouldn't you be aware if you walked over a mile outdoors at the end of March without any underwear on?

> MR. ACCARDO: Chloe.

Q   Are you aware that Mr. Bondurant took them when he left the room and has them now?

A   Sure. How do they fit?

> MR. ACCARDO: Chloe.

A   A gentleman would have returned them.

> MR. ACCARDO: Chloe.

Q   A lady would not have removed them in front of a man she barely knew, isn't that right?

> MR. ACCARDO: Objection, harassing the witness.
>
> MS. MAROVITZ: Oh, you'll see your high-priced lingerie again soon, Ms. Manning. They're beautiful. They'll have exhibit tags on them.

CHAPTER 21

WHAT IS THIS?

"WHAT IS THIS?"

"Just a little something," Jon said.

"What's the occasion?"

"Does there have to be an occasion?"

"No," Chloe said, "but usually."

"There is a minor occasion. Six months today since we started this thing at the Chop House."

"Oh, that is so sweet," Chloe said. "You remember everything."

"The calendar app remembers everything."

"Shall I open?"

"Sure. It's not much. You're pretty impossible to shop for, having everything and being able to buy whatever of the few things you don't have. And listen to me, I'm completely sincere: You can return this. If it's not you, or if it doesn't work with anything, you can take it back, I made sure of that."

"Oh my god! Is this – it's a Tory Burch!"

"Purses are pretty personal, I know," Jon said, "so please feel free –"

"No no no, it's beautiful!"

"I noticed stuff sticking out of the purse you usually carry. But now that you've taken it out of the box, it looks bigger –"

"Stop," Chloe said, "it's perfect! I'm five-ten-plus, look how this fits under my arm! And I use my purse like a brief-case, got all kinds of junk in there most women don't need and maybe I don't either but I print stuff out and jam it in my purse and this is amazing! Look at all the compartments and little secret zipper things! God, you – I'm tearing up."

"I'm glad you like it. But really, if you get it home and change your mind –"

"Stop. It's just – perfect – so thoughtful. I love it. I'm not returning it. I'm coming over and giving you a kiss, you sweetie."

"Happy anniversary."

"Six months. Happy anniversary to you, too," Chloe said.

"What do you want to do?" Jon said. "Phone in some Chinese or pizza or go out? Or I'm good with soup and sandwich here."

"I'm thinking Greek tonight," Chloe said.

"Not my style, babe."

"Greek *food*, you perv."

"Much more my style."

"I feel like talking in a booth over some food," Chloe

said. "Let's walk Greektown and try to find a fun little spot where we don't have to yell."

"Ah," Jon said. "*Fae ladi kai ela vrady.*"

"Wiseguy. All right, what does that mean?"

"Eat oil and come in the evening."

∽

Chloe: We need to do this sooner or later.

"Six months is a good time for taking stock, don't you think?"

"Sure, let's do it."

Chloe: That was easy. He's ready to talk. He's always ready to do whatever I want.

"Well, what do you think?"

"What do I think? I think we're doing great," Jon said. "I love you to pieces and I'm happy that things are working out the way we both hoped. But I have a feeling that you have had some thoughts on this, having raised the taking of stock."

"Not really. I mean, I have the same thoughts that you do. I love you and I have loved our relationship."

"'Have loved.' That's past tense! Or, I guess, present perfect, but it sounds past-ish. Is there a problem? Are you feeling that we're in a rut? Is that why we're having our talk?"

"No. No, not really. Not at all, I mean. But you raised the six months and I thought hmm, six months. That's a successful romance. Someday the plot will thicken, you know? Maybe we should explore."

"Sure, okay. Well, what are the things that could be

next? I suppose the most incremental thing would be to find some way to move in together."

Chloe: I was thinking the same thing. But . . .

"Yes, we could consider that," she said.

"We took that three weeks in New York," Jon said, "kind of a live-together trial run, I think we both thought. I did, anyway. Did you think that?"

"That did cross my mind at the time, yes it did."

"And think how great it went, babe," Jon said. "Together all the time, very close quarters in the room, stressful travel, a couple of hiccups with reservations and getting around the city. But we were cool together and didn't get uncool and worked around what needed working around. All was good. It was only three weeks, you know, but I felt really good about our long-term after we got back."

Chloe said, "I think I might have snapped at you a couple of times, or groused about something."

"Did you? I don't remember that," Jon said. "Whatever it was, it must been something minor or it got fixed. But that's the point: whatever issue we had, we worked it out and moved on."

Chloe: Of course you don't remember it. I complained about the rattly air conditioner in the room and you thought it was okay and I spoke sharply to you like you had something to do with it and you didn't say anything, you just went down and got our room changed.

"So you're saying . . . ," Chloe said.

"So I'm saying that I don't think we'd have any relation-ship problem living together if that's what we decided to do. Do you? At this point, not much difference between what we're doing now and living together, except that we wouldn't have to be hauling changes of clothes back and forth."

"No, I think the relationship would be fine," Chloe said.

"But I think we both know what the issue would be, right?"

"Yeah," Chloe said. "Yeah. I think I do. Logistics. Space. Taste, I suppose. I like my condo and looking at the city lights at night. You like your big townhouse. My condo has my stuff I like. Your home has more space but you have your stuff you like in all the rooms. Even in your bigger space, we'd be talking four animals."

"Six if you count us. I grew up with cats and dogs. They'd work things out. Not that worried about the pets."

Chloe: Nothing worries you.

"Okay, but the rest."

"The rest is a problem," Jon said. "Again, not a romance problem, a making-the-pieces-fit problem."

"There is a solution, Jon."

"Yep," Jon said, knowing where she was headed. "It's a big damned solution. Is it time to think about it? I'm willing."

"I'm willing, but . . . ."

"But house-hunting, deciding what kind of joint we want, city or suburbs – that's a big one – deciding whether to buy or build, house or big condo in the city with a view – I'd be fine with that, babe, I really would – selling our places, moving, decorating. Financial arrangements. A lot of big things, big changes, but that's kind of what 'taking next steps' means. But I'm game."

Chloe: Yeah, you are. Always.

"Well, that's right," Chloe said. "But as I think on it, Jon, I don't know. It's been a stressful time for me. The lawsuit, the trial coming up. We're still working on projects for the public offering when we get some resolution on Blake and the pressure is on to keep the numbers good."

Jon: Whoa. I thought we were headed somewhere, now she's finding reasons not to move forward.

"Babe, I know how tough it has been for you, but we've been strong together. If we don't want to wait, maybe I could take the laboring oar on some of the logistics."

"I couldn't let you do that, and you'd need me to tell you what I would be demanding in our love nest."

Jon: Making jokes. That's good. But kind of deflecting the problem-solving effort here.

"You have a point," Jon said. "The trial is in, what, six months? We can wait until it's over to start the process. And let me make a promise to you. Nothing that happens in the trial, nothing that happens with you, no worst-case scenario, is going to affect my love for you or wanting to be with you every day."

Chloe: Mind-reader. This is why this man drives me crazy. He wants me to know he's not just suggesting putting it off so he can do me until the trial and we see what happens to me. He does care about me.

"I know, baby," Chloe said. "I trust you."

"There's another thing about getting a new place," Jon said.

"That being?"

Jon: The word is going to come up one way or another. I'm not afraid of it. I can't imagine she is.

"The thing is, my dearest sweet angel-drawers: Doesn't that magnitude of commitment – the commitment to live together in a home we own, a home we picked out or built together, leaving behind the homes of the past – pretty much mean we are really – think about it – really committed in the most committed way we can be?"

"I – so we're skipping over just living together and moving right to – ?" She wasn't sure why she was having trouble saying the word.

"Does it make any sense to completely physically uproot and say goodbye to our comfy little individual lives and places so we can go living in a new place if there is even the slightest thought in the back of either of our minds that it might not last? Does it make sense to live on a 30-year note unless we are committed forever?"

"I would have thought we'd pay cash."

Jon: Jesus, she's stepping on my imagery. And another joke to evade the subject.

"Come on, you tease. It starts with 'm'," Jon said.

Chloe: He's right. Getting a place together is not something you do thinking you might undo it.

"Jon, I didn't intend to force a discussion of –"

"I know, I know," he said. "I wasn't thinking that you did. No, I don't think either of us intended this conversation necessarily to start down that road. And you said you were a little verklempt about the other things in your life right now that were throwing some cold water on the living-together step, so I'm thinking this is not a time to make any decisions about some step that's even more dramatic. But I don't want to be coy about the subject. I don't want you to think I'm afraid of it. I'm focusing on you, babe. You're the one crazy stuff happens to. I may be the only non-crazy thing in your life right now, and I know you know I'm here for you whatever step we're on."

Chloe: Why did I start this conversation? What did I expect to come out of this? Not me moving in with him, not him moving in with me, not getting a house together, and sure not a proposal. What was I hoping for out of him? He's saying a lot of right things. He's gone through every door I've opened. Just like he always does.

"I appreciate that, love, I really do," Chloe said.

Jon: What does she want? This is her relationship talk, and it sounds like status quo city right now. I'm fine with that for now, but I need to know now that we've started down this road.

"Honeypop, what do you want?" Jon said. "Ideally, where do you want us right now – geographically or otherwise?"

Chloe: I want YOU to open a door. I want you to take what YOU want. I want YOU to say SCREW the trial and SCREW your Q3 numbers and SCREW your stress, give that stress to ME, I will drown it in my Jon Rider pool of calm and reason and we are going to be together all the time. I want you to say, yell, that you will MAKE it happen and nothing will stand in MY way to make it happen NOW and I will not let anything stand in YOUR way. I want you, Jon Rider, to STOP being a non-crazy thing in my life just once in a while.

"I don't know," Chloe said. "I mean, I'm very happy with where we are, I love you, I count the hours and then the minutes. But when I think about a big new change on top of all the uncertainty – it brings me up a little short, but not short in my feelings for you."

"I know, lover," Jon said. You haven't said anything that worries me about our relationship. But alongside that feeling needs to be a feeling that you're in as good a place as you can be with all you've got going on. It sounds like maybe we need to mull this over a little, talk again sometime, any time you want, any time you're comfortable. Maybe we'll come up with an idea. And we don't have any timetable for a decision, but let's keep talking."

"Thank you, sweetheart," Chloe said. "You're the absolute best."

Chloe: A boyfriend comfortable with relationship talk. Huh. Yeah. Comfortable with freaking everything.

Jon: That was strange.

CHAPTER 22

CHLOE STARED AT THE PHONE

CHLOE STARED AT the phone.

✦

—*The One is off, Gloria said.*

— You say I am the idiot cat, Bandit said, but I can feel her slow and quiet. Is it The Other?

— The Other has been himself, Gloria said. I do not know.

— The Other is good with Food and treats and talking to The One in a bright voice that makes her smile, Bandit said. He lets us walk on him in the morning.

— I favor The Other also, Gloria said. But on alone nights I think she is with him away.

— He knows how to touch me, Bandit said. His touch is strong and he picks me up under my belly and rolls it strong

with his hands. He brushes me hard and pets me hard like The One does not do.

– I do not know a part of The Other's smell, Gloria said. The Other comes from other smells from wherever it is when he is not here.

– Maybe The One does not like the other smells, Bandit said.

– The Other has always smelled that way, Gloria said.

– Something hard for The One that we do not know, Bandit said.

– We know nothing about The One beyond what we see, Gloria said, and she knows nothing about us. That is why it is so good that she cares for us.

– It can only be something about The Other, Bandit said. He has been with us long but he is the only different thing from all the back times when The One was herself.

– I am sorry I call you the idiot cat, Gloria said. I will clean your head.

– What is she looking at? Bandit said.

✍

Jon had called her that morning. He asked her to look around for his phone. He was pretty sure he had left it on the island in her kitchen. The phone was hard to see against the dark granite.

Yes, she said. Right here. He said he'd be by that evening to pick it up. That night was not supposed to be a sleepover night, but the Bondurant trial was set to start the day after tomorrow and he had subtly increased his attentions over the past month. Not so subtly that she didn't notice. She appreciated his thoughtfulness, but the truth was it had not calmed her stress and, increasingly, her fear of what might happen.

The Rockwell Morton team could not have been more aggressive in getting ready for trial. Brian and Oona had prepared her for her testimony when they called her in defense. They had been over it and over it. They had prepared question-and-answer scripts to study, not to steer any testimony away from the truth, but to rehearse her for the questions she was likely to face in her direct examination by Brian and her cross-examination by Jolene Marovitz. They did the same with Myra Altobelli. Their strategy was to tell the strict truth about the hotel incident, and to consistently bend the arc of the trial back to the steep decline in Blake's performance, the time gap between the hotel episode and his termination, and Barbiron's strict observance of its pre-termination policies favoring performance improvement, policies he had ignored. Even if the jury found for Blake, if the record clearly showed his termination was justified on performance grounds, they always had a chance on post-trial motions and appeal. And they had Chloe's charisma and her sincere and believable version of the events of that night at the bar and hotel to mitigate the shocking implications of Blake's lying version.

There was no way of knowing if all of that was enough. She had built her success on controlling every detail in her fight for success. In this most critical of fights, she controlled nothing.

It had been a while since Jon and Chloe had the talk over Greek. They were aware of the passage of time with no change in their relationship. Which relationship was good, very good. But – there is always a "but" – since the talk, their awareness that there was no change or growth in the thing was always a ghostly presence in the room. Chloe had acted oddly after having brought up the subject of next steps in the restaurant and in the months since; on several occasions, it seemed to Jon, she had tried deliberately to provoke him. He never rose to the bait; he did not want to upset her as her other concerns loomed larger as the trial approached.

Besides, Jon thought, none of it was important enough to fight about.

⊰⊱

Jon never forgot things, especially not his phone.

She looked at it a long time. Gloria groomed Bandit on a nearby counter.

Had he left it so she would open it and see certain things? Would it be okay to look at it because that's what he wanted? No, that wasn't the way he operated.

Had he left it to see if she was a snoop, if he could trust her? No, not that either.

Okay, how about this: He's the one who brought up marriage. If we're sort of like married, shouldn't it be okay for me to see what's on his phone? It was another bad argument, but as she pondered Jon's old Samsung sitting there, the little Lisa devil walked across her shoulders and kicked the little Lisa angel right in the throat and out of the argument.

She peered at it for a long time, still not quite ready to conclude the ethical argument with herself with a ruling in favor of prying.

But she knew all along what she was going to do.

She picked up the phone. It was not locked. She turned it on and swiped it open.

❧

She tapped the Gallery icon to bring up his history of photographs. The phone was scratched and dented and she counted on him having had it a long time; Jon was not a guy who replaced gadgets that were working perfectly well for him. She began to scroll.

Jon did not take a lot of phone snaps. She didn't have far to go.

When Chloe came to the first of the images she was looking for, she felt her face warm, and then get hot. She was shocked into disbelief. Her heart had no idea what direction to turn.

Amelia was plain.

Amelia was plain as a bank.

Amelia in a pantsuit, Amelia in her PhD gown and mortarboard, Amelia in shorts and a buttoned top at a picnic, Amelia taking a bite of pizza.

She was not pretty, but she was not unpretty. Pleasant. Shorter than average, maybe 5-4, 5-5? 5-4. Just the tiniest bit plump, although phone snaps are not always trustworthy;

no, she was clearly just a little heavy. Not busty; just average woman-size. Her features were undramatic, about as helpful at fixing her identity and character as a police artist sketch. If she wore makeup, she didn't wear much. Her hair was a streaky blond, parted on one side, and worn flat down the sides and back down to her chin. In about half the photos she wore glasses.

She looked like anyone. She looked like everyone. She was a one-woman crowd scene.

She looked happy. She looked very happy. Even when she was not posing. She looked like someone Chloe thought she might like to have known. Very happy.

Amelia's ordinariness was shocking enough.

The images of Jon were devastating.

Selfies with Amelia.

His smile was broad, he was *laughing*, they were *laughing*, in snap after snap. God, the man was showing teeth, gums! His eyes crinkled in true delight, shining, reflections at the surface of some wellspring of deep satisfaction. In some he was looking at her like she was the most desirable woman on earth, the answer to all his prayers.

It got worse.

Amelia or someone must have used his phone or sent him the images.

There was Jon doing a cannonball into a hotel pool.

Jon in a Santa suit tossing a small child in the air, both of them howling with delight.

Jon mooning a busload of Green Bay Packer fans.

Jon being a volunteer assistant to a magician who was pulling a condom out of Jon's front pocket.

Jon on stage at the Chicago Bar Association Bar Show made up *in drag* as freaking Nancy Pelosi and *singing*.

Jon at a big round table with his mouth open talking and everyone else convulsed.

His images were a rainbow of the many shades of happiness; delight, ecstasy, excitement. Laughter, so much laughter.

And, even in the crummy old phone snaps, a fire in his eye.

She scrolled down as far as their wedding.

Amelia was no more distinctive.

But even the lousy cellphone image couldn't disguise it: It was a cliché, but clichés are clichés because they're true, and it was true here – she was radiant, incandescent with love.

So was Jon.

He looked like a different person, her Jon turned inside out.

She couldn't look at any more.

She turned the phone off and returned it to the island.

⁂

When Jon arrived they exchanged their usual mouth peck, but he instantly knew something was ajar in the room. "Ah," he said, spying his phone on the island. He walked over and put it in his pocket. "Thanks for taking good care of it, the three of you."

"I didn't take such good care of it," Chloe said.

"Why, what happened to it?"

She sat down in one of the overstuffed chairs in her great room and indicated that he should sit.

"Separate chairs," he said. "Serious business."

"Jon," she said, "tell me how you really feel about me, about us."

"You know how I feel," he said. "Why do I have to say it? I love you very much."

"There's something missing, isn't there?"

"What? What's missing?"

"I don't know how to describe it."

"Well, if you don't, how do you expect me to?"

"Are you aware," Chloe said, "that we never take selfies?"

"Sure we have," he said.

"Maybe a couple. But generally, we don't."

"You're not what I'd call a selfie kind of gal," Jon said. "You never suggest it yourself, you never pull out your phone to take one, so I don't. Maybe I'm a little oversensitive about not wanting you to think that I think of you as –"

"But aren't you a selfie kind of guy?" Chloe said. "Wouldn't you like some informal pictures of the two of us out on the town or having fun?"

"You know something?" Jon said. "I almost never go back and look at any pictures I have. But yeah, now that you mention it, I would. I'd love to have some nice shot of the two of us to put up in the house somewhere. But I'm thinking that selfies is not what you're thinking is missing in our relationship so I'm not sure why we're talking about them."

"No."

"Well," Jon said, "I'm out of answers pending

clarification of your concern. I'm crazy about you and I'm crazy about us."

Pending clarification of your concern. Like I'm a client.

"Are you?" she said. "Are you crazy? I don't mean certifiable, I mean isn't there something in there" – she reached over and tapped his chest – "I don't know, something that shines, that's full of delight, that wants to take chances, that wants to go batshit once in a while? Something that inspires you to fight for what *you* want, maybe even disagree with me once in a while, light a fire under this thing."

"We don't always agree," Jon said.

"That's not true, Jon. It's just that when we do disagree, you always let me have my way."

"What's for you to not like about that?" Jon said, his voice rising some. "If it was something I cared about, I'd tell you. Obviously, the things we disagree about are things I don't care enough about to make a fuss with you."

"Okay, we're now kind of getting to the point," she said. "I don't know what you do care about! I don't know what brings you joy! I don't know how to make your eyes sparkle and spark!"

"I care about you. You bring me joy. My eyes . . . ."

"Do you remember the time we were going to that cookout and you put on these socks that went to your knees and they didn't match anything else you had on, and I told you I wouldn't be seen with you in those socks?"

"What's this got to do with my eyes?"

"Do you remember?"

"Yeah, I do remember that."

"You liked those socks, didn't you?"

"Well, yes. I still have them."

"And what did you do when I said that?"

"I changed them."

"Did you agree with what I said? Did you think my tone with you was appropriate?"

"It was just socks. I didn't mind changing them. You were probably right about the matching. Maybe the length, too, I don't know. The tone, I don't remember your tone. It was just socks."

"Socks you liked. Socks you chose to wear."

"Chloe, it was just socks! I always want you to be satisfied with the way I look when I'm with you, babe, and if you thought I was going to look like a colorblind old man wearing support hose, then I needed to fix that. I care what you think. Why are we arguing about socks?"

"We're arguing about them now because you wouldn't argue about them then."

"Now we're arguing about having arguments?"

"We're arguing about caring. We're arguing about emotion. We're arguing about passion."

"I should have passion about socks?"

"You should live this one life you have with passion. You should be passionate about us."

"I never thought I'd hear you say that I lack passion."

"I'm not talking about sex," Chloe said.

"What are you talking about?"

"I'm talking about taking chances with your feelings, digging deep and exposing them to me, *all of them*, to me and the world. Or maybe I'm talking about having those feelings for me in the first place."

Jon shook his head. "Look, babe, I know you have been under tremendous stress with the trial about to start, so maybe this isn't the best time to be having –"

"Don't patronize me!" she said. "I'm perfectly capable of divorcing my feelings about us from this stupid trial! I am perfectly capable of exposing *my* emotions independent of this stupid trial! I am perfectly capable of telling you to stuff that 'I'm mister understanding man' attitude, because *that is the problem.* I'm accusing you of awful things and you're sitting there shaking your head."

"I don't know what to say," he said. "I don't know what you're talking about or why you're so angry."

"I'm talking about you showing me and giving me *all* of you, including all of the things I've never seen before."

"What of me don't you think I'm showing and giving? Christ, you won't even tell me your real first name! I have no idea how to respond to any of this. Where is this coming from, Chloe?"

She was shaking. She took a deep breath and calmed herself.

"I looked at your phone."

"You looked – you thought I was cheating? That's ridiculous, Chloe, and you know it. You actually thought you'd find some evidence that I was unfaithful?"

"No," she said.

"How did you interpret that message telling me my dry cleaning was ready? How about the one from the appliance repair guy saying he'd be there in 15 minutes? What did you conclude from all the texts from you with smiley faces blowing kisses?"

"I looked at the pictures, Jon. The photos."

"You opened my phone to look at the photos."

"Yes. It was wrong, but I did it. I'm sorry, I'm a jerk for doing it, I hope you can forgive me. But we need to talk about it."

Jon was quiet. He was angry at this breach of privacy, but showing his anger wouldn't rewind what she had done. Although . . . .

"I'm not happy about this, Chloe," Jon said, "but I'm going to hear you out. I'm trying to think. There's nothing on there, just old pictures, nothing illegal, no porn, just everyday stuff. Vacations, parties, events."

"Your wedding. Selfies."

"Amelia," Jon said.

"And you with her, and during your time with her."

"Mm."

"I'm sorry," Chloe said. She was ashamed of what she had done but she needed to know.

"I'm going to factor out the fact of your snooping so let's just discuss what you saw that has upset you."

"You *shouldn't* 'factor it out.' You should be furious with me! I – I breached your trust."

"There are different ways of expressing fury," he said. Chloe felt a chill enter the conversation. "What you say is true about looking at my phone being wrong, but really – again, putting aside your spying – I'm trying to be rational about this. I ask myself what's the real issue in you seeing these old photos?"

Jon now spoke softly and doled out his words slowly and evenly and with care. "You know I was married. You know I was happy. You know I was devastated when she died. You know it took me a long time to get over it. But then you walked into my life and hit the play button on my heart. Now I'm very happy with you. I thought you were very happy with me, and I can't imagine what you saw in years-old pictures that could change that."

"You were crazy about her."

"What makes you think I'm not crazy about you?"

"Because you're not crazy about anything!"

"You want a man who's crazy? You know that's not me. But wait a minute. Wait a minute. What do the photos have to do with this?"

"I said, I don't mean insane. I mean – I mean alive to me in the same way that you were alive to her. The look in your eyes. The laughter. All the crazy things you were doing in those photos. Santa Claus, Nancy Pelosi, flashing your butt at that tour bus. There was some feeling there for her, and some feeling you had about yourself, that you don't have for me or with me."

"You are an entirely different person. Can't a man express love differently to different types of women? I react to you in ways I never reacted to her because you have qualities that she didn't."

"What? Big tits? Money?"

"Chloe, that is a terrible, terrible thing to say to me."

She retreated. "I know I know I know. That's not me. I should not have said that, I know that's not you. I'm so sorry, I really am. Another thing I hope you can forgive.

"But Jon, it's not just your feelings for her, although they were clear enough. I could see that there was something there with her that I don't think we have. What scared me was that *you* were a different person *with* her. Yes, it shocked me to see it, but I really liked the person I saw in those pictures. He excited me. When I got over my shock, I laughed as thought about those pictures. I guess what I should say is that I liked that part of the person I thought I already knew. But obviously I didn't because I never see that Jon Rider. That Jon Rider moved me in a new kind of way. I found myself feeling his joy and wanting that feeling for us. She must have had something that I don't. Something that really turned you on, something that excited your passion. Why don't *I* make you completely happy like that? Or why *can't* I?"

"You do! It's just a different kind of happy."

"Yeah, a less happy kind of happy."

"I can't believe we're having this conversation," Jon said. "I've done absolutely nothing wrong, nothing to mess up our relationship, but you're really really upset with me over bad-quality snapshots of a woman who's been dead for years and an old version of a man who has moved on to a different kind of woman."

"Do you deny it? Do you deny that you felt differently about her than you feel about me? That you're capable of fire and passion that you don't show around me?"

"You and she are two entirely different people!"

"You're not denying it," Chloe said.

Jon considered himself a patient man, but he was fuming. "You want me to fight with you? Here's a fight: I consider your position unfair and entirely ridiculous. No foundation for it at all other than your apparent need for perfection in my expression of my feelings for you down to the molecular level, and you know something? That is not attractive."

"But it's true even now, Jon! With that Japanese woman at the animal function you were making sex jokes and everyone was falling on the floor! You've never done anything like that with me, nothing even close."

"You want me to make dick jokes in front of your friends? You want me to moon a bunch of Packer fans when we're out?"

"No, but I want you to show me all of your feelings, the crazy energy stuff just like the brilliant, thoughtful stuff. I want to know that you love me enough to show me that flame even when we're not making love."

It can't end this way, Jon thought. *But, shit.*

"I think I know what's going on here," he said. "You think that because you're beautiful and she wasn't that she had to offer some amazing thing that you don't have, and that amazing thing brought out something in me that you don't. Of all the things I never thought I'd see in you, it's insecurity. Or, Jesus farking Christ almighty, jealousy – of Amelia?

"All right, dammit. You know what she had that you don't, or don't seem to have based on what I'm hearing now? She had the self-confidence to know she was a person of value who deserved happiness with me, and she trusted me enough to know that I felt that in her and loved her for it. She had the love not to impose conditions on my feelings that I cannot possibly meet, which is what you are doing to me right now, and I don't even know what those conditions are! Well, what are they, Chloe? What do you want?"

"I want all of you! I want everything!"

"Chloe, there is nothing about the man I am now that you don't have. Maybe that's the answer: I don't have everything you seem to want . . ."

He rose from the chair.

". . . and I don't think I ever will."

"No, Jon! Are you dumping me?"

"The question is, Chloe, are you dumping *me*?"

"Is that what you want?"

"Is that what *you* want?"

"No! No! No!" she cried, "I don't want that!"

"The one thing that is over is this conversation," he said. "This is your home and I'm walking out of it. I'm not going to start a new argument on what 'dumping' means, although apparently having that stupid discussion might be one way that I could demonstrate the passion over meaningless things you seem to think this relationship needs and that I lack. But this" – he spread his arms and shook his head – "I'm not going to pretend to shoehorn *anything* about my life with Amelia into what we've got. Whatever that is."

"Jon!"

He could hear the tears in her voice behind him as he walked out the door.

⌀

Gloria sang:

  – *Ah, O One, be still so we may sit with you. We wander,*

we look away, but we know. We see your glow shrink and grow dim. But you are a cat and you will hide your hurt and your hurt will be with the forgettings as the suns rise and rise again.

— *That is a good song, Bandit said.*

CHAPTER 23

JON RIDER NEVER DRANK ALONE AT HOME

JON RIDER NEVER drank alone at home.

Jon Rider almost never drank alone at home.

It was the night after the night before.

When he had returned to his home the night before, that night where he believed he and Chloe had ended their romance forever – no, not "believed," its end was surely an accomplished fact – no, not "surely," but an actual accomplished fact, not to be revisited – he felt like there should be some way to mark it. Memorialize it. Put a bow on it. Slide a bookmark into it. Shouldn't a lifetime recognize the milestone failures as it does successes?

He arrived home from the breakup so conflicted, so convinced the parting was absolutely necessary to who he was but so sad he would never again bask in the bracing cool tide of Chloe Manning's female genius, that he went to bed in a state akin to fear. He closed his eyes and lay in the dark, empty bed, hoping sleep would reconcile these warring emotions.

He wondered when he would be squared-away again. He feared he never would be. He slept that night, but his dreams were stupid, embarrassing stuff, with fleeting appearances by people he hadn't thought of in years and for whom he cared nothing, and random events of such suffocating dullness that they seemed to mock the seriousness of what he had just done to another human being. And to himself.

The sun had risen and was about to set again.

He had aimed his day at directing his mind away from Chloe Manning.

He had tried watching television. All those satellite channels he paid for and never visited.

A History Channel show on space aliens visiting ancient earth civilizations. Must have been pretty dumb aliens, they certainly didn't help out those civilizations, all of which eventually went to shit and none of which even managed to invent gliding.

The Discovery Channel showed a suspiciously well-groomed naked couple trying to survive in some kind of jungle – nope, too close to home.

Comedy Central established that there was clearly not enough comedy in the world to fill a day's broadcasting.

MeTV repeated shows from the early Sixties, serving mainly to illustrate why the late Sixties had to happen.

Three channels featured programs on how the Nazis' plans for world domination were foiled by their sexual perversion, their occult interpretations of Norse mythology, and their failure to capitalize on technological advances learned from UFO time travelers. No mention of a two-front war or a demented absolute dictator.

TV was not helping.

Maybe household chores.

Cleaning his refrigerator took ten minutes.

Some milk that was plainly threatening to solidify.

Two cans of diet Mountain Dew.

Four Original Recipe thighs and drumsticks still in the bucket left over from a KFC dark-meat special some – too many – weeks back.

A half-carton of tuna salad from the Jewel deli – whoops, something fuzzy on that, out she goes.

Three doggy bags with carried-out leftovers he had trouble remembering and respected the dogs too much to ask them to consider.

Wait, here's something fun in the freezer: A Sharing Size bag of Peanut M&Ms. Frozen M&Ms don't melt in your mouth, they just rattle around in there spreading the sensation of that M&M goodness until you just can't help crunching down on them, unleashing yet another wave of chocolatey-peanutty delight. And no sharing! But there are some sadnesses that chocolate, even with peanuts, even that you don't share, just can't elevate to anything happier.

He wiped out a couple of barbeque and marinara and grape juice stains and was done.

Squaring away his already-squared-away fridge just reminded him that he was, after all, after the days and nights of Chloe Manning, a bachelor.

Exercise always made him feel good. He ran up to

Fullerton and back along the lakefront. He watched the women as they jogged with their ponytails bouncing up and down, sprouting from their scrunchies. In the years after Amelia he had forgotten the sheer inexplicable greatness of women that had reawakened with Chloe, and as he watched the joggers, he thought *I used to have one of those*. How can they be half the world's souls, billions, but still so special?

Odd that he felt good, but not better. Maybe some new shoes, new fitness tracker, new personality.

He cranked up the water temperature on his shower. Maybe a long steamy drenching would blast off that crust of loss and cauterize the tear in his heart.

It didn't do either of those things. The sweat washed away, but he felt unclean, damaged.

They use alcohol to clean wounds, don't they?

And it's okay that scotch ages, right? He had no idea how long the bottle of Macallan's 18 had been reposing against the wall at the back of the top shelf of the pantry, or why it was there. Hell, it might be Macallan's 25 by now. Someone brought it to the party Amelia had thrown to celebrate his ascension to the partnership at Rockwell Morton but he wasn't a big scotch drinker and it had remained unopened.

He opened it now and poured himself a couple of fingers. Then poured a couple more and capped the bottle.

He let it sit there for a little while and swished it around the glass. Was he supposed to do that? Was scotch supposed to breathe? How can a man believed to be successful at everything have failed at women and drinking in the course of two days? How much is a finger?

His first sip evaporated into his sinuses and crept behind his eyes, untangling the ganglia and spreading warmth into his brain. With each sip, his mind seemed to soften and grow more flexible, arranging itself to consider new things.

To see things that other people didn't see.

And one of those things that other people didn't see was his own heart.

And so, he faced a thought that had first tried to pierce his fury as he slumped in the back seat of his Uber ride home the night before, a thought he had brushed away then:

Wasn't she right?

∽

He opened the Gallery on his Samsung.

He saw what she saw.

He *had* been a different man then. His heart *had* been different, or somehow revealed itself more vividly. It was true that to a camera Amelia and Chloe could hardly have been more different, but he could see his feelings in those old photographs and he felt those times seep forward into his memory. He did things he wouldn't think of doing now. He reacted to Amelia in a way he was not reacting to Chloe, a way that most people would recognize as love-struck.

He identified his feelings for Chloe as love. So what was the difference now? Was he more focused on naming his feelings than feeling them? Some typical Jon Rider BS? Maybe he was a little in awe of her? Maybe he kept the love-sick-pup gazes bottled up out of respect for her position?

Maybe a little intimidated by her celebrity, throwing some cold water on hijinks and off-color gags?

He had not thought any of those things were the case with him, but he was Jon Rider. Start at the beginning. There is a reason for everything, you just need to be still and observe and think.

His heart was full.

Why was he afraid to show it to her, to show her everything that was in it, to let it speak freely and completely? And, when his heart was absurd, absurdly?

What would it say to Chloe Manning?

Here was a better question: What earthly benefit did he ever get out of being self-protective?

He took another sip of the Macallan's, more of a swallow, and this one hit his gut.

You've never been a mope.

You're moping, you mope.

You've never given up on a problem.

Problems of the heart are susceptible to resolution.

Ergo, snap out of it.

What do I want?

I want to be happy. I want to be a good man, a better man than I am now.

So: What is there about being with a brilliant, beautiful, slightly crazy woman who loves me that would have any result other than my happiness?

So: What could be the result of opening my heart to welcome new emotions, experiences, and yeah, even problems – and to let that open heart release to her and to the world everything that is in it — other than to make me that better man I want and need to be?

Nothing.

And nothing.

Jon Rider stood, excited.

He suddenly understood what this woman, this sometimes difficult, sometimes crazy woman, had tried to do the night before.

She had tried to set him free.

Not free from her.

Free from himself.

She tried to free him to show his love for her in any way that moved him.

Free to respect their relationship enough to stand with her as an equal in emotion, in self-respect, in being *out there* in the world.

Free to express himself fully as he would were she not the extraordinary Chloe Manning but a woman, a plain woman who did truly love him.

She had tried to show him that when you love someone it is okay — no, it is necessary — not to be squared-away all the time just for its own sake and the sake of your imaginary self-portrait.

I love her, he thought.

It's that simple.

And if I love her, I must be with her.

Amelia, it's okay.

You're at peace.

My living peace cannot be the same. My peace is the peace

of knowing, the peace of the clear path. Seeing the way through
the knotted underbrush of my useless self-image.

 And you know . . .
 You would like her.

 She's brilliant
 and she's goofy
 and she wants what she wants
 and she hides a thousand delights within
 but not from me
 and she's beautiful.

 Just like you.

He took another swallow, and poured the rest down
the drain.

❧

He needed to see her, to tell her. To be with her.

Then, in that window of clarity that opens oh-so-briefly
in the moments after the liquor finishes its journey up the
spine and settles in the mind, he thought two things:

First thought: Her trial was set to start tomorrow. Her
time outside the courtroom would be taken up with trial
preparation and consultation with counsel. She would
be under the stress of the possibility that the jury would
come back against her and Barbiron. Not a great time for
confessing the fullness, the release, of all of his love. And
if she lost, would she be emotionally prepared to receive
his confession?

Second thought: Her worst fear, exposure of her hotel escapade with Blake Bondurant, would be realized tomorrow. An account of that episode had not appeared in any of the pleadings; the discovery in the case was not public; Chloe certainly had not told anyone except him and her lawyers, and probably Lisa the Flamethrower. And the board of directors. All of whom had a strong interest in keeping her secret.

But plaintiff goes first. Blake was the plaintiff. He would undoubtedly be his own star witness. Her shame would be in the online headlines in all its naked glory before court adjourned for the day.

But: *I love her.*

And: *I am Jon Rider.*

And: *I see things other people do not see.*

And: *I have a big love problem and she has a big law problem.*

And: *Holy sh – the sun will rise in about ten hours and I'm sitting here all warm and happy and just buzzed enough and she's sitting somewhere all miserable and alone because I've been a fraidy-cat jerk and she's about to be crucified and I'm doing a big fat nothing.*

His mind raced. He had no authority to represent Chloe. He had no access to any of the discovery record. He had no idea what to do, or what it was even possible to do.

All he could do was think. Think fast. Think and see.

He thought about her story of what happened that took her to Blake's arms and hotel room. He thought about what she had told him about his deteriorating stewardship of his department. What else? Just that amateur demand letter

Blake had sent. He couldn't recall anything of substance in that piece of –

Whoa whoa wait. Not so fast.

Weren't there two demand letters? Yeah, the one they all looked at in the conference room, and that first email way earlier one she said was the same, the one she'd mentioned when she came in his office to confess. He'd asked her to send that one to him and he seemed to recall that she had done so. But by that time he was out of the case. He had not given it any thought and a demand letter isn't evidence of anything anyway. He did not recall having read it.

But he had nothing else. And nothing to lose. He thanked whatever Providence looks after foolish men that his independent work for Rockwell Morton included access to his firm email.

He fired up his laptop and found Chloe's forward of Blake's first demand email. Looked like she had not copied Brian or Oona or Nelson. The trial team had never seen this and didn't even know of its existence.

He was not hopeful. This tiny shred of the case – really, not even a part of the case at this point, just Blake's first shot across the bow – was not going to produce a boulder that could block a major trial set to begin in mere hours. Battles are not decided by the first shot fired.

He read the email from Blake addressed to Chloe. He read it though once quickly, the second time with the focus of a scanning electron microscope. There was something there struggling to attract his attention.

Chloe had been right – it looked a lot like the second demand she brought to the meeting at Rockwell Morton.

Almost identical; it looked like Blake had just cut and pasted the earlier email to create the second letter they'd reviewed in the conference room.

Almost identical.

He squinted. He stared. He scratched his nose. He looked at Teeko and Bridey and reminded himself they needed to go out.

He started to read it again.

He stopped.

Suddenly, he knew why Blake's complaint had been filed under seal so that it was secret from the public.

He summoned Google to his screen.

Tap-tap, tap-tap-tap, ach, backspace to correct, dammit, more keytaps, and click on the little magnifying glass to search.

Please, please, please.

The smallest of smiles grew on his face.

Did the universe want him to be with Chloe Manning? Is that what was happening here? Through his fatigue and the dying scotch buzz, he chose to believe *yes.*

He reached for his phone.

In one way, he was glad he got almost no sleep that night. Impaired judgment was a blessing for what he had to do, and some damage to his usual rationality was a good start.

Quick shower, shave, best dark suit and shoes most recently shined. Brooks Brothers button-down, yellow? – no, white.

And a perfect tie. Got the dimple on the first try. Gotta be an omen.

It was a day to run.

He ran.

He grabbed his documents and notes and ran for the door. He ran to his car and when his hand hit the car door he thought of something he needed and ran back to get it.

⟨⟩

— *Shortest walkies ever, Goodboy said.*

— *Not even walkies, Goodgirl said. Just out, poop, in, Man go.*

— *What is happen, Goodboy said.*

— *Man is crazy, Goodgirl said.*

CHAPTER 24

CHLOE MANNING WAS UNHAPPIER

CHLOE MANNING WAS unhappier than she had ever been. She was unhappier than she could imagine ever being.

Her life, she felt, had begun anew in a roomful of lawyers not so very long ago. Now it might end, as she knew it, in another roomful of lawyers.

She was sitting in a courtroom as a defendant and as the face of her beloved baby, Barbiron.

She was being accused of sexual harassment and of wrongfully terminating Blake Bondurant.

She was not guilty of those things.

She was guilty of some stupid things that were going to be made public for the first time.

Blake Bondurant was a putz and she had gotten naked with him.

She didn't know which was worse, that she'd gotten naked with a subordinate or that the subordinate was a putz.

She might be removed as CEO of the company for the sake of the public offering. It depended on how the trial came out, and how the evidence played in the press. She would look incredibly foolish, but maybe investors would laugh it off.

Yeah, people putting huge cash at risk are a light-hearted, forgiving bunch.

Nelson had filed a motion seeking to close the court-room to spectators and seal the transcript. When Judge Achebe learned of the nature of Barbiron's claimed need for secrecy during an argument in chambers with Blake's lawyers, he ruled that although the information was embar-rassing, it was not competitively sensitive and was highly relevant to Blake's claim. The trial would be public.

Chloe's secret would be a secret no longer.

And no Jon Rider to reach out his hand.

∽

There were lawyers all over the place.

There was a jury who might believe him instead of her. Mostly married women. None was a CEO of a major corporation. None had ever been profiled in *Vogue*.

And a big black judge in a big black robe in a big black chair, some kind of superlawyer god who was in complete control of everything.

She was in control of nothing.

And that morning she couldn't find any sensible mid-rise pumps like her lawyers ordered her to wear, at least none that didn't make her look like Hillary Clinton. And no conservative suits that didn't make her look even more like Hillary Clinton. She pulled her hair back as they had recommended and went way easy on the makeup.

Damn — Bill Clinton.

This is what hell must be like. Devils with briefcases poking you with pitchforks and you just had to sit there and take it in your meeting-his-mom heels and Calvin Klein suit, the kind you got at Macy's, or you did when there were still Macy's. *Pitchforks — note to self – talk to Product Development about feminizing farm tools.*

And Jon Rider had left and not returned or called or texted or sent out detectable vibes. She was alone again.

❧

Alone at the counsel table. Brian and Nelson were there, but she was alone.

She thought back to the events of the night before last. Jon left; her apartment seemed suddenly cold. She walked around. She sat. She poured a glass of wine, took one sip, and sent it down the drain. Even Gloria and Bandit interrupted their pre-bedtime begging to look at her in what passed for cat puzzlement.

After Jon left, she was sad, then mad, then sad again. Then mad again.

She called Lisa the Flamethrower.

"Late," Lisa said. "Not good."

Chloe told Lisa everything that had happened, everything that had been said.

Lisa the Flamethrower let her have it.

"He's not enough of – what – something? – for you?

That's two breakups! All right, I'm officially declaring him fair game."

"Lisa!" Chloe said. "No! Don't talk like that, even to tease."

"Oh, you still think you want him?" Lisa said. "You pitch a tantrum and when you get the totally predictable result of him taking a walk, then it's all 'boo-hoo, I want him back'! All right, now you listen to me, Chloe Marie."

"What on earth makes you think that my middle name is Marie?" Chloe said.

"Nothing," Lisa said, "except that I'm going to scold you a little and when you scold a girl she needs a middle name."

"You're going to scold me?"

"A little, gently," Lisa said. "I would never tell any woman to settle and I'm not telling you to settle. But you think, girl: You say you want everything, but when you don't even know what everything is, you need to think real damned hard about what is enough and whether you have it with him. I'm going to forget about the right and wrong of you looking at his phone –"

"That's what he said," Chloe said.

"Yeah, let's put that aside. You're freaking out about some old twinkle in his eye or look on his face or hijinks in public when he's married to his plain jane on some three-four-five-year-old phone snaps. You're saying 'mmm, how odd he doesn't look and act that way with me?,' right? So now you're wanting to think he has to be twinkly and puppy-dog and goofy around you and your friends to meet your requirements. But answer me this, Chloe Marie, *is that the man you fell in love with?*"

"No," Chloe said. "No."

"No, of course not. So how is it fair for you to ask him to put on some kind of old clothes you might not like at all? What if he did the same to you? Think about it, it's not so wild: What would *you* have thought if he'd said to you, 'Hey, baby, why don't you give some thought to dialing down the temp on that makeup, start shopping at Dillard's and, oh yeah, see if you can't pack on 15-20 pounds. And brush up on your quantum mechanics while you're at it.' He didn't fall in love with his wife all those months ago, he fell in love with you!

"Now, that's not a hard thing for a man to do in your case, but look at it the other way. Think of every other man you have ever dated, ever. Where does Jon Rider fall on that scale?"

"He's not even on it," Chloe said.

"That is the correct answer," Lisa said.

Chloe couldn't find any words.

Lisa spoke slowly: "*He isn't trying to turn you into the wife he loved, so why are you trying to turn him into some man you don't even know?*"

Chloe said nothing.

"Chloe, are you there?"

Chloe was there. She was taking deep, measured breaths.

"I have been a girl," Chloe said, "like you said, bratty little Chloe Marie."

"Well, let's not be too hard on ourselves," Lisa said.

"I need to be a woman, a woman who lives in this real world. The real world changes. People change."

"All right, all right, I've made my point," Lisa said.

"Don't get all Big Sur mindfulness self-improvement BS on me. I might have to start listening to my own advice on my own man-scene. Hey, is your middle name really Marie?"

"No," Chloe said. "Thanks for the scolding."

"You're welcome," Lisa said. "But I was being a little selfish because I've already picked out my dress for your wedding."

Chloe laughed. "Oh, man," she said. "Thanks for the giggle, I needed something to bust up this mood."

"Get some sleep," Lisa said. "Big day tomorrow. I'll be there. Amy and I will be right behind you." They said good night.

Chloe's weary, crowded head was shutting down as the dramatic night moved toward morning, but one thought pierced the fog of approaching rest: She loved *her* Jon. Her steady, supportive, always there, never spoiling-her-spotlight, always answering, always loving Jon. Who didn't care about Blake or Barbiron or money or *Marie Claire* covers or anything else if he could be with her. That is a man to love, and that is the man she loved.

He walked out of her door having heard something different from her. He needed to know she knew she had been wrong.

But it was midnight. He'd have been long gone by 10:30. She couldn't hit him with all of this now.

And she was due at Rockwell Morton at seven the next morning for final trial prep and instructions from Brian and Oona.

When her alarm went off at 4:30, her pillow was wet.

❧

She barely noticed Brian and Nelson mumbling next to her at the counsel table about what was to come that morning.

She thought back to that first day when she had been unhappy in a roomful of lawyers at Rockwell Morton. And how happy, crazy-happy she had been by the time that Rider-man had seen into the case, and, she now knew, into her heart, saw almost at once what she really needed.

But she tried to concentrate on what was going on in the courtroom.

There had been some preliminary skirmishing with the lawyers. The judge had denied Rockwell Morton's motion to dismiss the case several months ago, and in the runup to the trial he sided with Bondurant's lawyers on most of the evidentiary motions and jury instruction disputes. With all that underbrush cleared, the trial date was not going to move.

Chloe was not in the habit of questioning herself. Now, though, with Blake Bondurant's testimony just minutes away, she tried to imagine what it would be like to hear his account – any account, but especially his – of their saloon mashup and sleazy hotel encounter. Never mind that she'd had more thrills sitting on a barstool with a short leg. What in God's name is he going to say? And she still wasn't convinced he didn't have pictures, although his lawyers had not produced any in discovery.

She found it hard to focus. How mad was Jon? How hurt was he at her harsh accusations? Would her latest tantrum be the straw that broke his squared-away camel's back?

She thought about a lifetime to come without Jon Rider, but as she composed herself at the defense counsel table it passed completely through her mind without slowing down and vanished into the harsh fluorescent flicker of the courtroom's aging fixtures. No. No. Somehow, that was not going to happen. No matter what happened in that courtroom. But with so much to occupy her that morning, she could not see a clear path to reconciliation.

Blake Bondurant was smooth and looked good at plaintiff's counsel table. His dark jacket, pressed chinos, and an open-collar button-down shirt that bespoke respect for the process, but suggested neither affluence nor an unseemly pandering to the jury with a too-pathetic wardrobe. He would be a good witness. His poor performance at Barbiron involved technicalities of the sourcing and manufacturing processes that were not easy to explain. Her own performance in allowing their flirtation and taking off her clothes did not involve technicalities and was easy to explain. Those twelve honorable men and women might be taken in. Like she and the Russian River pinot grigio had been taken in.

She was sorry that Amy, faithful, adoring Amy, who was sitting in the front row behind Chloe's counsel table, was going to hear for the first time that her boss wasn't always strong, but could lose the battle against loneliness and longing and flattery and alcohol and boredom with a man nowhere near her equal. Amy – who was looking truly lovely with new makeup and clothes, and who had snagged some considerable male interest out and about – had been joined by Lisa the Flamethrower, along as promised to lend moral support and also to eye-flirt with Judge Achebe.

Yet through the fog of Chloe's unhappiness, the dreariness of that courtroom, the prospect of days of sitting there in her sensible shoes and straight-up-and-down girl-suit and buttoned-up pleated blouse with the prim little tie at the top and pulled-back hair and makeup she wouldn't wish on a nun, having to listen to the testimony of Blake the lying dick, she felt a kind of providential light shining on her, bathed in a glow of good fortune that had always been her companion. As though she could will good things to happen. Because Chloe Manning could always find a parking space, always charm a customer to pay off a big receivable so she could meet Barbiron's cash-flow forecasts, always carry on an extra bag. That same feeling that had inspired her early ideas for Barbiron, that had made it easy to knock on the doors of big money to get the startup cash, that told her Walmart and Home Depot and Amazon would eventually come around to doing business on terms she could live with.

The same feeling that had told her there was something wrong with that Philbrick case in Rockwell Morton's conference room.

She needed to stop thinking about that day.

Focus, now.

She focused on Blake's lead counsel, Jolene Marovitz. Chloe disliked and admired her. She wasn't a beauty, but she was tall and slim and exquisitely put-together for her trial performance. A short and not-quite-severe haircut went well with her large black-rimmed glasses. Chloe recognized the flattering designer suit she was wearing. (Why, Chloe asked, couldn't she doll up for trial if Blake's lawyer could?

Because, Oona explained, plaintiff lawyers want the juries to think they're successful and win all their cases; Chloe needed to look like someone who might have been taken advantage of and not like someone who had imperiously ordered Blake Bondurant to get to stripping. Yeah, good luck with that, Chloe thought; the female jurors – and, she was thinking, a couple of those male jurors – probably saw her on "Oprah" or the cover of *People* and won't be buying this Eleanor Roosevelt schtick.) Marovitz was finished off with a beautiful speaking voice, low and musical, bell-clear and insistent without being pushy. No one likes a pushy broad, Chloe thought, unless the broad has large breasts, is Chloe Manning, or both.

But in this setting, she was not even allowed to push. She just had to sit there and look oppressed and wrongly accused and about as stylish as Mrs. Mao.

The lawyers had picked the jury yesterday morning and after lunch, and both sides had delivered their opening statements before adjournment in the afternoon. Now it was the turn of the Rockwell Morton lawyers to be clever. They continued to dangle some hope of settlement before Blake's lawyers, so that in her opening statement Jolene Marovitz continued to dance around Chloe's mistakes, avoiding a description of that wild night. Blake's team was taking their bargaining chips, their claims of drunk-naked-Chloe harassment of virtuous Blake, right to the brink of testimony.

"All rise," the bailiff called as the door behind the bench opened and the imposing figure of the judge appeared. "The United States District Court for the Northern District of

Illinois is now in session, the Honorable Judge Cleon Achebe presiding. Please be seated, turn off your cell phones, and I mean completely off, and come to order. Anyone with a cell phone making noise the judge can hear will be removed from the courtroom."

"Case number 19-CV-08345, *Bondurant v. Barbiron Inc., Manning, and Altobelli*," the clerk read, "for trial."

Chloe had been impressed with Judge Cleon Achebe. He ran a snappy courtroom and did not take much nonsense from the lawyers, who clearly respected his authority. They were a little afraid of him. She thought maybe he didn't much care for her or Barbiron – he'd been a plaintiffs' employment lawyer in a prominent all-black firm before Obama appointed him to the federal bench – but she had a sense he knew his stuff and Barbiron would get about as fair a shake as it could expect. Lisa the Flamethrower knew him from his private-practice days – seemed to know him pretty well for being a one-time competitor, Chloe thought – and told Chloe he could be a hardass, but Barbiron could have done a lot worse in the judge lottery.

"Good morning, ladies and gentlemen of the jury," the judge said. "I hope you all got a good night's sleep." A few of the jurors nodded. "Good, good. We'll go until about 11:45, break for lunch, back at 1 for the afternoon session.

"You have heard the parties' opening statements, now it's time to see what the evidence says. Let me remind you to keep an open mind and carefully consider all the evidence. I will be instructing you on the law you are to apply to the facts that you determine based on the testimony and other evidence that you find credible and believable. As I mentioned to you at the outset, and as I will tell you again when I give you instructions before you begin your deliberations, what the lawyers say is not evidence. Witnesses, documents, other evidence that I admit into the record, that's what you'll have to go on."

"Counsel," he continued, "anything else before we get started?"

The attorneys all shook their heads no.

"Excellent," Judge Achebe said. "Ms. Marovitz, please call your first witness."

"Plaintiff calls Blake Bondurant to the stand."

Blake had been sitting at his counsel's table. He smiled at the jury as he walked to the witness stand. Several of the female jurors, and one of the male jurors, smiled back. *Damned charmer*, Chloe thought. *I was such a moron to fall for his act, even drunk. And now he's going to be slinging it at the jury.*

The bailiff instructed him to put his right hand on the Bible. "Do you solemnly swear that the testimony you are about to give in this cause is the truth, the whole truth, and nothing but the truth, so help you God?"

"I do."

Blake sat down. Jolene Markovitz moved to the podium and spread out her notes.

"Good morning, Mr. Bondurant."

"Good morning."

"Mr. Bondurant, would you please state your full –"

Chloe heard a noise from the back of the courtroom.

She heard Amy suck in her breath behind her.

She heard Lisa the Flamethrower whisper *fuck BALLS*.

She saw the female jurors sit up like a single animal.

Judge Cleon Achebe looked up over his glasses to the back of the courtroom and his eyes got big.

Jon Rider had burst into the courtroom, his hands over his head full of papers, pursued by men with guns, and he jogged up to stand with Jolene Markovitz at the podium.

"Your Honor," he gasped, "may I be heard?"

CHAPTER 25

JON RIDER WAS NEVER LATE TO COURT

JON RIDER WAS never late to court. At least, not back in the days when he went to court. He always arrived well in advance of the hearing time to get the feel of the courtroom, chat up the clerk, go over materials for the hearing in the quiet of the big empty room, away from phones and colleagues. Maybe work a little diplomacy – or mind games – on his adversary for the day.

But today, the day of what he judged to be his most important trial appearance ever, he was way behind where he needed to be to be of any use at all. That is, of any use at all to one Chloe Manning. His mind was full of her. This was it. This was the day he would be happy forever or just a footnote to the myths of the gods of romance and federal civil procedure. He had only received what he needed the night before and spent until the early morning hours reviewing pages of material, checking the law, and trying to figure out how he was going to make it all fit together.

He was still thinking about how he was going to play everything when he headed to the Dirksen Federal Building on South Dearborn. He hadn't been to the dreary Mies van der Rohe box in several years, and he hadn't missed it. The courtrooms were kept dim, every other cold fluorescent square shut off out of some unnecessary energy-saving initiative, like working underwater. But he was going to light that courtroom up today, if only – damn, now the parking was somewhere else, or the entrance had been moved, or something. Valuable minutes lost looking for that.

He ran from the parking garage and after he figured out where the blasted stairs to street level were going to dump him out, he oriented himself to the Dirksen and ran to the Dearborn entrance. The line to go through security was short and he still had his federal court ID card which got him waved through quickly after his papers had gone through the X-ray machine. Good, good, a good sign. He ran to the elevator and punched in the floor for the courtroom of the United States District Court Judge for the Northern District of Illinois, the Honorable Cleon Achebe.

He might make it.

When the elevator doors opened – goddam, took forever – he ran to the courtroom's swinging double doors and could see through the slit windows that Blake Bondurant was settling himself into the chair at the witness stand.

He could also see two large federal marshals blocking the doors. Guns, badges, carb-gut overhangs, the whole rig.

"I'm late," he said. "Sorry."

"I'm sorry, too," said the more senior of the two. "Judge Achebe's rule. No one allowed in after witnesses are sworn."

"I know," Jon lied, "but look, he isn't sworn yet."

When the marshals turned to peer through the slit windows, Jon slipped between them and pushed through the double doors and into the courtroom, on the last leg of his run for the day.

∾

The marshals were right behind him, guns drawn. Some combination of adrenaline and endorphins had put Jon's concentration into overdrive, and he sensed they were assuming his intent was lethal. He raised his hands, holding all the papers and notebooks, as he sprinted down the aisle to the podium and Jolene Marovitz and what he thought might well be the end of his legal career, if not his life.

Or the start of something better.

∾

Chloe Manning thought *I knew it, I can always feel it!* But even as that thought crossed her mind, she was deleting it. *This isn't my luck. This isn't my will power. This is just my goddamned princess moment. My knight in shining armor just stumbled into this room and is about to unsheathe his mighty tongue!* She giggled inwardly at a more personal version of that image.

She felt Brian and Nelson rising next to her. "Sit *down*," she hissed at them. "Sit *down*. Let him go go go."

They stared at her.

"We'll be out of here in in thirty minutes," she said.

∽

"Your Honor, may I be heard?"

The courtroom exploded in shouting and bodies not knowing what to do with themselves in the face of what looked like certain violence. Most trials did not call for much spectator interest, but the start of this one had attracted not only the usual collection of retired old men who passed their days watching courtroom proceedings, but also some representatives of the business press who had learned a Barbiron trial had been scheduled with a personal appearance by Chloe Manning, juror relatives, friends of the parties, and the curious strays. All of them were making some kind of noise. Even the seasoned court-watchers were hollering.

Jolene Marovitz was shouting *objection, objection*, and a couple of her colleagues at the counsel table threw in a couple more *objections* for good measure. The distinguished jurors dove into their chairwells, thinking Jon was about to pull out a Thompson submachine gun and dial up the kind of Capone-style justice for which Chicago was known worldwide.

Judge Achebe banged his gavel. "This Court WILL come to order or I will order the bailiff to clear the courtroom." He banged his gavel again. "I don't think I've ever had to say that before," he muttered.

The Barbiron counsel table was an island of calm, although Nelson's and Brian's jaws had dropped to their chests and they couldn't decide whether to look at each other, at Jon, or at their delighted client.

By that time the furious marshals had pushed Jolene aside and each grabbed one of Jon's arms and were starting to put him on the ground.

The judge spoke sharply: "Hold up, marshals."

"Your Honor," the senior marshal said, "we know your rule and we were at the door and had barred him from entering, but he tricked us and squirted through. We apologize and it won't happen again. Security has been alerted and an arrest team is on its way."

Chloe stifled a laugh. *A first! Jon Rider tricked someone! Told a lie! Told a lie to an authority figure! Two authority figures! Two armed authority figures! "Omigod, marshals, looky over there, it's Brad Pitt coming out of the men's room with Beyoncé and his shirt's buttoned all funny!" And then he – what – "squirted" through the doors? Jon "the Big Squirt" Rider!* Another naughty giggle stifled. *This is good. This is too good. The grandkids are going to love this.*

And her heart cracked a little.

"Your Honor," Jolene Marovitz said, "this is outrageous. An obvious trick of the defense to prevent the orderly presentation of very damaging testimony."

"I know, I know, Ms. Marovitz," the judge said. "It is an outrage, and this gentleman came very close to getting capped by these very large and angry federal marshals. But let's not be too hasty with our accusations against counsel. They seem as surprised as everyone else, although I note that Ms. Manning seems somewhat amused by the whole thing."

Chloe dropped her smile and shook her head vigorously *no, not amused.*

"The marshals are telling the truth, Your Honor," Jon said. "I did trick them. But the information I have is of the utmost importance to this Court and this case." He turned his head to the senior marshal. "I'm sorry I tricked you."

"You're gonna be sorry at the MCC in a few minutes" the lesser marshal said as a phalanx of armed marshals blasted through the doors into the courtroom.

"Hold on for a minute, marshals," Judge Achebe said. "Marshals Jackson and Lopez appear to have this miscreant under control." Judge Achebe looked Jon over carefully. He had seen him before. "Who are you?"

"My name is Jon Rider and I am admitted to the bar of this Court and I'm in good standing in the Northern District. Maybe not for long. I apologize profoundly for this interruption. I am well aware of the potential consequences and I would not have barged in here unless I had information critical to this Court's jurisdiction in this case. Your Honor may not remember, but I had a couple of matters before you some years back shortly after your appointment."

"I thought you looked familiar," the judge said. *I knew I'd seen that tie dimple before.* "Well, you obviously got through security downstairs, but you're a tricky guy, so let me ask you: Are you armed?"

"No, Your Honor. Only with information in aid of justice."

"Marshals, better frisk him. And you, Rider, cut the wisecracks."

Jackson and Lopez gave him an almost comically vigorous frisking, as though to atone for letting the trickster Rider squirt through. The Judge told them to release their hold on him, but to stand by "in case he tries any more tricks."

The jurors had begun to emerge from their chairwells and edge back warily into their seats.

Jon Rider took a moment to readjust and smooth out his jacket. He buttoned the middle button. He was always buttoned up when he addressed a judge. He felt the knot on the seven-fold Robert Talbott tie with the muted red design he had selected for the day's labors and, in the absence of a nearby reflective surface, satisfied himself by touch that it was – well, perfect. A tie should always be ready for battle.

"Well, Mr. Rider, you said the magic word, jurisdiction. But before you say another word: Bailiff, please conduct the jury back to the jury room while we get this straightened out."

"With all due respect, Your Honor," Jolene Marovitz said with all the indignation she could summon, "there is nothing to straighten out. Mr. Rider has no involvement in this case. To the best of our knowledge he does not represent a single soul in this courtroom and has no standing to address the Court no matter what he has to say. Not only that, his questioning of your unquestionable jurisdiction before the jury is highly prejudicial and may require the declaration of a mistrial."

"We'll deal with any potential prejudice to the jury later. But you raise a good point, Ms. Marovitz. In what capacity do you purport to address the Court, Mr. Rider?"

Jon Rider turned to the Barbiron counsel table.

"Well, Mr. Rider?"

Amy stood up in the front row and waved a dollar bill with gusto.

Chloe heard the crinkle of the currency. She turned and snatched the bill from Amy with a muted *thanks*.

Chloe stood up before Brian and Nelson had any chance to rein her in, not that reining her in would have been a realistic possibility with their client entirely focused on Jon Rider. She held out the dollar and gave it a shake. "Mr. Rider, would you please represent Barbiron and me and Ms. Altobelli as co-counsel with my attorneys here for the purposes of this trial?"

"Permission to approach the defendant, Your Honor?" Jon took the Judge's silence as consent and walked the few steps to Chloe Manning and her wrinkled dollar. "It would be my pleasure," he said, and took the bill. Their eyes met briefly, but they both knew they had to behave. He thought about winking, but instead pocketed the dollar and turned quickly back to the bench.

"Oh, come on," Jolene said. "Really, Your Honor. Mr. Rider is nothing *but* tricks, and now it appears he's in cahoots with the defendant."

"Judge," Chloe said, "I had no idea Mr. Rider would be here today and I have no idea what he's got up his sleeve. But whatever it is, I fu – I promise you it will be worth your while."

"Sit down, Ms. Manning," the judge said. "Do not address the Court unless asked to do so. And watch your language."

"Your Honor," Jon said, "I will file my formal appearance with the clerk over the noon hour. For the time being, I would ask that I be permitted to conduct a preliminary examination of this witness in the nature of a *voir dire*."

"Your Honor!" Jolene said.

"Hold on," the judge said. "First things first. I confess I've never seen trial counsel hired from the podium in the midst of trial, but as I sit here, I can't think of a single reason that Mr. Rider isn't presently a co-counsel on this case. Now, if it transpires that Mr. Rider and Ms. Manning have conspired to defraud – or trick – the Court I may take a different view of things. But I'm sensing there may be some fire behind all this smoke."

Judge Achebe remembered Jon Rider more clearly than he let on. One of those early cases was an antitrust case where Jon had demolished the plaintiff's damage expert on cross-examination. Another was a difficult securities fraud case where Jon's colorful and elegant charts of the inter-related companies and who said what to whom and where the money went earned his client the only not-guilty verdict among a dozen defendants, the rest of whom the jury hit for several hundred million. Although it may have been his easy charm before the largely female jury. Or the tie dimple. He recalled that Jon's lucid explanations of these areas of law that the newly-appointed Judge had not encountered in his private practice had hugely aided the Court in these early complex cases. "What's your jurisdictional argument, Mr. Rider?"

"May it please the Court, it would be immeasurably easier to explain to the Court if Your Honor could indulge me on my request to present the facts in an orderly fashion in open court. I respectfully repeat my urgent request that the Court permit me to get certain critical facts on the record through the sworn testimony of Mr. Bondurant."

Judge Achebe considered that this Rider had just about caused a bloodbath in his courtroom, but he remembered Jon's brilliance in the early days of his judgeship. "Ms. Marovitz?"

"Strongly object, Your Honor. Many reasons. No notice, no discovery. Mr. Bondurant already sworn and ready to begin his testimony. Jury exposed to this preposterous carnival. No prior contact of Mr. Rider with this case."

"I will concede that his entry was rather abrupt," the judge said.

Oh, yeah, you betcha. Chloe was so tickled she could hardly stand herself. *He is one abrupt enterer.* Judgie *had* to let him go go go.

Judge Achebe looked up. "Mr. Accardo?"

"Your Honor, this is as much a surprise to us as it is to the Court. Ms. Manning has assured us, as she has assured the Court, that Mr. Rider's appearance here was completely unexpected and she has no idea what he's proposing to advise the Court, nor do Mr. Gilles or I. I will say, however, that while we do not condone any interference with the judicial process, and certainly do not condone interruptions of this nature, Mr. Rider is a former colleague of ours and we have extremely high regard for his analytical skills and, to put the matter bluntly, his investigational skills."

"Sounds like you're telling me I'm kind of living in an old Perry Mason episode," Judge Achebe said.

"Except in color," Brian said. "And 3D. And HD."

"This isn't funny, Judge," Jolene said.

"No, Ms. Marovitz, it is not. But I have before me a member of the bar of this court who has been retained by the defendants before my very eyes, who tells me that he has information going to my authority to hear this case. Whether it should have been brought up before today, whether defendants may be deemed to have waived the argument, remains to be seen. As for his request to conduct an examination at this point . . . ." Judge Achebe pursed his lips and smiled a little. "Well," he said, "I like Perry Mason."

Jolene Marovitz was shaking. Judge Achebe noticed her growing distress and held up his hand in a calming gesture.

"Mr. Rider, how long would you anticipate your examination of Mr. Bondurant to take?"

"Ten minutes. Fifteen tops."

"Counsel," Judge Achebe said, "I am noting that Ms. Marovitz's objections have been adequately preserved for the record. She may have other objections upon hearing the examination that I will also deem preserved, and the Court may find cause to discipline Mr. Rider on its own motion. But I am sufficiently intrigued by Mr. Rider risking his law license and a couple of holes in that nice suit and his gizzard here today that I am going to permit him to conduct a preliminary examination of Mr. Bondurant outside the hearing of the jury."

"With due respect, Your Honor," Jolene Marovitz said, "are you kidding? We've had no notice! We have had no opportunity to prepare for whatever Mr. Rider proposes put on the record here. He may be an old buddy of Mr.

Accardo and Mr. Gilles, and especially the starry-eyed Ms. Manning, but I've never heard of him!"

"I am not kidding, Ms. Marovitz," Judge Achebe said. "But I am aware of the potential for unfairness to the plaintiff here. I have no desire to be reversed on appeal in this case for any reason. But I also don't want to proceed in a case where I may lack jurisdiction, and facts pertinent to that need to be on the record. We will deal with the issue of due process for plaintiff when this little drama is over. And, Ms. Marovitz –"

"Your Honor?"

"I *have* heard of him." The judge made a show of looking at his watch. "Mr. Rider, you've got fifteen minutes to make your jurisdictional record and avoid contempt and, quite possibly, mortal peril to your ability to practice law. Mr. Bondurant, you're still under oath. Ms. Marovitz, I see you're taking a breath to say something. I've made my ruling. Let's move on."

Jolene Marovitz harrumphed and huffed and flounced back to her chair.

CHAPTER 26

CHLOE MANNING WAS BEGINNING TO TINGLE

CHLOE MANNING WAS beginning to tingle.

Jon Rider stood alone at the podium, his papers squared away before him.

He looked down at the neat piles he had assembled, then looked up at Blake Bondurant. A faint smile played across his face.

"Good morning, Mr. Bondurant."

"Good morning," Blake said. His tone did not suggest he wanted Jon Rider to have a good morning.

"Mr. Bondurant, in this case, you have alleged sexual harassment during your employment by Barbiron and wrongful termination by Barbiron, is that correct? You've sworn to it in your deposition in this case, too, have you not?"

"Objection," Jolene Marovitz said. "Mr. Rider has made

Mr. Bondurant his witness and should not be permitted to ask leading questions."

"Overruled," Judge Achebe said. "There's no jury here. I can determine whether or not the leading questioning is leading the Court astray. We'll get this over more quickly with leading questions, so lead away, Mr. Rider."

"The question was whether you are alleging sexual harassment and wrongful termination by Barbiron, and sworn to it in discovery," Jon said.

"That's correct."

"Before you filed this suit, you sent Ms. Manning a demand letter, did you not?"

"Yes."

"In fact, you sent two demand letters. You sent one earlier on by email directly to Ms. Manning, and a hard-copy letter hand-delivered to her some months later, correct?"

"Yes."

Brian and Nelson exchanged puzzled looks.

"You wrote those letters yourself. You did not have a lawyer at either time, is that right?"

"Yes."

"Your Honor, I have marked some documents here as exhibits denominated J-1 through J-4 for identification, indicating that they are to be used in this questioning relating to the Court's jurisdiction. For convenience and to move things along, I would like to refer to them in this fashion. I don't believe it will be necessary to admit them as evidence in the action at this point, since for the purposes for which I intend to use them in this particular examination they do not go to the merits of Mr. Bondurant's claim other than incidentally. I have copies of both sets of exhibits for counsel and the Court." He handed sets of pages to Jolene Marovitz, Brian, and the clerk, who passed them up to Judge Achebe.

"Go ahead, Mr. Rider."

Jon asked for permission to approach the witness, which the judge granted.

"Mr. Bondurant, I'm showing you what I've marked as Exhibit J-1, and I ask you whether that is a true and correct copy of an email you sent to Ms. Manning accusing Barbiron of wrongful termination and harassment. I will represent to you that it has my name at the top because I printed this email off of my home computer last night because it had been forwarded to me some time ago, as you can see from the dates. You have to look down to the to-and-from to see who the original sender and recipient were. Does that look like a copy of your first demand letter to Barbiron, in email form?"

"Yes, it appears to be a copy of that email."

"In that email, you state: 'Also, the sexual harassment that I suffered while I was working at Barbiron and the hostile sexual environment there of which you are very very aware was very stressful to me and caused problems with my marriage to Charisse including my divorce.' Did I read that correctly from your email?"

"Yes."

"And just for the record, let's take a quick look at what I've marked as Exhibit J-2, and ask if that is a copy of the second demand letter you sent to Ms. Manning."

"Yes, it is."

"You sent this very shortly before you filed suit in this case, did you not."

"Yes. When I didn't hear anything from Chlo – Ms. Manning, I hired Ms. Marovitz's firm right away because I understood I was under some time limits to start a lawsuit. And she sued right away."

"Mr. Bondurant, do you see that in this second demand letter you didn't make any reference to any problems with Charisse?"

Blake looked over the page. "Looks like it. Come on, who cares what's in my letters?"

"The way this works, Mr. Bondurant, is that I ask the questions. In fact, Mr. Bondurant, your wife Charisse sued you for divorce about six months before you wrote that first email, did she not?"

"Yes. I also sued her for divorce."

"Yes, you did. Now, this was not what is referred to as an amicable divorce, was it?"

"You could say that."

"Well, Mr. Bondurant, you and your wife had some significant disagreements about how to divide up your property, and maintenance, and child support, all of the financial aspects of the divorce, did you not?"

"We worked it out."

"Eventually, yes. But before that there were some pretty serious fights about your property, and the attorneys did quite a bit of wrangling on that subject, did they not?"

"Yes."

"In fact, the parties took quite a bit of discovery on the subject of your and your wife's assets, did they not?"

"Sure seemed like it."

"And do you remember that your lawyers convinced the divorce court to order expedited discovery, so your case moved rather quickly? You wanted that divorce fast, didn't you?"

"Sure."

"And at that time, it was strongly in your interest to, shall we say, minimize the value of assets you owned or controlled – in fact, the value of all the community property. The less you have, the less you have to contribute to a settlement, right? The less your wife gets, the better you end up when it's all over?"

"Yeah, of course. That's the way it always works," Blake smirked. "I don't know what that's got to do with anything."

"And after all that discovery was over, you finally made a deal with your wife, right?"

"Right."

"And the divorce decree entered by the divorce court embodied that property agreement, correct?"

"I don't remember the exact terms. It was a long document."

"We'll come back to that in a bit. Now Mr. Bondurant, in the course of that discovery we were just talking about, do you recall that your wife's lawyers took your deposition?"

Blake paused. "This all was a while ago. I think – I don't remember."

"Really? You don't remember sitting in a conference room getting grilled for several hours by Charisse's lawyer? Permission to approach the witness, Your Honor?"

"Go ahead."

"Mr. Bondurant, I am handing you what I have marked as Exhibit J-3 for identification. I will ask you to examine that document, flip through it as you like. It's long, you don't need to read any of it, you just need to be able to identify it for the Court." Blake took the document and for the first time, he straightened in the witness chair. He traded his expression of smug disdain for Jon's questioning for one of emerging concern.

"Mr. Bondurant," Jon said, "does that appear to be a copy of your deposition taken in your divorce case on Wednesday, November 29, 2017?"

"Objection!" Jolene Markovitz shot to her feet. "Your Honor, we've never seen this document before, we've had no opportunity to review it, and we would have no basis on which to challenge its authenticity. Moreover, it was never produced by defendants in the course of discovery in this case."

"Your Honor," Jon Rider said, "this document is Ms. Marovitz's own client's deposition. Defendants and their counsel never had a copy, and I would be surprised if Ms. Marovitz served any discovery requests on Barbiron that called for it to produce documents that were Mr. Bondurant's own words sworn and recorded in a matter in which Barbiron and its lawyers had no involvement whatsoever."

There was a ripple of quiet laughter in the courtroom.

"Overruled. Let's let Mr. Bondurant look at the document and identify it if he can."

"You trying to bogart my fifteen minutes, Jolene?" Jon asked, directing his most disarming smile her way.

"Mr. Rider," Judge Achebe said, "you know better than to address counsel directly. Kindly address all of your remarks to the Court. And apparently Ms. Marovitz has no idea who you are, so your form of address to her strikes the Court as presumptuous."

"Beg the Court's pardon," Jon said, "and Ms. Marovitz's. Mr. Bondurant, if you've had a chance to flip through that, does that appear to be a copy of your deposition taken in your divorce case?"

"Where did you get this?" Blake asked. "I never gave my lawyers permission to give anything out. How am I supposed to know if this is a copy of anything? I didn't memorize this thing. I gave it months ago."

"I got it from your ex-wife Charisse, Mr. Bondurant."

At this point there was one of those moments in testimony where you could have heard a *subpoena duces tecum* drop in the courtroom.

"I picked it up from her last night."

Blake looked at Jolene Marovitz, who had just picked up the transcript and started to skim through it.

"In fact, I had her write in blue ink in a blank space on the cover, see that? I gave you the copy with her original handwriting on it. 'On January 7, 2020, I delivered this copy of the deposition Blake Bondurant gave in our divorce case to Jon Rider. Signed, Charisse Bondurant.' And I had her initial each page at the lower right, see that? Doesn't matter. A couple of seconds ago you admitted that you gave a deposition a matter of months ago, having earlier testified that you didn't remember."

"OK, I remember, I gave one. I don't know if this is it."

"Flip to about two pages from the end. Is that your signature?"

"Looks like it, but – "

"And do you see on the next page that says 'ERRATA" at the top, where you could list any corrections, there's nothing there? You made no corrections to your testimony before you signed the deposition?"

"I don't remember."

"But you do remember that your deposition was taken, do you not, and do you also recall that at that time, you swore to tell the truth, the whole truth, and nothing but the truth, so help you God?"

"Yes, I did."

"Mr. Bondurant, I'm not going to spar with you on whether this is a true and correct copy of your deposition. Just turn to page 97 of the pages I've given you. You can follow along, starting at line 17 and continuing on for the next page or so. At your deposition, were you asked the following questions and did you give the following answers?

"QUESTION: All right, Mr. Bondurant, we've gone through the house and the cars and all of your other tangible property and your accounts, we're going to turn now to your intangible property.

"ANSWER: What's that?

"QUESTION: Well, let me put it this way. Does anybody owe you any money?

"ANSWER: Like a loan? No, nothing like that.

"QUESTION: Have you made a claim against anyone, or an insurance company, anything like that?

"ANSWER: No.

"QUESTION: Do you have a claim against anyone for personal injury, or breach of contract, any kind of a legal claim?

"ANSWER: No.

"I'm going to stop there for a moment, Mr. Bondurant, just to make sure you know what I'm asking. Were you asked those questions, and did you give those answers?"

"If you say so," he said.

"Oh, I do say so, Mr. Bondurant, but what's important is whether you say so, and while you're considering whether to lie about that – "

"Objection!" Jolene Marovitz shouted without rising.

"Sustained. Mr. Rider."

"Beg pardon, Judge. While you're considering how to answer that question, bear in mind that this Court can subpoena the court reporter, and your divorce lawyer, and the video that was made of your testimony. Were you asked those questions and did you give those answers?"

"All right. Yes. But those answers were all correct."

"Let's keep going. Were you asked these questions and did you give the following answers? Page 99, line 4."

Later, Jon would tell Brian and Nelson that he could have sworn he heard Jolene Marovitz whisper *oh shit*.

"QUESTION: I want to make sure I've been clear about my questions here. I'm not just asking about whether you have made any claims prior to this date. I'm asking if you have any claims at all that have arisen during the course of the marriage, whether or not you have actually made those claims yet.

"ANSWER: I'm not sure I understand. Actually, I'm sure I don't understand.

"QUESTION: Okay. Do you have any monetary claims against anybody or any business that you might assert, whether you have already made those claims or filed suit, or whether you might make a claim or sue in the future?

"ANSWER: Sorry. Could you repeat the question?

"QUESTION: Yeah, that was a little tangled, I apologize. My earlier questions may have been phrased so you thought I was referring only to some claim that you actually have made prior to today. Now I'm asking a broader question. Do you possess any claims against any person or business that you could make or file in the future? That you haven't made yet?

"ANSWER: No, not that I know of. No, I don't.

"I'll stop there for a moment, Mr. Bondurant. Were you asked those questions and did you give those answers?"

"Again, sir," Blake said, shifting in his seat, "I think those answers were all correct as I understood the questions."

"Do you? Let's go on, page 100, line 17:

"QUESTION: Mr. Bondurant, just to wrap this up and get a little more specific: You were terminated from your job with Barbiron in September, about two-and-a-half months ago, is that correct?

"ANSWER: Yes.

"QUESTION: But we learned earlier when we were talking about your sources of income that you never filed for unemployment. Why did you not file?

"ANSWER: Didn't qualify, supposively.

"QUESTION: Why?

"ANSWER: I wasn't laid off. I was supposively fired for cause.

"QUESTION: So are you saying that you also don't have a claim against Barbiron for wrongful termination or sex discrimination or something like that?

"ANSWER: Right. I'm not one of those guys that looks for some kind of BS excuse when the breaks don't go his way. Look, I really don't want to go into the reasons I was fired, it's not really relevant here. It was a disagreement and I thought I was right and the company was wrong. But, I mean, I didn't have a contract or anything and they had a bunch of documents supposively showing I'd screwed up. I thought it was total bull, but I wasn't so sorry to go. If they hadn't fired me I probably would have quit. I expected to get a better job. I still do.

"QUESTION: Well, let me be more precise: You are not expecting any money from Barbiron? You are not going to make a claim or sue for any money or severance or the like from Barbiron?"

"ANSWER: That's right. No offense, but I've had it with lawyers for a lifetime.

"Mr. Bondurant. Look at me. Look at me. Were you asked those questions, and did you give those answers?"

Blake Bondurant was silent for a quarter-minute.

"Mr. Bondurant?"

"I changed my mind."

"Yes or no, Mr. Bondurant?" Jon looked up at Judge Achebe. The Judge nodded *go on, I got it*.

"So you're testifying under oath here that after that rather detailed explanation in your deposition, under oath, of why you didn't have a claim against Barbiron, you" – air quotes – "'changed your mind.' By the way, I note that your answer did not mention sexual harassment or a hostile sexual environment. Well, let's look at the facts a little more closely. Mr. Bondurant, you testified that the property settlement in your divorce was based on the information exchanged during discovery in your divorce proceeding. You weren't sure if that settlement was incorporated in the court's final order. Remember that?"

"Yes."

"And that decree was entered on December 18, 2017, just a few weeks after your deposition, right?"

"I don't remember the date."

"It is hard to remember dates, Mr. Bondurant, so let me show you what I have marked as Exhibit J-4 and ask you if that is a copy of the divorce decree entered in your divorce case?"

Blake flipped through it without reading it. "It looks like it."

"There's a date stamped on the front, see that? Read that out loud to the Court."

"December 18, 2017."

"And that was about three weeks after your deposition, right?"

"Approximately."

"Just flip through that a moment, Mr. Bondurant, and tell the Court whether that decree incorporates the financial terms that were based in part on the value of your assets as they were established by discovery, including your deposition."

Jolene Marovitz stood, but spoke without much conviction. "Objection, the document speaks for itself, also argumentative and no foundation, beyond this witness's knowledge, no showing he ever read the document or had any role in drafting it."

Judge Achebe, who had been relaxing in his big judge

chair during the examination, sat up to his microphone. "The Court will take those factors into account in evaluating Mr. Bondurant's testimony, Ms. Marovitz, but I'm going to overrule your objection."

Jon rephrased his question: "Does the December 18 decree incorporate the financial terms based on the value of your assets disclosed during your deposition and other discovery, Mr. Bondurant?"

Blake looked to his counsel table, but none of them met his eyes. He paged through the thick document listlessly, stopping on one or two pages. "Yes," he said in a small voice.

"Right. Now let me show you Exhibit J-1 again, your first demand letter you emailed to Ms. Manning, in which you demand two million dollars from Barbiron, which is what your attorneys have advised the Court is the minimum they will be seeking in this trial. Please read the date on that letter, nice and loud."

"December 21, 2017."

"December 21, 2017, *three days* after this final divorce decree, the J-4 we just looked at, was entered, and only *three weeks* after you swore before the divorce court in your deposition that, for several good reasons, you had no harassment or termination claim that could be part of the value of your property. The value of your property that got incorporated in the divorce decree mere days later did not include this lawsuit, and that was to your financial advantage. Do I have that timing right, Mr. Bondurant?"

Chloe had resumed bouncing in her chair.

Blake Bondurant's tan had grown pasty and blotchy.

"The dates are on the papers," he said.

"Indeed they are," Jon said. He spoke quickly now to get the next point out before Jolene Marovitz stopped him. "And speaking of dates, don't they give us the reason you were so all fired anxious to get this divorce out of the way? Because you knew you had a deadline to file a harassment complaint with the Equal Employment Opportunity Commission after your termination, so you had to get that divorce final and that order entered before you filed, and before you sent that first email to Ms. Manning, right? And since you knew you were going to file with the EEOC when you and your divorce lawyers expedited that case, every single answer in your deposition was a lie, was it not? You couldn't have 'changed your mind' – you had to know you were going to file all along."

"Objection!" Jolene Marovitz said. "Grossly argumentative, privileged, calls for a legal conclusion, compound question, and harassing."

Judge Achebe thought about it. Rider had it figured. But it had been argumentative and compound, and he needed to throw Jolene Marovitz a bone. "Sustained," he said, "but you may rephrase the question if you wish, Mr. Rider."

"I'm mindful of my own deadline, Your Honor," Jon said, "so we'll pass that point for now."

Jon looked down at his notes; looked like he had covered everything. Then he thought of something. "By the way, Mr. Bondurant. You recall, do you not, that your lawyers filed a motion asking this Court to allow you to file your complaint under seal, so the public could not see it, and the Court – this Court – granted that motion, agreed with your lawyers to let you do it?"

"Yes."

"And isn't it correct that the reason you didn't want the public to see it, Mr. Bondurant, was that your ex-wife Charisse is a member of that public and you didn't want her to know that you were suing for millions of dollars, for the same reason you didn't want her to know that you were going to sue Barbiron for millions of dollars when you gave your deposition?"

Jolene Marovitz objected on privilege, relevance, speculation, prejudice, and one or two other grounds, but her heart wasn't in it. Judge Achebe had heard the question and could not unhear the implied argument that the motion to the Court to file the complaint under seal was part of a scheme to defraud the former Mrs. Bondurant.

"I'm happy to withdraw that question, and I'll conclude by saying that I'm happy to agree with Ms. Marovitz on something else," Jon said, gesturing to all of the documents he'd offered. "These documents do speak for themselves."

He looked at his watch. Thirteen minutes.

"Thank you, Your Honor. No further questions."

✍

Jolene Marovitz was on her feet. Judge Cleon Achebe was faster.

"Ms. Marovitz, you will get your say, but I need to clear a few things up with Mr. Rider. Mr. Bondurant, you may stand down for the time being."

Jolene sat down. Blake appeared to stagger a bit under the almost palpable glare of his attorneys.

"Mr. Rider, as interesting as those passages are, they sound to me like more-or-less standard impeachment material – extremely damaging impeachment material, but just garden-variety evidence tending to demonstrate this one witness's lack of credibility. You could just as easily have provided Mr. Accardo this material for his use in cross-examining Mr. Bondurant in the testimony he was about to give before you busted down the courtroom doors. This testimony did not require the noisy and – what word are we using? – tricky invasion of this courtroom followed by drawn guns and I am inclined to hold you in contempt."

"Your Honor, with all respect due this Court, Mr. Bondurant's testimony goes well beyond whether his allegations and evidence are entitled to be believed, well beyond issues of his credibility as a witness. Recall that the value of Mr. Bondurant's assets, including potential litigation claims he possessed that accrued during the marriage – if any – was critical to the property division embodied in the final judgment in the divorce in the state court proceeding. He swore to the state divorce court several times that he had no such claims, that in fact *he did not have the very claims he is asserting here*, and the marital assets were accordingly divided to Mr. Bondurant's advantage, since these potentially hugely valuable claims were completely unknown to the divorce court and to Mrs. Bondurant's counsel. He now swears to *this* Court that he *does* have such claims, worth millions of dollars, that he doubtless expects to put into his own pocket and not share with the former Mrs. Bondurant."

"So . . . "

"So under the doctrine of judicial estoppel, a litigant may not take a sworn position in a first case that is to his advantage with the intent to deceive the first court, and then take the opposite position in a subsequent case. Swear one thing to the first court, and swear the exact opposite to the second court. Especially here, where the deception in the first case – basically perjury – did not relate to a side issue or a minor dispute, but to the very existence of a claim against Barbiron. This kind of deception is regarded as an attempt to manipulate the legal system and to defraud the court. It vests the second court with the discretion to dismiss the case in its entirety. For which I hereby move pursuant to Rule 12(b)(6) of the Federal Rules of Civil Procedure."

Judge Achebe nodded. Jon's argument attacking the entire case and not just whether Blake Bondurant was a truthful witness was starting to sink in.

Jolene Marovitz broke the uncertain silence. "But Barbiron never pleaded any of this as a defense in any of its papers," she said, standing again. "Too late to bring it up now. Defendants have waived this argument."

"Incorrect," Jon said. "In *Davis v. District of Columbia* decided by the D.C. Court of Appeals in June or last year, it was held that because judicial estoppel goes to the integrity of the judicial process, it may be raised at any time, including by the Court itself, and in that respect is similar to objections to jurisdiction, which also may be raised at any time. Passing copies of the case to all counsel and the clerk."

Judge Achebe flipped through the case. He was a little

embarrassed he hadn't caught the issue Jon Rider was raising.

"Ms. Marovitz," he said, "Mr. Rider jogs my memory that in cases like this, the second court does have the discretion to dismiss the case. However, since you were taken by surprise, fairness requires that you be given time to respond. I will order simultaneous filings of briefs in fifteen days on the application of the law Mr. Rider is claiming, whether the defendants have waived the argument, and all the rest. The clerk will advise the parties of a date for a further hearing on this, at which time, Ms. Marovitz, you may cross-examine Mr. Bondurant if you wish to seek to rehabilitate him. And now I'd like all counsel to approach the bench. Madam court reporter, we're going off the record for a moment."

Brian, Jolene, and Jon lined up in front of Judge Achebe, who was peering down at them. He spoke quietly. "Mr. Rider, frankly, I should discipline you in some way. You came in here shouting 'jurisdiction,' but your questioning did not raise a jurisdictional issue. My actual statutory authority to hear the case is unaffected by anything you presented. It just gives me discretion to dismiss this case if I feel like it. That has nothing to do with jurisdiction. I could just shrug my shoulders and deny your motion and continue to try the case."

"Just what I was thinking," Jolene said. "Another trick."

"Here's why I'm not doing that, Ms. Marovitz," the judge continued. "Your client is a liar. It could not be more clear that he hid the fact of his claim from his ex-wife – worse, he denied that he had any such claim or that he intended to make one – with the secret intention of raising it after the divorce was granted so he could keep one hundred percent any settlement or trial damages and she would get none of it." Judge Achebe paused, and his voice took on some additional heat. "And he – actually, your firm, Ms. Marovitz – used this Court's good offices to hide his filing by moving to file under seal."

"Well . . . ," Jolene said.

"And if I deny Mr. Rider's motion to dismiss and resume the trial, now or in the future, Mr. Accardo will take those papers from Mr. Rider, thank you very much, and, when he cross-examines Mr. Bondurant in front of that jury, he will insert each one of them roughly in a bodily location dear to Mr. Bondurant to which judges should not be explicitly referring before distinguished counsel. By the way," he said, glancing up into the courtroom, "I see Mr. Bondurant has slid almost entirely under the counsel table.

"Ms. Marovitz, I'm absolutely going to consider your response to Mr. Rider's argument with all the fairness to which it is entitled, but if I'd had this material before trial I'm not at all sure we'd be having a trial. I'm simply not going to waste a jury's and this court's valuable time if the record shows, as it is apparently going to, that Mr. Bondurant unambiguously swore to the honorable state divorce court in his deposition that he has no claim against Barbiron. And Ms. Marovitz . . . "

"Your Honor?"

"'I changed my mind,' he said?" Judge Achebe shook his head.

"Obviously we need to look into this with some care,

Your Honor," Jolene said. "We don't want to waste our own time, either. After we have reviewed the situation, perhaps I can be in touch with Mr. Accardo on a possible resolution."

"That would be a splendid outcome, Ms. Marovitz, and I'm sure Mr. Accardo will be pleased to hear from you." Brian, who was happy with the way things were going without having to say a word, nodded perhaps a shade more vigorously than he had to. "If you need more than the fifteen days I just gave you, notify the clerk and any reasonable request will be accommodated. Now," the Judge said, "I can't keep this jury tied up for weeks. I suppose this will technically be a mistrial, so I'll need to tell them what's happening and discharge them. Mr. Rider, I may not be done with you. I haven't decided."

Jon Rider didn't care what The Honorable Cleon Achebe was going to do to him. Fine him, report him to the Illinois bar, suspend his federal court privileges, or kick him in the ass. Didn't care. He was ecstatic. For the first time since Amelia died, he felt completely alive, that he was about to be complete, his life was going to be wonderful beyond all imagining, absolutely stupid wonderful. He didn't feel like a man who had made a professional error, or who was in contempt of Judge Cleon Achebe's ill-lit courtroom, or who had risked a bullet in the back from a federal marshal.

He felt like Ebenezer Scrooge on Christmas morning. *That glowing, shimmering female spirit did it to me all in one night!*

He felt like a naughty little boy with all the joy that naughtiness brings to naughty little boys, especially naughty little boys who are being naughty for the entertainment of some cute girl who he's hoping might be a little naughty herself. He wanted to laugh out loud.

"I understand, Your Honor," he said.

"You don't seem too shook up about it," Judge Achebe observed. "You're grinning in a way some might think is inappropriate."

"Oh, Your Honor. Oh, Your Honor. I have done several *very* inappropriate things today, much to my own surprise I assure you, and I expect to do at least one more very inappropriate thing," Jon said.

"Mr. Rider," Judge Achebe said, "what is that you have in your hand?"

"One more inappropriate thing, if it please the Court."

CHAPTER 27

CHLOE BARELY HEARD THE NEWS OVER THE ROAR

CHLOE BARELY HEARD the news over the roar from her heart.

Brian was telling her what Judge Achebe had said and what it almost certainly meant: The case was over, or at least would never return in the form of a trial with live testimony. Most likely Jolene would call and they'd end up with a small-value settlement that would include a confidentiality provision prohibiting Blake Bondurant from making any use of the compromising information. Maybe the Court would dismiss the case entirely based on Jon's arguments, although a cheap settlement would be better so the confidentiality agreement could be a part of it. All that drunken blabbermouth puking nudity was never going to come out, and the price of that would not excite anyone thinking about underwriting a Barbiron initial public offering.

"Chloe, are you understanding what's happened here?" Brian asked. "You seem a little abstracted."

"Abstracted," Chloe said, looking around the court-room. "Sure. Sorry." Where had Jon Rider disappeared to? She was a bundle of swirling emotions that were not play-ing nicely together. The devastation of the breakup of two nights earlier was being chased and, yes, overtaken by the excitement of Jon's risky and yes, entirely absolutely nutbag crazy ride to the rescue. And now, after another of his magic acts, he's disappeared *again*. That man.

Wherever they stood now, she wanted to give him the hug of a lifetime and kiss her thanks all over his amazing mug and not stop forever and tell him she loved him for what he is and whatever he or she might ever become.

Judge Cleon Achebe asked the bailiff to bring the jury back in. When they were seated, he said:

"Ladies and gentlemen of the jury, I apologize for the delay in the proceeding caused by Mr. Rider's untimely and, I must say, unseemly invasion of the courtroom. We have held some additional proceedings, and I don't know if you will be happy or unhappy to know that on my own motion, I am declaring a mistrial and discharging you of your duties, with the Court's very deep gratitude for your patience and willingness to serve."

The jury seemed mostly unhappy. Several jurors shook their heads; a couple snorted or said "oh, jeez." One of them was heard asking about getting his parking validated. They looked at each other, uncertain of what to do next.

Jon Rider stood up.

He had been sitting in the back of the courtroom, slumped behind a row of spectators.

"Your Honor," he called out, "permission to approach the bench and address the Court?"

"Hello again, Mr. Rider," Judge Achebe said. "Much better this time. You may approach."

Everyone looked at Jolene Marovitz, but she kept her seat, and her mouth shut.

Chloe was ecstatic to hear that voice behind her, and overjoyed to see that tall man with the dry-ice seeing eyes glide up the aisle toward the podium, this time without running and without his hands in the air pursued by armed cops. She was delighted to observe that his tie dimple had been undamaged by the events of the morning.

Jon paused when he came even with the Barbiron counsel table. He looked at Chloe and smiled. She smiled back and a little bag of warmth broke inside him. He saw that her eyes were shining, glistening with feeling.

"Your Honor, I have caused the Court and the parties – and, most of all, this distinguished jury – considerable inconvenience today, and I apologize profoundly for that." He smiled at the jury and made a small bow. The female jurors nodded and smiled as though to say *that's OK, we have no plans for the rest of the day, or tonight and into tomorrow morning, for that matter.* This time they were joined in their return nods by two male jurors.

"I am hopeful to have the opportunity to make some things right with the Court and the jury, Ms. Marovitz, and other entities of importance to this case. To that end," he said, "before you enter the order of mistrial and the jury is discharged, I respectfully request leave to call one witness."

"No objection," Jolene Marovitz said.

"No objection," Brian Accardo said.

What? You've won this thing for me, Jon Rider. Don't do anything that's going to screw this up. What the hell are you thinking?

"We seem to have some time left before the noon hour," Judge Achebe said. "Call your witness."

Lisa the Flamethrower and Amy turned to one another. *Oh my god* they whispered together. *Oh my god. Oh my god.*

"Defense calls Ms. Chloe Manning," Jon Rider said.

❧

Chloe turned to Brian and Nelson, her mouth open and her eyes blazing with questions.

They smiled at her. "You've been called," Nelson said. "Better get up there."

She snatched a tissue from her purse and wiped her eyes. Took a moment to check her blush mirror and do a quick repair on her lipstick. A few jurors and spectators tittered. *Christ, I look like total crap.* But as she threw her shoulders back and walked to the stand, she thought:

I am Chloe Manning. I have been on the cover of Vogue and Cosmopolitan and the Chicago Business Reporter. I have survived being naked in a hotel room with idiot Blake Bondurant and dressed in this public place like Mamie Eisenhower. I have been in love and been loved back and been dumped. I'll get through this. Jon Rider, you unhinged trickster, don't you dare leave me again.

The bailiff held out the Bible. "Do you swear that the testimony you are about to give in this cause is the truth, the whole truth, and nothing but the truth, so help you God?"

She looked into those Jon Rider eyes as she had so many times before, so many times when his vision seemed to push gently into her and look around her thoughts and peer down into her heart. But this time – what was it? His eyes were soft. They weren't pressing insistently into hers, through hers. That Rider-man had banked his inner fire for this moment; the eyes were hopeful, defenseless, inviting her in to explore. This time, their topaz glow summoned and welcomed her.

"So help me God, I do," she said.

Jon Rider stood at the podium, Armani buttoned, hair combed back into place, tie tied by the tie gods.

"Please state your full name for the record," he said, pretending to look into his papers.

"Harriet Chloe Manning," she said.

"Ms. Manning," he said, a large smile growing on his face as he raised it to face her, "do you like that last name?"

"What, you mean my first – oh my god." As a woman in business she had always been conscious of trying to avoid doing girly things, but now she put her hands up to her face. "Oh my god. Oh my god."

"May I approach the witness?" Jon Rider said.

Judge Achebe said, "You may."

Jon Rider walked slowly up to the witness box and stood directly before her. There was something in his hand.

Chloe took a deep breath. Her eyes shone.

"Oh my god," she exhaled.

He dropped to one knee. "Harriet Chloe Manning," he said with a dash of theatrical resonance that shot his voice off the walls and around the courtroom, "will you marry me?"

The gasp from the jury and spectators threatened to suck all the air out of the room.

Amy went *woo hoo!*

Lisa the Flamethrower said, perhaps a decibel or two over a stage whisper, "Hell, this beats Proposal-Cam at Cubs Park." Judge Achebe looked her way and she winked at him. He winked back and pretended to wipe something from his eye.

Jon held the ring-box up to Harriet Chloe Manning.

Their initial shock behind them, the courtroom and jury suddenly understood Jon's actions of earlier in the day for what they surely must have been. This wasn't just some crazy suit who seemed a little overexcited about some arcane legal point; this handsome man had risked everything to save the woman he loved. There was a short outburst of whoops and applause and a few *say yes*es.

Judge Achebe banged his gavel. The courtroom was instantly silent.

"There's a question pending, Ms. Manning," he said, and it struck her for the first time that absolutely everyone except maybe that dirtbag Blake was in on this.

Jon Rider, you magnificent bastard, she thought. *I'm gonna make you sweat for a while.*

She took the ring-box and considered the ring, taking her time. It was a blinding emerald-cut rock, in the three-carat range, she was guessing, set in a galaxy of identical, distinct princess stones sloping away from it on either side in orderly twin rows narrowing to the back of the band.

None of the glittery beds of teeny spiky diamonds and intricate scrolly metal work the young women were wanting those days. The whole thing set in yellow gold. Just like him to avoid platinum, keep his distance from what everyone else was doing. An, elegant, blazing masterpiece. She held the box at different angles, pretending to consider its strobing fire and color and spark in the changing light.

Jon barely breathed while she was examining his offering in a rather more leisurely fashion than he had anticipated. Being Jon Rider, he had a little speech ready in case she displayed any hesitation.

Baby, get the commitment papers ready. You've shown me I'm as wheels-off and as looney-tunes and as free and as happy as I ever was and as any man could ever be over a woman. You released the rest of me and it's escaped to make me do this thing that Jon Rider would never have dreamed of doing before. Please let me share this part of me with you forever.

Surely he hadn't misread –

"Jon Rider," she said directly into the microphone, now fully invested in the theatricality of the moment, "this is one squared-away ring. I love it, I love you, and Your Honor, I love you, too, and in answer to the pending question I say yes, Jon Rider, I will marry you."

Jon almost fell over in relief. He had not avoided getting shot and losing his license for nothing.

"No further questions, Your Honor."

Judge Achebe said, "Since I don't believe Ms. Marovitz intends to cross-examine on this point" – Jolene shook her head, offering a small grudging smile – "you may stand down, Ms. Manning. Mr. Rider, you may stand up, if you can."

Jon placed the ring on her finger.

They kissed in a restrained, professional way intended to avoid outrage to the dignity of the Court. It was a kiss that carried with it the understanding that less civilized and more wide-ranging kisses would be forthcoming in the not-so-very distant future, like within the hour if they could get their newly-engaged asses out of there and back to his place or her place or any place.

Chloe said: "We'll talk about that 'last name' thing later."

Jon said: "You may have noticed I didn't actually make you answer that question."

Chloe Rider. Not so bad, really. Not bad at all. Kind of like it. Maybe name a lawnmower or geriatric scooter after it. She looked at Jon with a heart full of love, love and gratitude for whatever it was that had flipped his switch.

And hers.

We all need to be willing to make changes sometimes.

The courtroom was cheering.

The Flamethrower had turned her phone on and was snapping pictures and blasting a text to a reporter she knew at the *Tribune.*

Two of the female jurors began to chant: "RING, RING, RING," soon joined by the entire jury box. Chloe danced over and fluttered her left hand up and down the rows to the jurors' *ooh*s and *ahh*s and a few happy sobs.

One of the jurors said, "I absolutely love your suit. And cute pumps!"

Chloe said, "Oh, me too, thank you so much," and she found herself meaning it.

∽

"Well," Judge Cleon Achebe said, "since the defendant says she loves me, I may have to recuse myself from further consideration of this case. Counsel, get this case goddam settled, for all our sakes." He banged his gavel. "This Court stands adjourned."

The next ten minutes were hugs and handshakes. Jurors and spectators joined in. Cell phones were held high in the air to record the joyful chaos with the happy couple in the middle.

Judge Achebe descended from the bench to add his well-wishes. The Flamethrower touched his arm and whispered in his ear.

Marshals Jackson and Lopez came in to shake Jon's hand and to assure him that their threatening to shoot him in the back was nothing personal.

Amy found herself entertaining two of Jolene Marovitz's cute male colleagues.

Even Jolene Marovitz shoved her way through the crowd to offer congratulations.

She'd had to fix her makeup, too.

CHAPTER 28

Next Morning, Above the Fold in the *Tribune*

Next morning, above the fold in the *Tribune*:

The Mogul and Her Mouthpiece
***Dramatic courtroom proposal to Barbiron
CEO brings trial to a halt***

Lisa's call to her *Tribune* contact had brought photographers to the entrance of the Dirksen Federal Building in time to snap Chloe and Jon spinning out through the revolving doors. The shot they used had caught the noonday sun igniting her left ring finger.

Thanks to Lisa's work with her *Tribune* reporter friend, the accompanying story was heavy on Chloe Manning's local prominence and the romance of it all, and short on legal details. Jon's initial disruption of the trial was turned into a "surprise appearance," and the presence of firearms aimed at the exquisite Merino weave of the gallant swain's jacket went unreported. There was no mention of any of the details of Blake Bondurant's claim.

The reporter quoted The Flamethrower – whose photo in the article was captioned "Lisa Blazier / Attorney friend of CEO" – describing the proceeding as "a routine employment case that appeared to be on the verge of settlement on the eve of trial, as frequently happens." Lisa had also arranged for inclusion of the judge's official headshot ("U.S. Judge Cleon Achebe / Judicial Cupid").

Chloe Manning and Jon Rider never saw it.

Their eyes were elsewhere.

Elsewhere, closed in sweet exhaustion.

CHAPTER 29

CATS! GOODGIRL SAID

— CATS! Goodgirl said.

— I run to smell CATS! Goodboy said.

— Dogs, Bandit said.

— Aim for the nose, Gloria said.

⤬

THE CHICAGO WIND roamed the streets and found the lovers. It gathered and billowed against the window, whispering their story as they dozed.

At the Chicago Chop House, Jim adjusted the piano bench to begin his first set and warmed up with a quiet vamp of his own invention. He looked out at the room as he charged his tip snifter with a fiver. There were several young couples talking at the bar. Jim smiled at the thought of beginnings.

When his fingers settled on the keys, they played "That's All."

[End]

Made in the USA
Las Vegas, NV
18 December 2020